# Wildcat Bride

## The Quinter Brides, Book Five

## by

## Lauri Robinson

This is a work of fiction. Names, characters, places, and incidents either are the product of the author's imagination or are used fictitiously, and any resemblance to actual persons living or dead, business establishments, events, or locales, is entirely coincidental.

**Wildcat Bride: The Quinter Brides, Book Five**

COPYRIGHT © 2011 by Lauri Robinson

Cover Art by *Nicola Martinez*

The Wild Rose Press
PO Box 708
Adams Basin, NY 14410-0706
Visit us at www.thewildrosepress.com

Publishing History
First Cactus Rose Edition, 2011
Print ISBN 1-60154-891-5

Published in the United States of America

## "Eva!"

**His shout rose above the murmur of voices,** and hit target. The woman, with a blue green feather sticking out of her hat like a tail on a runaway mustang, twisted around. Her startled face transformed into happiness as her big, brown eyes settled on him.

"Eva!" he repeated.

"Bug? Bug!" She turned to a man beside her, and then spun back around, rushing forward.

His feet barely touched the floor. The crowded room might as well have been empty, for he saw nothing, heard less, as he crossed the room in record time. They met, and all of a sudden, Bug became as unsure as a chicken trying to fly. She'd changed. With her long, russet-colored hair that held the light brighter than a flame, and her slender, willowy figure, she'd always been pretty. But, here, tonight, dressed in finery and with tiny spirals of hair dangling beneath her lacy hat, she was breathtakingly beautiful. He didn't know what to do, where to start.

Eva, however, appeared to know just what to do. She wrapped her arms around him and fell against his chest.

"Bug Quinter! I am so happy to see you!"

He folded his arms around her. God, she felt good. Right. A deep sense of homecoming filled his soul. "It's good to see you, too, Eva girl. Damn good." His eyelids closed, and he held her tight, wishing his legs and torso had extra arms, so they, too, could wrap around her, for he never, ever, wanted to let her go.

# Dedication

To Jeannette,
Marriage made us sisters.
Love made us friends.

Chapter One

*New York City, New York*
*April 1888*

He must be seeing things.

Bug, named Brett Allen Quinter at birth, ducked and twisted, trying to see around the dozens of heads blocking his vision. He batted aside an ostrich feather fluttering and swaying as it stuck out of the top of a hat in front of him, and peered above the crowd to where he'd caught a glimpse of someone familiar.

The ostrich-feather-hat-owning woman spun about and glowered at him, once again blocking his view with the annoying fluff on her head. He glared back for a second, before stretching on his toes and pinpointing a location. Another feather, not unlike the one tickling the bottom of his nose quickly disappeared amongst the throng of people dressed in finery and anxiously awaiting for the clock to strike six.

There was nothing spectacular about the second feather either—blue-green with a large distinct dot. It was the rapid beat in his chest and the way his breath wanted to stop going in and out as it should that made him believe he saw more.

"Brett, what are you doing?" Jenny Staples pulled on his jacket sleeve.

He tugged the uncomfortable suit coat back in place. The sleeves weren't nearly long enough. They made him feel bunched up, and the ribbon tie she insisted he wear was choking the daylights out of him. The uncomfortable garment aside, he grabbed Jenny's hand and pulled her out of the long line waiting for the door half of a block ahead to open.

"Come on."

She followed, probably because she had no choice, he was stronger.

"Where are we going? We're going to lose our place in line."

"I thought I saw someone I know." Bug pulled her in his wake, stepping into the street to bypass the crowd filling the walkway.

"That's impossible. Who could you know in New York City?"

He didn't answer. For one, it was none of her business who he knew in New York City, and for two, he didn't want to waste the time explaining. They were practically running, the long line of people barely a blur. The carriage he'd seen the familiar shape step out of started to move. "Wait! Hey there! Wait!"

"Who are you shouting at?" Jenny asked, breathless but still at his side.

Waving both arms over his head, he shouted again. "Wait!"

"Brett!" Jenny once again pulled on his coat sleeve. "Stop it, you're making a spectacle of yourself," she whispered angrily.

The driver had seen him and stopped the team before pulling the hackney completely away from the curb. Bug brushed Jenny's hand aside and jogged forward. Pulling himself up on the side of the buggy, where he could face the driver, he asked, "The woman that just got out, where was she going?"

Tipping the edge of the stiff brimmed top hat that matched the rest of his black suit, the driver indicated the building the long crowd was waiting to open. "To the art show, Sir."

Art show? Bug's heart triple-stepped around in

his chest. It couldn't be. Could it? "Is her name Eva..." His mind, spinning with more thoughts than a rabbit had babies, went completely blank. Hell! She was just Eva to him. "Robertson!" he half shouted when the name planted itself in his head. "Eva Robertson," he repeated for himself as much as the driver. "Is her name Eva Robertson?"

The driver shrugged his shoulders. "I'm sorry, Sir, I'm not at liberty to say."

"Not at liberty—"

"Brett, get down from there!" Jenny interrupted, now tugging on his pant leg.

"Sir," the driver said while Bug tensed his leg, wanting to shake off Jenny's hold. "Sir. Please, you're holding up traffic."

The noise of the city penetrated his thick skull. Shouts and curses, as well as all consuming sounds of traffic and folks in general. More people graced the city streets and boardwalks than Bug figured lived in the whole state of Kansas. All in all, it reminded him of just how much he missed the peace and quiet of home.

"Brett, get down!"

"Sir?" The driver, though not sounding nearly as annoyed as Jenny, looked at him questionably.

Bug glanced left and right, acknowledging the traffic and ignoring it at the same time. He set his stare back on the driver. "Just tell me, was that woman Eva Robertson or not?"

"Sir, I'm not—"

"I know," Bug said, "at liberty." He settled his eyes on the man, and wished like hell he hadn't complied when Jenny said he had to leave his Peacemaker back at the hotel. Didn't matter though, he didn't need the pistol. Bug fisted his fingers into the front of the driver's starched collar. "Let me tell you about liberties, Dodge City style."

The man's eyes bulged out of their sockets, and

his Adam's apple bobbled against Bug's knuckles. There was something about Dodge City that caught an Easterner's attention every time. They were either as curious as a cat about the cow town and those who lived there, or scared witless. He'd go for witless with this driver.

"Was that Eva Robertson?" he asked again.

"Yes," the man mouthed.

He knew it! Though he'd barely got a glimpse, something deep inside him said the woman he saw was his... Clearly defined memories of him and Eva spun in his head faster than a Kansas dirt devil. Eva was his what? She was Ma's neighbor, a family friend, but he didn't have a claim on her. Well, sure she was his friend, too, but it wasn't like he could say she was his...As in *his*. Yet he had—for years—and probably always will.

Bug let go of the driver's shirt and patted the white material back in place for good measure. "Thanks," he offered, jumping down the ground. What the hell was Eva doing in New York City?

The driver leaned over the edge. "Sir?" he whispered.

Bug wasn't sure if what the man had to say was a secret or if he just hadn't gained his voice yet, either way, Bug once again grabbed the rail and pulled himself up to hear what the man had to say.

"Are you really from Dodge City?"

"There about."

A faint grin formed on the man's face. "Nice to meet you, Sir." He glanced around before adding, "Here, in New York, she's to be referred to as Eloisa Reynolds."

Bug frowned with confusion. "Eloweesa Raynoids?" he asked, trying to repeat the name the driver had said. He was close, but couldn't get his tongue around the sounds the way the other man had.

The driver nodded.

Eloisa Reynolds? Bug's heart hit the ground before his feet did. Eva was married. His Eva had gone and gotten herself hitched to some fella named Reynolds. A shiver raced up his spine. Bug slapped his thigh with one hand. *Damn it, Ma!*

His mother had made it a habit of marrying people off—usually in the middle of the night with the assistance of her shotgun. But, why would she have married off Eva? To someone else? He was supposed to marry Eva. Someday. That's why he was here.

The hackney pulled away from the curb, finding its spot in the long train of wagons, coaches, and buggies of every shape and size. Bug would never get used to how the city traffic never stopped. Even in the dead of the night, wagons rolled up and down the streets, squeaking and clanking to the point a man couldn't get a good night's sleep no matter how tired he was. And the stench—even to someone used to mucking out barn stalls—was disgusting. The street sweepers couldn't keep up; the traffic never slowed long enough for them to pick up the refuse before it was ground deep into the road. Not even Dodge, in the rainy season and with pens full of cattle, smelled this bad.

"Brett? Brett? What has gotten in to you?"

He spun about. Jenny, looking about as happy and flustered as a wet kitten, stared up at him. The pink, lace covered hat, which once had been perched perfectly on her blonde curls, now hung over one ear. The cockeyed hat, along with the red flush covering her cheeks, made her sweet little face, all the cuter. A twinge of guilt caught his guts. He shouldn't have pulled her down the street like that. That wasn't very gentlemanly. His mind caught up with him, and he spun back to the building. There wasn't time to dwell on his actions now. The doors had opened.

"Come on." He grabbed Jenny's wrist and pulled her toward the front of the crowd.

"We can't budge." She planted her feet on the boardwalk. "We have to go to the back of the line. Hopefully, we'll still be able to get in." A pout sat on her lips as she stared at the line stretched from block to block. "I never imagined there would be this many people."

"We'll get in," he insisted and hooked her elbow, so he wouldn't lose her amongst the crowd. "Excuse us," he offered, shouldering his way through the mass of people. Jenny stuck at his side as he elbowed and pushed his way forward. Folks were huddled up like cattle at a feed bunk. "Excuse us," he continued, seeing the door.

"Hey!" A man grabbed his arm. "You can't—"

Bug shot the pipsqueak his best menacing glare. He'd learned the stare from Buffalo Killer. The brave could make a diamondback cower with one look. Not that it mattered. Right now Bug could have stared down a rattler—and spit in its eye.

Tugging a derby hat lower on his heavily greased hair, the little man stepped aside.

"Excuse us," Jenny offered in their wake.

Several minutes later, Bug tapped his toe, growing more impatient as another man ahead of them fumbled with admittance tickets. The ticket-taker, in a suit of red and blue so brightly decorated with gold that Bug wanted to holler *the British are coming*', finally took the tickets, and Bug handed out the two he'd drawn out of the pocket inside his suit coat. Glad to get away from the crowd, Bug shot from the door and strolling across the room, he searched for Eva.

"Brett Quinter!" Jenny came to a screeching halt, her hand once again pulling on his coat sleeve.

Short of dragging her across the room, he stopped.

"I demand to know what has come over you. It took me two weeks to talk you into attending this show with me, and now you're practically knocking people down to get in the door." She followed up her demand with a little squeal.

He spun about, half expecting to see someone ready to throw them out. Instead, he realized Jenny had just caught a reflection of herself in one of the mirrors lining the back wall.

"Oh!" she gave him an icy glare and stomped forward, plucking the long pin from the back of her crooked hat as she moved. He followed, taking in the room with each step.

Of course he hadn't wanted to attend another 'show' with her. The last one had men dressed in their underwear bouncing across the stage like deer frolicking in the meadow. And the women on stage with the men...He shivered. They had singing voices that drove through his eardrums like three penny nails. The mere thought made his ears start to throb again.

After Jenny had restored her hat and poked and pinched and patted every inch of skin on her face, she spun back around to face him.

"Are you ready?" His eyes returned to scanning the space, looking for the ostrich feather he'd caught a faint glimpse of outside.

"Am I ready?"

"Yes," he repeated.

"Brett Quinter—"

"Eva!" His shout rose above the murmur of voices, and hit target. The woman, with a blue green feather sticking out of her hat like a tail on run away mustang, twisted around. Her startled face transformed into happiness as her big, brown eyes settled on him. "Eva!" he repeated.

"Bug? Bug!" She turned to a man beside her briefly and then spun back around, rushing forward.

His feet barely touched the floor. The crowded room might as well have been empty, for he saw nothing, heard less, as he crossed the room in record time. They met, and all of a sudden, Bug became as unsure as a chicken trying to fly. She'd changed. With her long, russet colored hair that held the light brighter than a flame, and her slender, willowy figure, she'd always been pretty. But, here, tonight, dressed in finery and with tiny spirals of hair dangling beneath her lacy hat, she was breathtakingly beautiful. He didn't know what to do, where to start.

Eva, however, appeared to know just what to do. She wrapped her arms around him and fell against his chest. "Bug Quinter! I am so happy to see you!"

He folded his arms around her. God, she felt good. Right. A deep sense of homecoming filled his soul. "It's good to see you, too, Eva girl. Damn good." His eyelids closed, and he held her tight, wishing his legs and torso had extra arms, so they, too, could wrap around her, for he never, ever, wanted to let her go.

She leaned back far enough to tilt up her feather-decorated head. As adorable as ever, her big eyes searched his face, as if she was making sure it was him. He grinned.

She giggled and hugged him again. "What are you doing here? I thought you were in Pennsylvania."

"I am. I'm just visiting the city for a few days. What are you doing here?"

Eva attempted to step out of his hold, but his arms didn't want to let her go. She patted his shoulders. He had no choice but to ease his hold, let her go.

With one hand, she gestured around the room. "I'm here for the art show."

For the first time he noticed the paintings

covering the walls. More stood on easels. People flocked the framed art work. One picture in particular held his attention. It was a soddy, surrounded by the rolling plains he knew and loved so well. Memories lassoed his mind, mystically dragging him into the scene.

Eva held her breath. Not only was her blood pounding hard enough to steal her hearing permanently, her heart threatened to explode. Ever since Jack had said they were going to New York, she'd hoped to see Bug, but had feared the opportunity wouldn't materialize.

He looked fantastic. Extremely handsome in his black suit coat and tie. Then again, Bug, with his coffee colored hair and even browner eyes, was always handsome. Even in work clothes, covered in wheat dust, grease from oil seeps, or crusted Kansas dirt he was the best looking man around. Always would be. From the moment she'd seen him, eight years ago when she was fifteen and he sixteen, she'd lost her heart. Since then she'd thought they would be together, as in man and wife, but over the past two and a half years, she began to fear that wasn't meant to be. He most certainly was her true love, but oil was Bug's true love.

"That's your soddy, Eva," he said, sounding in awe.

"Yes, yes it is." Her breath sat tight in her lungs again. That painting was one of her favorites, even though she'd painted it five years ago—when Willamina still took pride in having the brightest whites in Kansas. Memories, including the bitter scent of Willamina's strong lye soap washed over her. Things that would last forever yet would never happen again.

"Why? Why would you paint your house..." Bug glanced at the people fawning over the painting. "And put it on view for all these people to gawk at?"

9

His tone was so sharp the air gushed out of her chest.

"I—" she started.

"Eloisa!" Jack interrupted her explanation. "What are you doing? You can't start socializing until after we make your introduction." He took her arm. "Come along, my dear."

"Jack, this is—"

"Excuse us," Jack interrupted again. "Feel free to explore Miss Reynolds's work," he said, barely glancing at Bug. "She'll be free for questions later."

Bug stepped forward, as if he was going to stop Jack from leading her away, but a blonde woman wrapped both of her hands around Bug's arm. Eva's heart constricted. The woman's touch looked unmistakably familiar, like she was used to touching Bug.

Jack kept pulling. Eva had no choice but to go with him. "I'll see you, later?" It was most certainly a question. Then again, maybe it was a plea. She didn't want Bug to leave. Not without a chance to visit. It had been so long since she'd seen him. Almost three years. Ever since that day he'd stopped by to say good-bye and kissed her. He'd said he was taking a sample from one of his oil seeps to Pennsylvania—and would be back in a few months. His kiss had lingered well beyond the months, and lasted throughout the years. Even right now, in the middle of the crowded room, if she closed her eyes she'd be able to remember how astonishing it had been.

Jack whispered sharply in her ear. She didn't make out what he said, but he kept dragging her away. Her feet were getting tangled in her skirt. She'd have to turn about or fall. "Bug? I'll see you, later?" she asked again.

Bug's eyes hadn't left her, but he didn't answer either. Jack tugged abruptly, spinning her about.

When she caught her footing, she spun back. Bug's head was bent down as he listened to something the blonde said. The happiness of this—her first art show—shattered.

Chapter Two

The exhibition was scheduled from six to nine, and Eva found herself wishing it wasn't happening at all. The pretend smile on her face hurt, as did her feet in the tight, pointed tip and spiked heeled boots that now had to be three sizes too small. She wiggled her toes, wondering if blood still flowed to them. Needle sharp stings raced along her feet and up her shins.

"Smile," Jack whispered in her ear. "This turnout is tremendous. Even better than I hoped."

"I am smiling," she insisted quietly, nodding her head at those passing by.

Jack patted her cheek. "Try harder."

She would have responded, but just then he waved at a man entering the room.

"Mr. Cannon." Jack moved swiftly, away from her to cross the room and greet the man personally.

Eva let out a sigh. The gallery was packed from wall to wall already, and yet more people shuffled in the open doorway. When Jack had first described tonight's event, she'd been thunderstruck, never imagining anyone would attend a show featuring her artwork. Then again, when Jack first arrived at the soddy, a few months after Bug had left, explaining how he'd seen her painting hanging on the wall of the Majestic Hotel in Dodge City, she'd never imagined he'd sell the number of paintings he already had.

The picture in Dodge that Jack had seen was of Bug's brother, Hog and his wife Randi. The couple had built the hotel and restaurant a few years ago, which was on its way to becoming famous. People flocked into the establishment. Hog claimed it was because everyone wanted a piece of refinement in their lives. She'd painted the picture as a gift, as she had for all of Bug's brothers and their wives, Kid and Jessie, Skeeter and Lila, Hog and Randi, and Snake and Summer. The Quinters were the only family she'd had—besides Willamina—since her parents died while traveling west.

She'd been fifteen when her family left Missouri for the silver mines in Colorado, but they'd only made it as far as Dodge City before she'd been orphaned. Her mother to disease, her father to an outlaw. Willamina had taken her in, and afraid the outlaw would return, they'd left Dodge. In some ways it was all a blur, how quickly everything had happened. But happen it had. The oldest Quinter brother, Kid and his wife Jessie, were friends of Willamina's and lived eighty or so miles west of Dodge. In no time, Eva and Willamina were settled in the soddy that had belonged to Jessie before her marriage. In even less time, they were accepted by the Quinters as part of the family.

"Miss Reynolds, can you tell me about this picture? I just love it! Is it really of Dodge City?" A woman dressed in a shimmering black dress, set a large painting on the floor in front of her feet.

"Yes, that is of Dodge City," Eva answered.

"Oh, my." The woman leaned closer. "My friends are going to be green with envy. Please tell me all about it. When did you paint it? Who are the people?" She pointed to the four men on horseback, wearing large hats and long dusters.

"I'm afraid they're not real, just images I created. That's how most men dress in Kansas." Eva explained. "I painted it three years ago while I was staying in Dodge for a few weeks."

"Oh," the woman said. "I was hoping they were

outlaws or something."

Feeling the woman's disappointment, Eva leaned closer and pointed to the big white house in the background of the picture. "I can tell you that house is Danny J's."

"Danny J's?"

Eva wondered if she should go on, not really sure why she admitted that was Danny's house. It really didn't matter and might give the woman something to tell her friends. "Yes," she whispered. "It's a brothel."

"Oh!" The woman slapped one hand over her excited shout.

Eva cowered. She really shouldn't have shared that. "I'm sorry. I'm sure you don't want to purchase it now."

"Are you serious? Of course I want to purchase it. Even more now that I know more about it." She picked the painting up. "I absolutely love your work. It's magnificent!"

"Thank you," Eva offered. It never failed to stun her at how people marveled over her creations. To her it was just something she had to do. Therefore, she'd been painting for as long as she could remember.

"No, thank you, my dear. I must continue browsing, I'm sure there are more paintings I need to purchase." The woman, clutching the framed work to her breast, moved on.

Eva, smiling at the strong sense of self accomplishment hovering around her heart, turned to gaze at the people examining her art work. Men and women elbowed each other aside to get closer looks, while others stood on the tips of their toes, peering over the heads of those in front of them.

It was all due to Willamina. Not long after they started living together, Willamina learned of Eva's passion for painting. The woman insisted Eva took time to paint every day, even when there were other chores needing attention. Eva had seen to the chores first, of course, she wouldn't have Willamina doing them all herself. Not that Willamina couldn't have, even old and bent over, the woman had had more energy and gumption than people half her age.

She scanned the room then, searching for Bug's tall figure and remembering many happy times. She'd seen him earlier, while Jack was making her introduction, and the crowd was clapping and flocking towards her like birds gathering up to fly south. Bug hadn't congregated forward, instead he'd hung back, leaning against an open space on the far wall and frowning.

He was nowhere to be seen now, and neither was the blonde who hadn't left his side. Was she, the petite, prettier than pretty blonde, the reason he hadn't returned to Kansas? May never.

Like a fly, buzzing from one spot to another, Jack appeared at her side again. "Come along, my dear, there's a couple making a very large purchase who has requested a private conversation with you."

"What?" she asked, still searching for Bug.

"Snap out of it, Eva. You'll never have this chance again if you don't devote your time and attention to these people. They'll become your best fans, and assure your paintings sell worldwide." Jack, always serious, squeezed her elbow. "We haven't worked this hard for some pretty boy in a three piece suit to screw it up."

Miffed, she scowled at him. "Jack, you—"

"Just smile, and come with me." His fingers dug into her flesh as he led her to a private room near the back of the gallery.

Knowing now wasn't the time, Eva breathed through the anger building in her chest as Jack haughtily described the way Bug had entered the event. Ignoring him, and his attitude, she held her head high, and strolled into the side room with a fake smile glued on her lips.

The elegant couple was from France, and interested in what other paintings she had that weren't on display. They insisted people in Europe were starving for art work from the Wild West, especially those like hers, the ones that depicted everyday life and people.

Eva had no idea how someone could be hungry for paintings, but following silent instructions from Jack, she visited with the man and woman until they seemed satisfied with her answers. An agreement was settled, Jack would send them a dozen more paintings he had in storage, and provide the couple the first opportunity to purchase a few specific others as she completed them.

The conversation had been lengthy, and when she re-entered the gallery, the darkening windows suggested evening had turned into night. Eva scanned the room again, praying Bug hadn't left. Her eyes found him almost immediately.

A grin formed on his face. Relief flooded her chest. He pushed away from the wall. The room, in her mind anyway, was empty as she made her way across it. Bug, just like his brothers, was as tall, strong, and sturdy as an oak in a storm. The thought of basking in his protection made her pace increase.

He caught her hand, but instead of folding those brawny arms around her, he fell into step beside her, leading her toward a hallway that led to the back of the building. Once out of the room, he spun her about.

"Why, Eva? Why would you put our lives on display?"

"Lives on display?" she repeated, confused by his angry tone, and disappointed that he didn't hug her.

"Yes. That's Willamina washing clothes next to the soddy in that painting. And that other one, that's

Buffalo Killer. How do you think he'd feel to know someone's buying him to hang up for people to stare at every day?"

"Well, uh—"

Jack, once again, was there to interrupt her explanation. "Eloisa!"

Bug, with blood boiling and temples pounding, glared at the man who attempted to step between him and Eva.

"Excuse me," the man's eyes roamed up and down Bug's suit before he said, "my good man. Miss Reynolds is needed elsewhere." The man planted an elbow, none too gently in Bug's ribs.

Snatching the irritating fellow, even though he was good sized, by the back of his stand up collar, Bug lifted the man off his feet. "Jack is it?"

The man, toes dangling, nodded.

"Jack, my good man," Bug growled, "don't ever elbow me again. Not unless you want to see what happened to the last man who did."

Jack nodded, and eyes blinking, turned to Eva. "Eloisa, please tell your fri—"

Bug, still holding the man an inch or so above the ground, tightened his hold. He'd taken the time, while Eva visited with the patrons of the show, to discover that she and Jack weren't married. A fact that had made his heart sing, and his mind was relieved, too, knowing he no longer wanted to hang his mother. Yet, the man, husband or not, still irritated the pants off Bug. "Her name is Eva, not Eloisa."

Eva set both hands on his chest. "Bug, please put Jack down."

He'd never been able to deny her anything, and madder than a cross-eyed bull or not, now wasn't any different. Bug relaxed his hold and the man slipped from his fingers. A smile cracked Bug's lips as the heels of Jack's kid-leather shoes hit the floor with a thud.

"Elo-Eva," Jack started, tugging the lapels of his jacket straight.

She held up one hand, but her gaze stayed locked on Bug's. "Leave us alone for a few minutes, Jack."

Bug didn't look aside either, but knew the moment Jack moved away. Perhaps the man wasn't a fool after all. Bug tossed the thought aside. There were so many other questions swimming around in his mind, he could barely make one out from another. "Why does he call you that?"

"What?" she asked, frowning.

He wrapped his hands around her fingers still settled on his lapels, and gently removed them. Holding her fingertips, massaging the knuckles, he asked, "Whose Eloisa Reynolds?"

"Me." She gazed at their fingers for a moment. "Jack says Eva Robertson is a fine name for a girl from Kansas, but not for a world renowned artist."

"World renowned?" Her paintings were the best he'd ever seen, and the prices of them had astonished him, but when had she become world renowned?

"Yes, I'm not world renowned yet, but Jack says I will be in a few years."

"Who is this Jack guy, anyway?"

"He's my agent. He sells my painting and sets up shows like this for me to display my work."

Bug's guts churned. "How many of these shows have you done?"

"This is the first."

"So, Jack says you're going to be world renowned?"

She nodded. There was a happy glint in her eye.

He didn't want to disappoint her, but the whole thing smelled like rotten eggs to him. "And Jack set up this show."

Again, she nodded.

"And Jack says you have to call yourself Eloisa instead of Eva?"

"Yes, he said—"

"I know, you already told me." Bug ran the ball of his thumb up and down the inside of her wrist. "How much does Jack make off your paintings?"

"Fifty percent"

Bug choked on his own saliva. Swallowing, so she wouldn't notice, he repeated, "Fifty percent?"

"Yes, that is the going rate."

"Eva," he said, shaking his head.

"What?"

"When did you become so gullible?"

Her big, brown eyes snapped up, alive and alarmed they gazed at him. "What?"

"Gullible. You can't believe—"

"I can't believe what, Bug Quinter?" She tugged her hands out of his.

He reached to recapture her, but she stepped back.

"Who do you think you are? Storming in here." She held up a hand as he stepped closer. "Jack told me about the commotion you caused in line." Her icy glare held him from trying to reach out to her. "Scowling at the other guests like they're trespassers. And then!" She threw her arms in the air. "You not only accuse me of exploiting my family and friends, you tell me I'm gullible for believing in myself? Gullible for believing I, Eva Robertson, an orphan from Kansas, could become a world renowned artist."

Damn. None of it seemed that bad in his head. "Eva," he started. "You don't understand."

"Oh? And what part don't I understand? That you're a brute? That you don't care about anybody but yourself?"

"A brute?" How'd she turn it around on him?

19

"Yes. A brute." She held one finger under his nose. "Let me tell you something, Bug Quinter. I'm a very good artist. Those people out there are paying good money to purchase pictures I painted. And yes, they may be of people and places I know, but you know what else?" She continued before he could answer. "I have permission from those friends and family to paint them. To exploit them!"

She poked his chest with her finger now. It didn't hurt, but it was annoying. "Buffalo Killer gave me permission to paint him. He was proud that I wanted to, and he was proud when the other six I've done of him have sold for substantial amounts of money."

"Buffalo Killer knows..."

"Yes!" She hit him one last time with her finger, as if for good measure. "He knows and he's proud of me."

Her tantrum had lit ire to flame in his chest. It bothered him to think that everyone else knew about her paintings being sold—for substantial amounts of money—and they were proud of her. He was, too, but he had the right. They didn't. Especially not Buffalo Killer. "What about Willamina? How does she feel about being on display for everyone to see? She's worked hard her entire life, and to be displayed as a wrinkled old wash woman, well, that's just wrong."

The resounding crack of her hand hitting his cheek was more shocking than the contact itself. Stunned, he stared at Eva.

Tears glistened in her eyes. "How dare you insinuate I'd ever illustrate Willamina as anything less than the caring and wonderful woman she was!"

One word pelted him with icy rain. His breath welled in his lungs, making them flame. "Was?"

"Yes, was!"

The thought of Willamina being gone turned his blood into ice. He grabbed Eva's upper arms. "What?

When? Why didn't someone tell me?" This time he didn't give her the time to answer before he continued, "Everyone writes to me, Ma, Jessie, Lila, Randi, Summer, hell even the boys, including August writes now and again. But no one mentioned that!" He tightened his grip. "Not even you!"

She shook her head.

"Why?" The pain inching its way from his gut to his heart blistered his insides. "Why didn't someone tell me?"

"I asked them not to." Her fingers shook as she wiped the tears from her cheeks.

"Why would you do that?"

"Because there wasn't anything you could do. She was old and tired. It was her time. She didn't suffer, nor was she ill. She just didn't wake up one morning. I didn't want her death to interfere with your dream of becoming an oil man."

He wanted to pull her close, to ease the pain twisting her face, but he couldn't, his own pain was too severe. Willamina had been like a grandmother to him. He loved her as dearly as he did the rest of his family. "That wasn't your choice to make. It should have been my choice. I should have been there. I should have dug her grave. Said my good-byes."

Eva chewed on her bottom lip. Tears trickled down her face, dripping off her chin. Bug spun about from the sight. "That wasn't your choice to make, Eva." Shaking his head, forcing the tears from pressing their way out from behind his eyes, he walked through the room. His blurred gaze landed on the sod house picture. An old woman—Willamina—was bowed over a wooden wash tub, scrubbing clothes on a tall wash board. Her gray hair, falling from the bun at her nape, floated on the breeze as did the line of garments hanging from a rope stretched from a pole to the corner of the house.

He stomped over and snatched up the picture. The little price card in the corner fluttered to the floor. It didn't matter, he'd already seen the number, knew buying the painting would empty his pocketbook.

"Sir?" A man dressed just like the ticket taker blocked his path.

Bug hitched the painting under one arm, and dug out his purse. Pulling every last bill out, he slapped the money into the hand the man held out.

Jenny appeared at his side then. "There you are. I've been looking everywhere for you. There are a few paintings I'd like to purchase, too."

"No." He tucked his wallet back into his pocket, and took her elbow.

"No?" She tugged her arm from his hold. "Yes, there is. I'll show you."

"No."

She fell in step beside him as he walked to the door. "Brett Quinter, I'm not leaving here without my paintings. Now, quit being so grumpy."

Jenny tried to make him stop or turn around, but he shook her hold off like a fly on a cow's back. "Suit yourself," he said, without missing a step toward the doorway.

Chapter Three

Eva, unable to keep up with the tears flowing down her cheeks, shivered as Bug walked out the door. She'd never wanted him to learn about Willamina's death this way. The pain, the hurt, on his face remained before her eyes even when she closed her lids. How could she have been so callous? So uncaring? That wasn't like her.

She bowed her head, burying it in both hands, and leaned against the wall. Yes, he'd hurt her. How could he believe she had no idea what was happening, that she didn't know what was going on? She wasn't gullible, nor was she stupid. Of course, fifty percent sounded like a lot, but Jack had taken a chance on her, and she owed him for that. Paying him with money was better than paying him in other ways. And using a false name had been partially her idea. She didn't like the idea of everyone knowing who she was. When the time came, and she wanted to settle down and raise a family, no one would know that she was Eloisa Reynolds. She'd once again just be Eva Robertson.

Willamina had liked the idea. And she liked that painting of herself. She said it showed her soul. Being a washwoman that is. It demonstrated how she'd dedicated her life to keeping the world as clean and bright as she could.

"Eva?"

She wiped at the tears still flowing and glanced up. "I need to leave, Jack. I just need to leave."

"All right, sweetheart," he took her arm. "Come this way. We'll go out the back. It's only two blocks to the hotel."

Words wouldn't form, so she nodded, thankful for his kindness. It was always there, just below the surface even when others didn't see it. The jaunt to the hotel didn't take long, yet, by the time they arrived, she'd dried her tears and regained control. In the front lobby, she stopped Jack.

"I'm fine. You don't need to see me up."

"Are you sure?" He patted her cheek.

"Yes."

He glanced over his shoulder. "I should get back. I'll explain you came down with a headache."

She rubbed her temples. "You won't be lying."

"I know," he said. "I met him."

The smile that touched her lips was real. "He's a nice person. It was just—"

"Don't try to explain it all now. We'll talk at breakfast. I really need to get back to the gallery. Benjamin Cannon is very impressed by the event."

"I'm glad." She was, but it didn't resonate in her chest as it should. "Go on. I'll see you in the morning."

He brushed a gentle kiss to her cheek. "Sleep tight."

She waited until he'd walked back out the double glass doors etched with huge roses before she turned and made her way to the front desk. There she inquired about having two meals sent up to her room. With the assurance the food would be delivered in half an hour, she went to the long stairs, and taking one at a time, prepared herself to face her traveling companion.

September Quinter was only fourteen, but a more mature, insightful young girl probably didn't exist. The Quinters—Bug's family—had been very supportive of Eva's painting career, but when it came to this trip to New York, they'd been adamant she wasn't going alone. Every one of the brothers, as well as their wives, had offered to travel with her. Their offers had been sincere, it had been their abilities to comply that she questioned. The men were very busy with their businesses, and their wives, just as busy with their families and children.

It had been Ma Quinter who suggested September, and Eva hadn't been able to say no to the girl, for it was evident September looked at this trip as the chance of a lifetime. It had been so far. Jack had made sure they had a private car on the train ride, and the hotel they stayed at was the best in the city.

Whenever they'd had a spare moment the past two weeks they'd explored fancy shops or gone sightseeing, including the newly structured Statue of Liberty, for which every Quinter family member had made a donation. Joseph Pulitzer had sent out a fundraising plea in his *World* newspaper, asking every American to step up and contribute to the cost of building the base for the statue. Pulitzer said, "The statue was not a gift from the millionaires of France to the millionaires of America, but a gift of the whole people of France to the whole people of America." As soon as she'd read the article, Ma Quinter had set about collecting donations from all of western Kansas.

A smile touched Eva's lips as she recalled how folks had asked Ma why she was so passionate about funding something she'd never seen. Ma, in her no nonsense way, had said she didn't have to see something to believe in it.

September, as well as Eva for that fact, had been thoroughly impressed with the statue, and couldn't wait to tell Ma all about it. The thought made her pause. Fingering the key she'd pulled from her pocket, Eva glanced down the hall. It was empty. The red, plush carpet had been recently swept, not a foot print could be seen in the pile. Eva thought of

September and how the girl had taken notes about the hotel, things she wanted to tell Randi and Hog about.

They weren't scheduled to leave until next week, but Eva was ready to leave now, tomorrow at the latest. September wouldn't mind, the girl was ready to be home. She hadn't wanted to attend the art show, and Eva hadn't forced her. Though September would have loved to have seen Uncle Bug. They hadn't discussed it, yet Eva knew the girl had hoped as badly as she they'd run into him.

The key slipped from her fingers, hitting the floor silently. How was she going to keep the fact she'd seen him from September?

\*\*\*\*

Bug held the door for Jenny to enter the hotel. The four block walk from the art gallery hadn't eased the pain in his chest. Matter of fact, the air, which he had imagined would be cool and refreshing, had coated the back of his throat as soon as he'd stepped out the art show door. Hot, stuffy, and disgusting, the air had made its way into his lungs, where it still hung like dust-coated cobwebs.

Without looking his way, Jenny marched through the door. Her fancy heeled boots echoed off the tile covering the foyer floor. He'd told her he wasn't fit for company, and that she should go back and buy her paintings, even offered to send a bellhop from the hotel back down to fetch her. But, silently, angrily, she'd refused and stomped down the boardwalk beside him.

They'd stopped at the street corners, waiting for a break in the never ending traffic before crossing, and even then, when he tried to take her arm, she kept it tucked to her side, letting him know just how unhappy she was with him.

She didn't pause now, waiting for him to catch up as she stormed toward the staircase like a thundercloud rolling in from Colorado. He wasn't none too happy himself. Bug let her climb the stairs by herself as he made his way to the front desk. There he asked the man about having the painting wrapped and shipped.

Happy to assist a guest, no matter what the task, the man assured Bug all would be taken care of and relieved him of the painting. At a cross roads, and not knowing which way to go, Bug spun around, and rested his back against the tall desk with his elbows on the top.

"Brett, my boy," Chester Staples greeted, stepping off the wide staircase. "I just passed Jenny. She didn't appear to be in a good mood. The art show wasn't what she expected?"

"No, I guess not, sir," Bug answered, pushing off the desk.

Chester frowned deeply. "I've seen Eloisa Reynolds's work. It's brilliant. What was the problem?"

Hearing that name made Bug wanted to shout— *It's Eva Robertson, not Eloisa Reynolds*—but he couldn't. Nor could he say he was the problem, not to Jenny's father—his boss. The man, though fair and honest, loved his daughter and catered to her every whim—most of which drove Bug batty.

"Come on, join me for a drink," Chester gestured to the room across from the desk. "Did you get a chance to eat? I know you didn't before you left for the show."

"No, sir, we didn't eat."

"Well, Jenny will send Charlotte down to get something. I'll have a drink while you eat." Chester turned, walking toward the dining room, and Bug, knowing the man expected it, followed.

Poor Charlotte, the household employee from the Staples's Pennsylvania home that traveled with Jenny as her fulltime maid, would get an earful.

27

Most likely about his boorish behavior. Bug liked Charlotte, she was a feisty little thing when she wanted to be, but there wasn't a whole lot he could do to ease what she'd have to put up with tonight.

After they sat, and Bug asked for whatever the evening special was and Chester ordered his bourbon, the man let out a small chuckle. "Did you tell her she couldn't buy anything?"

"Excuse me?"

"Jenny. Did you tell her she couldn't buy any of the paintings?"

"No, sir, I didn't. Matter of fact, I told her to buy whatever she wanted. I said I'd send a bellhop down to help her carry it home." It was the truth, minus some other serious pieces, but still, the truth.

"She's a lot like her mother was. Stubborn and strong willed. They don't make them like that anymore." Chester smiled at the waitress who set a glass down in front of him. "One more after this, darling."

"Yes, sir," she agreed, and then turned to Bug. "Your meal will be out in a few minutes, sir."

"Thank you," he acknowledged, doubting he'd be able to swallow a bite. It stirred his stomach just thinking how no one in his family bothered to write him about Willamina. Hell, he didn't even know when she'd died. Was it last month? Last year? That kind of news was important. His family had told him about new babies, each one of his brother's had had one of those since he left home, and they'd told him about other friends that had passed on. Why not Willamina?

Something snapped. He blinked, looking to see what it was.

Chester held up his hand and flicked his thumb over his finger, making the sound again. "What's the matter, boy? You were miles away."

He couldn't lie to the man now anymore than

he'd been able to a few minutes ago. When he'd arrived in Pennsylvania with his oil sample almost three years ago, Chester had been one of the first men he'd met. The man was part owner of the American Refinery Company near Bradford, Pennsylvania. The company produced over eighty percent of the country's oil and had the world's most prolific oil fields.

Upon hearing about the oil sample Bug had brought in, Chester had contacted him and invited him to visit the fields. Their relationship grew steadily, and before long, Chester offered him a job. Bug was resistant at first, since he'd come to learn enough so he could go back to Kansas and create his own company, but Chester had been insistent, and eventually convinced Bug he'd only know enough to make him dangerous by just visiting the fields. If he worked for the company, learned every aspect of the oil business, when he returned to Kansas, he'd be destined to succeed. Chester had also implied the American Refinery Company would be interested in financially backing Bug's oil business.

"Did something happen, tonight, Brett? Something between you and Jenny?"

Bug shook his head. "No, sir. Nothing more than usual. Jenny gets frustrated with me on a weekly basis."

Chester laughed and swallowed the last of his bourbon. The waitress was there with the second glass before he set the empty one down, and she also placed a plate of food in front of Bug.

"Let me know if you need anything else, gentlemen."

"We will, darling, thank you," Chester answered.

Bug didn't even bother to pick up his fork. The food wouldn't do his stomach any good, so there was no sense sticking it in his mouth. He met Chester's gaze, "Sir, I received some news tonight. A dear,

dear person I knew back in Kansas has died. I need to return home."

Chester bowed his head in respect. "I'm sorry to hear that, Brett. And I understand. How long will you be gone?"

"How long?"

"Yes, when will you be returning?"

"Returning?"

"Yes, to Pennsylvania. How long do you plan on staying in Kansas?"

Bug didn't need to contemplate an answer. "Forever, sir. That's my home. I won't be returning to Pennsylvania."

"Oh." Chester took a sip of his bourbon. He took his time swallowing. "I knew this would happen someday, but..."

"I never said I'd stay in Pennsylvania, sir. You knew my plan was to return to Kansas from the beginning."

"Yes, yes, I did. It's just that since you and Jenny. Well, I guess I'd hoped she'd convince you to stay on the east coast. I don't see her settling very well in Kansas."

Bug practically swallowed his tongue. The danged thing had swollen to twice its size. "Excuse me, sir? Jenny settling in Kansas?"

Chester leaned back in his chair and folded his arms across his chest. "I must insist the two of you marry before you go. I can't allow her to go otherwise. Her mother would spin in her grave."

"Marry?" He could barely breathe around his swollen tongue.

"I know the girl has imagined a large, lavish wedding since she was a child. It'll take a few weeks to put it together." Chester glanced across the table. "Who did you say died? A family member? Would the rest understand if you can't return immediately?"

Bug's mind spun so fast his vision was blurred.

Marriage? The thought—that of marrying Jenny—
had never crossed his mind. Hell, maybe Ma wasn't
so out of the ordinary. It appeared every parent was
set on marrying their kids off lickety-split.

"It was a family friend, sir," he managed to say,
realizing Chester waited for an answer.

"So they'd understand if you aren't able to
return to Kansas immediately?"

"Yes, I mean, no. I'm returning immediately,
sir."

"That's impossible. Jenny—"

Bug's wits returned along with his upbringing.
"Sir, excuse me for interrupting, but, Jenny, is a fine
girl. A nice girl, and I haven't minded watching out
for her, now and again, but, sir, I never asked Jenny
to marry me. I can't marry her."

"Like hell you can't!" Chester roared loud
enough to startle the waitress on the other side of
the room. The sound of broken glass echoed in the
deepening silence.

Chapter Four

"What do you mean, going home?" Jack asked, coffee sputtering from his lips

"Shh." Eva pressed a finger to her lips. "September is still sleeping. She was up half the night packing her things."

Jack set the cup down and wiped his mustached mouth with the white napkin supplied by the bellhop who'd carried the breakfast to the room. Dressed in another impeccable suit, with his coal black hair neatly combed, and his shoes smartly shined, Jack looked as elegant this morning as he had last night at the art show.

"Eva, I know seeing your friend last night has you confused, but really, honey, running back to Kansas? That's not like you. You've gone head to head against me over trivial things. Trust me, I know how stubborn, persistent, and determined you can be." He frowned, then grew more serious. "Who is this Bug person? What aren't you telling me?"

"Nothing. Bug is the youngest Quinter brother. You've met the others."

"Yes, and it was like being interrogated by a Confederate brigade. I thought they were going to take me out back and tar and feather me." He twisted in his chair, as if shaking off an eerie feeling.

"It wasn't that bad and you know it." She ate the last slice of her orange, licking the juice from her fingers.

"Maybe not for you, but for me...Let's just say, I know where you stand with those men, and I'll never do anything to cross them. Especially not that

Indian." He shivered again. Then as if his worries were over, he picked up his fork and stabbed a sausage link. "This Bug is the youngest?"

"Yes."

"You never mentioned him before, nor did the other brothers. Why not?"

"I don't know. I guess he never came up."

Jack stared at her, extremely serious, for a long time. Her nerves peaked, tickling her skin from the inside. She reached for her cup of tea, but changed her mind, afraid her shaking hands would spill the contents across the white tablecloth.

Jack set down his fork and wiped his mouth once again. "It's a funny thing, you know."

"What?"

"What I've learned about love over the years."

"Love?"

"Yes. Love." He leaned forward and planted both elbows on the table. Touching the fingertips of both hands against each other, he continued. "Of love and women that is. You see, when a woman first falls in love with a man, it's all she can think of, all she can talk about. To the point others get tired of listening. But, later, when that love has settled deep inside her, she protects it like a baby. Oh, it's still all she thinks about, but it's so precious to her, she keeps it to herself, unwilling to share."

Eva folded her hands on her lap, squeezing the trembling knuckles against one another.

Jack sighed. "So, this Bug Quinter, he's the one holding your heart. I've always known there was someone, but I thought perhaps he'd died, and the memories were too painful for you to speak of him."

She couldn't deny his comprehension. Jack was smart and insightful. She'd known that from the beginning. He'd see through a lie in a heartbeat. She simply shrugged her shoulders, for in all honesty, she had no answers.

"So why are you running away from him?"

"I'm not."

He laughed. "Is he returning to Kansas, too?"

"No."

"I've never pressed you for information you didn't want to share. Have I?"

She shook her head. He'd never asked anything of her she wasn't willing to provide.

"I've always been honest with you. Right down to how I spend the money I make off your paintings. I know others questioned the profit margin, but with my fifty percent," he waved a hand, "I pay for all this. I don't expect you to."

He hadn't. Even September's expenses had been paid by Jack. Other than the incidentals they both purchased—like the miniature Statue of Liberty for Ma.

"You've made me a lot of money the past two years, I won't deny that, and the possibilities in the future are unlimited." His eyes asked her opinion.

This time she nodded in agreement.

"I'm saying all this, because I want you to know, what I'm about to say is from my heart, not my bank account." He leaned back, bracing both hands on the table. "I don't want you to give up your career for some man. Not because I don't want to lose your income, but because I believe in you. You are a gifted woman. Your paintings could grace the halls of the richest homes and buildings in the world. People are touched by your work. You have the ability to make your pictures talk to people. They evoke feelings, memories, hopes, and dreams. I've known this since I first saw that picture back in Dodge."

Silence fell upon the room like a gentle snowfall, clear and clean. She let it completely settle and took a moment to consider his confession before replying, "I'm not giving up my career. I'm just going home. I'll keep painting."

"But will your heart be in it?"

"Of course, nothing's changed."

"You came to New York hoping to run into Bug Quinter, didn't you?"

She knew even before he shook his head that her startled expression had given her away.

"Oh, Eva." He pushed away from the table and walked around it, stopping next to her chair. "I hope this Bug knows what he's missing."

"What he's missing?"

"You said he's not returning home." He lifted his brows. "Is he?"

"No." She shook her head and shrugged at the same time. "I'm sure he will someday."

"And you'll be there waiting for him."

"Waiting for whom?" September asked, poking her head out of the door that lead to the bedroom of the hotel suite.

Eva held her breath. She hadn't told September about seeing Bug last night, but she hadn't asked Jack not to mention it. She shot a nervous glance up to Jack.

Jack twisted about. "Good morning, sleepyhead," he greeted. "I almost ate your breakfast."

September, reed thin as most girls her age are, walked across the room, smiling. "Thanks for leaving some for me. I'm starving."

"As you usually are," Jack commented, patting her sleep tousled blonde curls.

"Waiting for whom? Who were you talking about?" September wasn't one to let a subject drop. Pushing up the floppy sleeves of her dressing gown, she sat down and lifted the cover off the third place setting on the small table.

"The carriage driver," Jack said, staring steadily at Eva. "He'll be here by two to take you to the rail station. Be sure you're ready for him."

"So we are leaving today? We're going home?"

September asked, clearly happy.

"Yes, young lady, as much as it pains me to say, you're leaving today." Jack moved across the room, picking his hat off the side table near the door. His gaze landed on Eva. "I'll go make all the arrangements and meet you for lunch downstairs at noon."

"Thank you, Jack. Thank you."

He nodded her way and then winked at September. "Don't eat too much; lunch is only four hours away."

"Don't worry. I won't." Looking his way, September took a big bite off the piece of toast in her hand.

Jack chuckled and pulled the door closed behind him.

"I like him," September said.

"I do, too," Eva agree, lifting her cup of tea.

"Enough to marry him?" September asked.

"No," Eva answered, sipping her tea.

"Me neither."

A fit of giggles struck them both.

****

It had been two days since the art show, but Bug felt as if it had been a year. Chester and Jenny Staples had left for Pennsylvania this morning. The event had left a mixing of emotions gurgling about in his stomach. Chester had been amicable enough. Yesterday, the man had cornered Bug in his hotel room for a good three hours. It appeared that Jenny had the same idea as her Papa. That she and Bug would get married. He apologized, both to her and to Chester. He'd never said anything, done anything to imply that action, yet, Bug sincerely didn't want to hurt either the daughter or father. They were good people, and he held great respect for both of them.

Spending time with Jenny had started about nine months ago. Bug had met her before then, at the mansion during holiday gatherings and such, but it hadn't been until last summer that Chester had asked Bug to escort her to a play. A troupe from New York was performing in Bradford, and Chester wasn't able to take her.

Bug had, and they'd had an enjoyable time. Since then, Jenny started setting up places for them to go once a month or so. Then it became more often, and the past couple of months, it had been every weekend. Some of the things she chose to do were fun, but others, like the screeching women and underwear-dancing-men were downright awful. She'd wanted to attend the art show, and at first Bug had refused. He had no reason to go to New York, but then Chester had suggested they all go, since he wanted to meet with some men at the stock exchange.

The price of oil was steadily climbing, and Chester was hoping to compile a group of investors to build a subsidiary company of American Refinery. Rockefeller and his Standard Oil Company controlled the market on refining the oil. Bug wasn't overly interested in the refinery business. His love was discovering the oil—knowing where to look and how to coax the black tar out of the ground.

He shook his head, and glanced about, making sure he was still on the right street. Once he started dreaming about oil, everything else took second fiddle. Except for Eva these past two days, not even Chester's offer to make Bug American Refinery's newest prospector enticed him enough to set thoughts of her aside.

Spying the hotel he'd learned she was staying at, he picked up the pace, jogging across the road, dodging a wagon or two while in route. He jumped onto the curb, and ignoring the obscenities the wagon drivers shouted his way, he brushed off his suit jacket, tugged his cuffs in place, and marched through the rose etched glass doors.

"I'm sorry, sir, I'm not at liberty to give you that information," the little eye-glass wearing man behind the desk said. A nasty smile sat on the man's lips, as if he enjoyed stating he wasn't at liberty.

Bug leaned across the desk, his fingers itching to grab the man's shirt—bow tie and all. "Not at liberty?" he repeated.

"Yes, sir." The man's head bobbed up and down.

Bug's hand was half way up, just getting ready to swing around and shoot across the desk top to snatch the man's shirt front, when someone grabbed it.

"Hold up there, my good man."

The voice was unmistakably unforgettable. Bug spun about, pulling his arm from Jack's grasp at the same time. "Where is she?" Bug demanded.

The man didn't answer, instead he started walking. Off to one side, Jack crooked a finger, signally for Bug to follow. Figuring it was the only way he was going to find Eva, but not too happy, Bug trailed Jack into the hotel's dining room. Jack took a seat at a table near the big window that displayed the never ending traffic and gestured for Bug to take the seat on the opposite side of the table.

Convincing his commonsense to overrule his ire wasn't easy. Exhaling through his nose, Bug sat.

Jack leaned back, arms folded across his chest. "I don't believe we've been properly introduced, but since you already practically choked me to death, a formal introduction isn't necessary, is it?"

Bug blinked, trying to decipher exactly what the man had said.

"Name's Jack Houston. And you are Bug Quinter. Also known as Brett Quinter. The youngest of the bunch."

The muscles in his neck were so tight, nodding was tough, but Bug did so, agreeing with the man's greeting—if it could be called that.

"You have four brothers, Kid, Skeeter, Hog, and Snake. And one half-brother, at least that's how he considers himself, Buffalo Killer."

Again, he nodded. Eva must have told Jack all about him.

"You left Kansas almost three years ago, to visit the Pennsylvania oil fields, hoping to learn enough to go back home and start drilling for oil. You only planned on being gone six months or so, but, Chester Staples discovered you, and convinced you to stay on for a bit longer. He offered you a chance to learn more about the oil fields and refineries."

Bug squirmed in his seat. "You got more you want to tell me?"

Jack shrugged, and then held up one hand as a waiter walked their way. "Shall we order?"

Bug simply shook his head when the waiter looked his way after taking Jack's order. He wasn't hungry, hadn't been for two days. Jack lifted his silverware off the sparkling white napkin and rearranged the utensils neatly on the table. He then flayed the napkin open and settled it on his lap, preparing for his beefsteak to arrive.

Tired of waiting, Bug asked, "Where's Eva?"

The waiter was back, setting a cup of coffee in front of Jack and a glass of water in front of him. When the young man left again, Bug glared at Jack.

"She left." Jack shrugged.

"I learned that much from the pipsqueak behind the desk. Where'd she go?"

Jack gazed out the window as if the never ending traffic held his attention. Bug clenched his fists. The man turned then, and met his stare with one just as serious. "I won't allow you to hurt her."

"Hurt her?" Bug slapped the table hard enough to jostle water over the rim of his glass. "Eva's the last person on earth I'd hurt. I—" he stopped shy of saying he loved her. He did, but Jack sure as hell didn't need to know that.

"You what?"

"Where is she?" His patience was running thin, but at the same time a heavy weight bore down on his shoulders. "Just tell me where she is."

Jack looked him over, as if sizing him up. Acting as if he had all the time in the world, the man took a leisurely sip of his coffee, and then returned the cup to its saucer. "Hold your horses, Bug. I'll tell you, but I have something else to say first."

Bug arched a brow. Who the hell did this man think he is?

"I'm the man who stepped in when you left," Jack said.

"What?" Bug exclaimed.

Murmurs filled the room, the people at every table stared their way.

He lowered his voice to seethe, "What the hell is that supposed to mean?"

Jack took another sip off his coffee cup, as unaffected as a duck in a rainstorm. When he set the cup down, he replied, "Just that. After you left Kansas, I became the man Eva needed."

Steam now boiled in Bug's head.

"Calm down," Jack said. "This isn't Dodge City. A temper tantrum will only result in getting you thrown out of here."

"After I break your neck," Bug growled across the table.

Jack cracked a smile—a sincere grin that took Bug aback. "I really want to hate you," Jack offered. "But try as I might, I can't seem to." He waved his hand casually. "Sit back and relax. I'll explain what I mean."

Even though his nerves jumped around like crickets in a corner, Bug leaned back and folded his arms. "Start explaining, but I gotta warn you, I'm finding it real easy to hate you."

Jack laughed. "I'm sure you are."

The waiter arrived and as he set the plate down, Jack pointed across the table. "Bring the identical thing for my friend."

Bug met the waiter's expectant glance with a nod. He still wasn't hungry, but if that's what it took to get the story out of Jack, so be it.

Jack cut a slice off his steak and rolled the bite size piece in the juice oozing from the inside of the meat. He poked the fork in his mouth, and chewed appreciatively. After he swallowed, he stated, "It's good. You'll like it."

Bug doubted, but didn't comment.

"The best steak I ever ate was at the Majestic in Dodge. Your brother Hog's place. I was on my way to Denver, and the train engineer highly recommended the passengers try the fare at the hotel during our brief layover." Jack poked another piece of meat into his mouth and chewed.

Bug's stomach growled, telling him he hadn't eaten in two days, and needed to.

"I never made it to Denver."

"Why?" Bug asked, hoping conversation would get his mind off his stomach.

"Because I saw Eva's painting. I spent a couple of days at the hotel, learning about her from your brother and his beautiful wife Randi. They're good people."

"Yes, they are," Bug agreed readily, feeling more than a touch homesick. Hog and Randi were the best cooks to ever grace the earth.

He had to wait until Jack swallowed again before the man continued, "I drove over to Eva's then. Willamina, hunched over and glaring at me behind the sites of a rusty rifle met me before I dismounted." Jack chuckled as if the memory made him happy.

Bug had to grin, too. Willamina was as protective as a mother bear and could be quite menacing if you didn't know her. The remembrance made his mind twist. He'd thought about wiring his family, asking about Willamina, but didn't think he wanted the information that way. "When did she pass?"

Jack set his fork down. His gaze was sincere. "No one told you?"

Bug shook his head, swallowing the lump forming against the back of his throat.

"I'm sorry," Jack offered. "It was about two years ago."

"Two years ago?" Anger zinged up his spine. He'd thought maybe it was just a few weeks or maybe months at the most. The fact his entire family held the news from him for years was mind boggling. Why would they do that?

"She was happy for Eva, you know. If anyone besides me, that is, saw the potential in Eva's work, it was Willamina," Jack said.

Bug nodded—it was the only reaction he could afford right now. Anything else might make him unable to control the stinging in his eyes and chest.

"I had to prove myself to all of your brothers, including that Indian who lived in the barn."

"What?"

"Prove that—"

"No, not that, Buffalo Killer lives in whose barn?"

Jack swallowed his food. "Eva's."

"Since when?"

"It appears your family hasn't kept you up on much have they?" Jack gazed over the rim of his coffee cup. His eyes held an inquisitive stare.

"No, it appears they haven't." The pain had grown dull, leaving Bug empty—and lonely.

The waiter set a plate in front of Bug, and he

stared at the food, his appetite once again gone.

"Eat up," Jack said. "You may not feel like it, but you need it. I have a feeling you'll be traveling for the next few days."

"Oh?"

"Why haven't you told Eva you love her?"

Bug cut off a large chunk of steak and shoved it in his mouth, rendering him incapable of answering, which is exactly what he wanted.

"It's written on your face larger than the Statue of Liberty."

The food in Bug's mouth could have been hooves and lips for all he tasted, yet he chewed as if he relished the flavor. Of course he loved Eva. His entire family did. He swallowed. "How long has Buffalo Killer been living in her barn?"

Jack chuckled. "I'll be honest with you, if you're honest with me."

Bug nodded. The food hadn't erupted when it hit his stomach so he tried another piece.

Jack accepted the silence and offered, "I think Buffalo Killer only stays there while I'm there. Kind of like a chaperone. But, I've only been at Eva's three times. The first time Willamina was still alive, so he wasn't there then, but the last two times, he showed up the same day I did. Eva was surprised to see him both times, so I can't imagine he lives there all the time, but I never asked."

"Why not?"

"Because it's none of my business."

Bug eyed the other man up. "What is your business?"

Jack sat back in his chair and tossed his napkin onto his now empty plate. "To see that Eva, or Eloisa Reynolds, becomes a world renowned artist. And I will. That is if you'll let it happen."

"Me?"

"Yes, you. You're the only thing in her way."

"How do you figure that? I'm not even in Kansas. Haven't been for three years."

"I know. I also find the fact that no one in your family or Eva mentioned you as very interesting."

Bug laid his fork and knife down. "No one mentioned me?"

Jack shook his head.

"Ever?" Hell, he might as well have been dead for all his family cared.

"Nope. And that says a whole lot more than if they had."

Bug tossed his napkin on the table as well. "How so?"

"If they'd told me about you, I would have known what I was up against. I'd have been able to learn what you were up to, tell Eva about Jenny Staples, and possibly convince her you no longer loved her. She'd have been crushed, but I'd have been there to pick up the pieces, and encouraged her to focus on her artwork, washing you from her mind."

Bug glared, his best menacing look, but it didn't seem to affect Jack.

The man cocked one brow before he continued, "By not telling me, they left the opportunity for you to walk back into her life wide open." He leaned forward, planting his elbows on the table. "I'm not your enemy, Bug. Even if I'd known about you, I wouldn't have tarnished Eva's mind against you, unless," he held up a finger as if making a point, "I'd felt it was in Eva's best interest. I'll always want what's best for her, so remember that."

"And you'll always want your fifty percent of her earnings," Bug replied, ready to get to the point of the conversation.

"Yes. I will. I won't deny that I make a lot of money off her work, and that I want it to last for a very long time. But let's be honest, the bottom line is if Eva's not happy, she's not painting. If she's not painting, there's no work for me to sell. Therefore, the base of my interest is in her happiness not in her work."

Bug let Jack's comment roll around in his mind for a bit. He finished his glass of water and pushed his plate aside. "And that's where I come in."

Jack nodded. "Eva's my oil well. I'm not in love with her, but I love her. Just like you love oil. Like I said, we aren't enemies if we both want the same thing. Eva's happiness. But…" he let the words settle before he continued. "If you aren't in love with her, and just out to hurt her, I won't think twice about eliminating you from her life."

Bug turned to the window, not to watch the traffic, but to decipher the thoughts rolling around in his head. He wasn't out to hurt Eva, never had been and never would be. What he was mulling was how respect for Jack had filtered into his mind. The man was honest, and Bug had to admit, Eva was lucky it was him peddling her works across the nation, or world for that fact. There were plenty of other shysters that wouldn't have her best interest at heart.

"I take it we understand each other," Jack said.

"Yes," Bug admitted, "we understand each other."

"Good. Now I can tell you that she went home."

Bug spun about. "Home?"

"Yes, she and September left for Kansas yesterday."

The paper crinkled as Bug dug it out of his pocket. A picture of one of Eva's paintings had been on the front page of the *New York Times* this morning. "This article says there will be two more shows."

"There will be. She just won't be at them."

"Why not?"

"Because she thinks you hate her. She didn't tell me why, or what had happened. All she said was that she wanted to go home."

"I don't hate her." Bug's guts rolled, remembering their last conversation. He had his apology ready. Had practiced it over and over again. "Damn it. Why'd you let her go?"

"Because going home is what would make her happy."

"Alone?"

"No, September is with her."

"Two young girls? You sent two young girls off on a train, alone? Anything could happen to them. They could get robbed or abducted or—"

Jack laughed.

"What's so funny?"

"Eva's twenty-three years old, Bug. She's grown up the last three years. She can take care of herself, has been for quite awhile."

Bug frowned. Eva had grown up. The girl he rode away from in Kansas would never have slapped his face the way the woman had the other night at the art show.

Jack rubbed a hand over his mustache. "Let me give you a word of advice, my friend. Don't go riding in to her place claiming you came back to protect or take care of her. You might get chased out faster than you rode in. With a load of buckshot trailing you."

Chapter Five

Eva stretched out on the bed and patted the space beside her. "Let's rest for a bit. That storm last night was impossible to sleep through."

September crawled onto the massive bed that took up most of the space in the bedroom of the luxury train car. "That lightning was something wasn't it?"

"Yes," Eva agreed. She pointed to the curtains pulled back and tied away from the glass windows. "But today the sun is shining."

"What's the first thing you're going to do when you get home?" September asked.

"Oh, I don't know, maybe visit Willamina's grave. Tell her all about our trip." Guilt stabbed at her chest. Bug had been so hurt by her actions. His family, especially Ma, wanted to wire him about Willamina's passing right away, but Eva had asked them not to. At that time, she believed he'd be home within a few more weeks and didn't think a wire would be the appropriate way for him to learn the news.

The two of them had been close, back before he left for Pennsylvania, and she knew how much he loved Willamina. Or at least how much he had. The man she met in New York was different in so many ways. He not only looked older, more distinguished, he acted different. The old Bug would never have suggested she was gullible. He would have talked to her, not acted like he knew everything when he clearly didn't. Perhaps it was a good thing he'd left three years ago, for she really didn't know how well she liked the man he'd become. Oh, she still loved him, would always love him, but right now, after she'd had plenty of time to think about it, she really didn't like him much. Or the tiny blonde that had been glued to his side.

For three years, Eva hadn't so much as looked at another man, but it seemed Bug was on very friendly terms with the blonde.

"You haven't heard a word I've said, have you?"

Eva turned her head. September smiled and asked, "Have you?"

"No, I'm afraid I haven't."

"That's okay. I was just rambling. Talking about how much everyone is going to like the gifts we brought back to them." The girl crossed her ankles, making the bed shake even more than the rambling wheels beneath did. "Do you think Mr. Hampton will like the ink pen you bought him?"

Eva let a pent up sigh escape. "Yes, I think he will."

"Me, too. A lawyer does a lot of writing."

Elliott Hampton had moved to Scott City a few years back, but Eva hadn't met him until Jack enlisted Elliott to take care of her financials. Jack also insisted the contract between the two of them be drawn up by the lawyer, and then Jack had Kid review it, before she signed it. Elliott Hampton had also handled the adoption that made September and her little brother August, legally Quinters. That alone was all it had taken for the entire family to like and trust the lawyer.

"Don't you?"

"I'm sorry, I wasn't listening again," Eva admitted, once again glancing at September.

"I said that I think Mr. Hampton likes you. Don't you?"

"I think Mr. Hampton is a nice man, and that he likes everyone."

"Not like he likes you. Even Dora says he has a crush on you."

"Dora needs to mind her own business," Eva supplied. Though four years older than September, Dora Zimmerman had been September's best friend for years. Eva smiled, hoping to soften the way she'd snapped.

September giggled. "I know. But that's just Dora. She'll always be a busybody." September flipped on her side and propped one elbow on the bed. Settling her chin on the heel of her palm, she continued, "Dora says all the girls in Scott have tried, but that Mr. Hampton isn't interested in them. The only person he danced with at the last social was you."

Piqued, Eva asked, "Really?" Now that she thought about it, they had danced together twice that night. And Elliott had looked quite handsome in his brown vested suit. But then again, it was the same suit he always wore.

September nodded. "Do you like him?"

"Of course I like him. Everyone does."

"Yeah, but do you *like* him?"

Eva wasn't willing to answer, not because she felt September's question was too personal, but because she really didn't know. She did like Elliott, as a person, she'd just never thought of him as someone she could fashion loving. Bug was the only man she ever thought of in those terms.

She pushed her head deeper into the pillow. "I thought we were going to take a nap."

September plopped back onto her pillow. "All right. It's going to be a long night. Our train arrives in Scott at seven fifteen, and then we'll have to gather all of our luggage and travel home. I know Pa will be at the station when we pull in, so we don't have to worry about waiting, but once we get home, everyone will be full of questions about our trip. I predict we'll be lucky if we get to bed before midnight tonight."

"Midnight, uh?" It was a game they played on the trip, predicting different things. They never wagered anything on their predictions, just being right was the only prize they needed.

"Yes. What about you?"

"I think Summer will say ten o'clock is your bedtime, no matter how many questions the others have."

September smiled and closed her eyes. "It sure will be good to be home."

"Yes, it will." Eva closed her eyes as well. The image of Bug appeared, not the one she'd met in New York, but the friendly, happy young man she'd fallen in love with years ago. She tugged her lids apart and turned to watch the great flat land of Kansas flow past the window. Would she be able to keep the fact she'd seen Bug from Ma? The woman had a way of getting information out of people without them even knowing it. September would be so hurt when she learned that Eva had seen Bug and she hadn't.

Eva closed her eyelids again, mainly so she could keep the tears prickling at her eyes at bay. Why did he have to change? Why had he ever left in the first place?

She twisted and rolled onto her side, wiping at the tears dripping onto her cheeks. It was life, she knew that. Nothing ever stayed the same. To do so would be impossible. Yet, she found herself wishing. Even after the deaths of her parents and Willamina, she hadn't wished to turn back time, for she understood death was a part of life. No matter what, everyone would some day die, leaving room for others to be born. Maybe that was it. Bug hadn't died, he just changed. No longer loved her.

She rubbed her cheek against the pillow.

Perhaps he'd never loved her like she'd thought he did. After all, he'd never said as much. Images of him, of them together, flowed across her mind. Her heart skipped a beat recalling the time out by the badlands that he'd been hurt, and they'd all feared he'd die. Then there was the big party in Dodge, when they'd danced together on the front lawn of the Majestic. Other memories emerged; happy, wonderful times, and the images, along with the constant chug of the engine and rumble of the train wheels, lulled her to sleep.

The blast of the train whistle, loud and long, brought her upright. Eva rubbed her eyes and glanced out the window. The land looked no different than it had when she'd fallen to sleep. Neither did the bright blue sky. Yet, she felt as if she'd slept for hours.

She scooted to the edge of the bed and carefully climbed off since September still slumbered. Quietly, she walked from the bedroom to the main part of the train car. The bright red velvet that covered most of the walls and all of the furniture had been a bit overwhelming when they'd first entered the car in New York, but now, days later, the décor seemed as natural as the continual swaying.

The train whistle sounded again, and she reached the car door as someone tapped on the other side. Pulling the door open, she smiled at the friendly porter.

"We'll be arriving in Dodge in five minutes, Ma'am."

"Thank you. How long will we be there?"

"Just long enough for folks to get off or on." He glanced down at the watch he held in one hand. "No more than fifteen minutes if we want to stay on schedule."

"Thank you," she said, stepping back to close the door.

The porter glanced into the room. "Will you or the young miss be needing anything? I could fetch you something during the stop if so."

"No," she whispered. "September is sleeping. We won't need anything. But thank you just the same."

"You're welcome, then Ma'am," he, too, lowered his voice to a whisper.

Smiling, Eva closed the door. It seemed the young porter was a bit smitten by September. It was no wonder, with faded blue eyes and hair so blonde Eva didn't mix any other color with yellow when she painted the girl's image, September was very pretty. And her sweet, caring personality only added to her beauty.

Eva's forehead crinkled with thought. September was close to the same age she'd been when she met Bug for the first time. The train jerked and rattled, slowing down for their arrival in Dodge. She sat on one of the thickly stuffed chairs. Why did everything remind her of him?

The whistle blasted again.

"Sheesh!" September said, making her way from the bedroom. "Has that whistle always been so loud?"

Jerking as it braked, one hard lunge sent September tumbling into the chair beside Eva. Laughing, Eva answered, 'Yes, it's always been that loud."

September stretched her hands over head. "Oh, well, I slept like a log. How about you?"

"My nap was wonderful as well. Thank you."

"We're in Dodge, uh?"

"Yes, we are. The porter said we'd be leaving again in fifteen minutes," Eva explained.

"I know. I read the schedule. I was hoping we could see Uncle Hog and Aunt Randi, but by the time we walked to the hotel, it would be time to leave."

"Yes, it would. Maybe another time." Eva grabbed the arms of the chair, bracing for the final lurch as the train stopped. It came as expected, and once again, she was shocked that everything in the car stayed put.

It seemed as if the train was still rocking on its wheels when a loud pounding happened on their door. They both stood, but neither she nor September had time to move across the room before the door flew open.

"Aunt Randi! Uncle Hog!" September screamed before the door was all the way open. Flying across the room, she landed in Randi's petite arms. Then after a long hug, she stepped into an embrace from her barrel-chested Uncle Hog that lifted her feet off the floor.

Eva, laughing with delight, accepted hugs from both as well. "What are you two doing here?" she asked. If there was one thing that held true for each of the Quinter brothers, it was that they adored their wives and their wives worshipped them, but the unique thing was how that loved flooded to include everyone else in their family just as strongly.

"Are you kidding?" Randi looked as beautiful as ever with her hair pulled back in a flounce and fluff way that made it puff out above her ears. The style always made Eva wish she could make her straight, brown hair look so elegant. "Did you think we'd let you pass right through town with saying hello?"

"Besides," Hog said, hugging September one more time, "my brother sent three wires making sure we knew exactly what time his daughter was traveling through."

"He did?" September asked. Smiling brightly, she added, "That sounds like Pa."

Randi held up three fingers. "Yes, three."

Eva laughed. Shortly after Snake married Summer, he adopted her younger siblings,

September and August. But to meet him, the way he loved those kids, one would think they were his from the day they were born.

"One wire," Hog started as he picked a large basket off the floor outside the doorway and carried it to a nearby table, "was to tell us to be sure and bring you something to eat."

No matter how many men Eva met, Hog would forever be the largest. He was the tallest and broadest of all the brothers.

His grin grew as he continued, "The next one was to make sure we got the first one, and to confirm the time of your train. And the third one was to make sure we got the first one, that we'd remember to bring you something to eat, to confirm the time of your train, and to give you this." He picked September up, hugging her all over again. "The biggest welcome home hug ever."

"Really, he did," Randi explained. Hog was still hugging September, and Randi leaned closer to whisper, "So, did you see Bug?"

Eva's throat constricted.

"You did!" Randi hugged her again, but kept her voice low. "How is he? As handsome as ever? When is he coming home?" Her questions, fired rapidly, stung Eva all the way to her toes.

She had to say something. Whispering, she admitted, "I saw him, but September didn't. There wasn't time. He's fine. But please don't say anything."

Randi leaned back and patted both of Eva's cheeks. The woman's big, brown eyes bore into hers as if she was trying to read Eva's mind, to learn more of what had happened. Randi hugged her again, "Don't worry, Eva," she whispered, "he'll be home for good soon. I know he will."

Eva wanted to say she wasn't worried, but it would be a lie, so she returned Randi's hug and then changed the subject by asking, "Where's Josephine?"

"She's home taking her afternoon nap," Randi said. "Believe me, when you get a two year old to sleep, you don't wake them up for anything."

"Ohhh," September groaned. "It's been ages since I've seen her."

"I know, but we'll be at your place next weekend." Randi gracefully slipped beneath the arm Hog folded around her shoulders.

"You will?" Eva and September asked at the same time.

"Yes, we will," Hog agreed.

"Why?" September giggled. "I mean, I'm happy about it, but it's not someone's birthday or anything."

Hog brushed his finger over the tip of September's nose. "Because your father says we have to be. He's throwing you a welcome home party."

"He is?" The girl's blue eyes sparkled with delight. Her cheeks grew red as she bowed her head slightly. "Goodness, I was only gone a couple of weeks."

"He's been planning it since you left. And says the fact you're arriving early only means you get to help with the final plans." Hog squeezed Randi tighter to his side. "And we wouldn't miss it for the world."

The whistle sounded again. "Oh, no, has it been fifteen minutes already?" Randi asked.

Her question was followed by the conductor's loud yell, "All aboard!"

"I'm afraid so, my dear," Hog answered. "Come here, kiddo, give your uncle one more hug."

September complied and Eva hugged Randi. "Thank you for the basket. I'm sure it will be delicious."

"And enough for the rest of the week,"

September added, switching places with Eva.

Hog gave her a bear hug. "Good to have you home, Eva."

"Thanks, Hog, it's good to be home."

Within minutes, Hog and Randi were gone, and the train was pulling away from the station. September hung her head out the open window, waving and shouting at her aunt and uncle, while Eva stood near her shoulder, waving as well. As the train picked up speed, September gave a final wave and pulled her head in. She wasted no time opening the basket and digging into the variety of foodstuff.

Surprisingly, she tucked the cloth back over the top and turned about. "Eva?"

"Yes?"

"I just had a terrible thought."

Concerned, Eva reached out and rested a hand on the girl's shoulder. "What? What is it?"

"If you were to marry Elliott Hampton, you wouldn't be in our family anymore."

Eva's mouth became so dry there was nothing to swallow. She licked her lips, trying to make her thick tongue work. "I'm not planning on marrying Elliott Hampton. Furthermore, I'm not a part of your family now. I'm your neighbor and your friend, and I'll always be that."

"But it's always been like you're my aunt." September shrugged her shoulders. "I've always felt like it was Uncle Kid and Aunt Jessie, Uncle Skeeter and Aunt Lila, Uncle Hog and Aunt Randi, and Uncle Bug and Eva."

The heart in Eva's chest weighed a hundred pounds. "Your Uncle Bug hasn't been home for almost three years."

"I know, but I still thought when he did come home the two of you..." September turned back to the basket. "Never mind. Are you hungry?"

"Not really," Eva admitted.

September turned away from the table and plopped down in one of the chairs. "Me neither." She waited until Eva sat down in the other before she added, "I sure do wish we would have seen Uncle Bug while we were in New York. One look at how pretty you looked that night of your art show and he would have hightailed it back to Kansas faster than you can say lickety-split."

Eva held her breath, hoping that would help ease the pain encompassing her chest. It didn't. And when the air gushed out, she could have sworn her heart flew out with it.

**\*\*\*\***

Bug stared at the walls surrounding him, wondering yet again how he'd came to be sitting in a jail cell in New York City. Yesterday afternoon, after eating lunch with Jack Houston, he'd headed for the train station. He hadn't acquired much the past three years, and what he had that wouldn't fit in his saddlebags, he'd left at the hotel. He really wouldn't have use for the three piece suit and it had been as uncomfortable as hell. The stuff he wanted from the boarding house he'd lived at while working for American Refinery would be sent to Kansas. Chester said he'd see to it, and Bug knew the man would. The one regret he'd had was his horse. It, too, had been left in Pennsylvania when he'd traveled to New York. Tenderfoot, as he'd come to call the animal when he first bought it, was a fine bay, but there hadn't been time for him to go retrieve the horse, he wanted to get to Kansas as soon as possible. Besides, Mrs. Whitesell, the boarding house owner, would find Tenderfoot a good home, maybe even make herself a nice stash of cash. She'd been good to him, and Bug didn't mind her gaining a profit at all.

What he did mind was staring at these gray walls and metal bars. The guard upstairs now had Bug's saddlebag and his Peacemaker. He better get them back.

There he'd been, minding his own business, walking across the platform, ticket in hand to give the porter, when some young gal started yelling someone stole her money. He'd turned around, looking for the thief when two constables bore down on him. They had him on the ground and his hands shackled behind his back before he had a chance to even get a glimpse of the girl, let alone the real thief.

One of the officers had reached into Bug's vest pocket and pulled out a little pink satchel. Bug had never seen it before and swore he had no idea how it got in his pocket, but the constables didn't give him an ounce of attention. They wouldn't give the girl the pouch either, they said it was evidence, and she'd have to come to court on Monday when a judge would oversee the trial.

A paddy wagon had arrived shortly thereafter. They'd taken his boots, shackled his ankles, and then shoved him inside. The barred wagon stunk of urine and sweat, just like the cell surrounding him did. Even worse was the noise—men yelling and pounding on the bars. Bug rubbed his forehead. The men had carried on all night.

They'd even taken his hat, so he had no way of muffling the sound or blocking the view. He flipped around, throwing his legs over the edge of the cot and braced his hands on his knees. The bottoms of his socks were crusted from walking on the filthy floors.

When Kid had been arrested several years ago, Scott City, then known as Nixon, didn't even have a jail. They'd just lowered Kid into an old dried up well on the edge of town. Glancing around, Bug determined his brother's accommodations beat the hell out of his.

His internal clock said it had to be morning by now, but since he was in a deep dungeon, under the police station house and without windows, he had no way of checking. Yesterday, one of the men upstairs, a large, dark haired man with such a deep accent Bug had a hard time understanding, had asked if there was anyone Bug wanted notified of his arrest.

The only person he knew in the city was Jack Houston, so that's whose name he'd given the man. Which was another thing he couldn't check on—if the man would try to get a hold of Jack or not.

The shouts around him increased, and included a loud banging noise. He stood and moved to the barred wall of his tiny concrete cell.

"Quinter!"

He pressed his face to the bars, attempting to see where the sound came from. It was useless. His fingers barely fit through the openings between thick metal.

"Quinter!"

"Here!" he yelled. "Down here!"

A constable, dressed like the others, in blue from head to toe with shiny buttons and a big badge on his fat chest, stopped near Bug's cell door. "You Quinter?"

"Yes," Bug assured. "Why?"

The man waved a hand. "Down here!" He turned back to Bug. "You got company."

A moment later, Jack Houston appeared. Much taller than the constable, Jack had to duck so his head didn't hit the gas lantern hanging from the ceiling. Bug had stared at the light and the way it flickered all night.

"What the hell happened?" Jack asked, stopping at his cell door.

"I don't know, Jack. Some gal at the train station said I stole her money. I didn't, but damn if they didn't find a frilly little pink pouch in my vest pocket. I swear, Jack, I have no idea how it got there."

Jack stared at the constable who stood nearby. "Could we have some privacy please?"

The constable laughed but then moved. Bug had a feeling the pot-bellied man was leaning against the wall just out of sight.

Jack turned back to Bug. "Tell me what she looked like."

"A little thing. Bright red hair." Bug shrugged, he hadn't really cared what the girl looked like, figured it didn't matter. "I really didn't get a good look at her, but she spoke funny. Like a bunch of the folks in here."

"Irish." Jack nodded and leaned closer, whispering, "Irish immigrants have infiltrated the police department. There's not a one of them that isn't beyond taking a bribe. Start over and tell me everything from the moment you left the hotel."

"I walked straight to the train station."

"Did you talk to anyone?"

"No?"

"Bump into anyone?"

Bug started to say no, but then recalled a minor incident. "Just outside the hotel door two boys ran past me. One fell down and I helped him up."

Jack shook his head. "He probably planted the pouch on you then. You didn't feel anything?"

"What do you mean, feel anything?"

"The streets are full of pick-pocketers. Many are orphans, but some aren't, they're part of a ring. Usually though, they take things out of people's pockets, not put them in." Jack glanced up and down the hallway that Bug couldn't, but wanted to see. "You went straight to the station then?"

"Yup, and I was just about to step onto the train when the girl started yelling."

"How much money was in the pouch?"

"I don't know. No one ever said."

Jack scratched the back of his head. "It's

Saturday morning. They won't set bail until you see the Judge on Monday. I can't get you out before then, but I'll call in some help, and see if we can get the whole thing figured out before you go in front of the Judge. I'll also find a way to get your hearing the first one heard that morning."

The thought of staying in the small cell two more days and nights was about the worse thing his mind had ever conjured up. But from what he'd experienced so far, he believed Jack was right—there was no chance he'd get out before Monday.

"What do you mean, call in some help? My family can't get here that quick."

"I'm not calling in your family. I'm calling in mine. You just sit tight, and I'll see you Monday morning." Jack glanced around again. "I'll see about getting you a decent meal."

"I'm not worried about eating." He'd go hungry before eating the stuff they'd set on the floor this morning. "But, clean water in a clean glass would go a long way down here."

"All right. I can't come again. Visiting hours are Monday through Friday only."

"How'd you get in today?"

"I told you, there's not one of them that's not open to a bribe. But you gotta know the ones to ask." He tapped on the cell door. "Don't worry, I'll get you out."

"Thanks, Jack. Thanks for coming. I appreciate it."

"You can thank me on Monday."

With that, Jack was gone. The constable, too. Bug stood there, his hands wrapped around the bars, and stared at the flickering light. This may prove to be the longest weekend of his life.

\*\*\*\*

On Monday morning, he was in the exact same spot, waiting for someone to shout his name. The days had been long, as if time had stopped, but the nights had been worse. The haunting eyes of the rats scattering about had glowed red and peered at him from every angle all night. For some reason, and it couldn't be because daylight filtered in since none did, the creepy critters weren't quite as daring during the day.

He leaned his head against the bars. Jack really had no reason to help him, but during the long hours Bug had hoped like hell the man was true to his words—still did. There was no way he could live another day in this cell. Fresh water had arrived not long after Jack had left, delivered in a Mason jar so he could replace the lid. He'd also been given some bread, wrapped in brown paper instead of left open to the air like the other food that had been delivered.

"Quinter!"

"Here! Down here!" he shouted in response. "Down here!"

Chapter Six

Monday morning arrived sunny and clear. Barefoot, Eva padded across the floor of her bedroom in the home she still considered new. It had been built over a year ago, on the same property the sod shanty sat. After selling several paintings, she'd bought the place from Kid and Jessie. Her main regret was that Willamina hadn't ever lived in the new home.

Then again, Eva surmised as she plucked fresh undergarments from her dresser drawer, it wouldn't have mattered to Willamina, she'd been happy no matter where she lived. She had that ability. Something Eva just couldn't muster up right now.

She dressed quickly, listening to the morning birds twittering outside the window and the wind rustling the leaves on the windrow of trees next to the house. Memories and thoughts intermingled in her mind. She'd been happy in the soddy, too. Couldn't help but be with Willamina and the Quinters nearby. Why did that seem to have been so long ago?

After donning a day dress, she made the bed, her fingers smoothing the covers while her inattentive mind carried thoughts about as easily as if the wind outside was blowing to and fro in her head.

The homecoming on Friday night was wonderful. The entire Quinter clan, along with most of the town had met her and September at the train station. It was bittersweet. She was happy to be home, yet September's musings had hovered in Eva's mind until they grew so heavy she couldn't concentrate on anything else. It was silly, no matter whom she married, if she ever married at all, the Quinters would still be family to her. Yet a chunk of doubt sat in the base of her mind, asking her if she could manage to remain close with the family when Bug brought his new wife home.

He eventually would, there was no doubt there. Family meant too much to all of them for him to remain out East permanently. Would she be able to witness his happiness—married to someone else?

These were the thoughts that had followed her home from the train station and took residency in her mind all weekend. Whether he'd hurt her or not during their brief encounter in New York, she still loved him. That would never change. It was different, the way she felt about Bug compared to the rest of the brothers, always had been.

Leaving the bedroom door open, so the morning breeze could waft through the house, she made her way down the hall to the staircase. Her house wasn't large in comparison to Snake and Summer's or Kid and Jessie's, but it was a mansion in relationship to the soddy. There were three bedrooms upstairs, and a water closet that boasted hot and cold running water and an indoor privy.

The stairs delivered her to the ground floor, and she crossed the open space to the doorway that led to the kitchen, where she filled the coffee pot with water from the pump at the sink. She lit a burner on the oil burning cook stove and then strolled past the stairway to the front room. Each room, including the bedrooms had oil burning heat stoves. The brothers had been instrumental in convincing her to install them instead of fireplaces or woodstoves. Last winter, when the snow blew into three foot drifts, she was very thankful to not have to haul wood in several times a day.

There was no need for heat now, wouldn't be for a few months, and she continued through the room to her studio. Her favorite area. It was large and encompassed the entire west side of the house. Windows started a foot off the floor and stopped at about the same distance from the ceiling. They made up most of the three outer walls, filling the room with natural light even on gloomy, cloudy days. Easels stood with paintings in different stages of completion, and dozens of canvas frames, some done and others simply a sparkling white, leaned against the wall and windows. The back wall was filled with shelves from bottom to top, holding paints, brushes, books, and all the other materials she used on a regular basis.

Center and forefront was the painting she'd been working on last night. A covered wagon, with its tarp mended and torn and buckling against the wind, was the focal point. But to her, it was the girl being escorted off the bouncing wagon seat by the dark haired young man. It was the day she'd arrived at Kid and Jessie's. The day she'd met Bug.

Her heart beat slow and steady in her chest, as if it too was remembering and cherishing the simple, yet cosmic moment of her life. She sighed, closed her eyes, and then took a deep fulfilling breath. If she'd known what the future would bring that day, she'd have fenced in her heart with barb wire.

The jingle of a harness and clop of hooves interrupted her meditation. Out the window, a black buggy rolled down the driveway, driven by a tiny woman with her long, blonde hair neatly plated into a braid that hung to her waist.

Eva twisted about and scurried to the front door. The wide, covered front porch ran the length of the house. Stopping short of walking down the steps, she waited beneath the edge of the wide awning for Jessie to bring the buggy to a stop.

"Good morning!" Jessie called, wrapping the reins around the brake.

"Hello. What are you doing out and about so early?" Eva asked. "My coffee isn't even done perking yet."

Jessie laughed. "Good because I haven't had any yet." She climbed the stairs. "The children were still sleeping and Kid said he'd make them breakfast when they did wake up."

They wrapped their arms around each other's waist, a familiar greeting between the two of them, and walked side by side into the house. "Are you on your way to town?" Eva asked as they crossed the threshold.

"No, I came to visit you. We barely had a chance to talk the other night. I want to know everything about the art show, about New York," Jessie caught the door with her free arm, as it snapped shut she added, "and about Bug."

Eva stumbled, but Jessie's hold held her upright. "How did you know?"

"Eva Robertson! I consider myself your best friend. Your sister. Do you honestly think I wouldn't be able to take one look at you and know you saw Bug?" Jessie pulled her toward the kitchen. "Besides the fact you arrived home a week early."

Jessie led Eva to a chair and set her down. Then the other woman gathered cups from the cupboard and filled them from the steaming pot. She set them on the table and took a seat next to Eva. "You wouldn't have left early if you hadn't seen him. The art show wasn't the only reason you went to New York. I knew that from the beginning so don't try to deny it."

Eva's resolve shattered, breaking apart in big, painful chunks. "Oh, Jessie, it was awful."

"The art show?"

Eva shook her head, knowing if she opened her

mouth she'd wail like an infant.

"Bug?"

She nodded.

"Why, is he hurt? Looks awful?"

She shook her head. A sob burst from her chest. "He hates me."

"Hates you? Now, that I don't believe." Jessie handed her an embroidered hanky. "Here, cry your eyes out, and then tell me everything that happened."

Eva didn't need the instructions to let the tears flood, they were already doing so. After the storm eased, she blew her nose, and feeling a touch better, smiled at her friend. "Thanks, I needed that."

"Yes, you did. We all do once in awhile." Jessie dumped out the cold coffee in Eva's cup and refilled it. "Now, what happened? Where did you see Bug?"

Wrapping her hands around the cup, Eva absorbed the heat. "He came to the art show."

"I suspected he might."

"Why, did you write to him about it?"

"No, no one did. Just as you asked." Jessie sipped her coffee. "So what happened?"

"Oh, Jessie, it was so good to see him. He looked so handsome, and strong, and tall, and..."

"And?"

"And he had a beautiful woman at his side."

"What?"

Eva swallowed, nodding.

"Who was she?"

"I don't know. I didn't ask. There wasn't time, right after we met," she paused, remembering how wonderful his arms had felt around her in that moment. Knowing Jessie waited to hear more, she continued, "I had to make my introduction and then there were people who wanted to talk to me. It wasn't until later in the evening that I saw him again. He was so angry then."

"About what?"

"Everything. He felt I was exploiting our family with my paintings, and he thought I was gullible by letting Jack oversee everything. We had a terrible argument, and..." Painful guilt bubbled in her stomach. "I told him about Willamina. Just like that I blurted out that she was dead, and that I wouldn't let anyone write to him about it. He was so hurt and so mad. He told me that wasn't my choice to make and then he left."

"Did you see him again?"

"No, we left the next day."

"Why?"

"Why?" Eva repeated.

Jessie nodded. "Why?"

Eva searched for an answer. Pain, raw and oozing, twisted her insides, and blocked her mind from recalling the reasons that had determined she should return home that morning. Not a single one surfaced.

"Why not? There wasn't anything I could do." She shrugged. "I just felt I had to come home."

"Without a fight?"

"We had a fight."

"No, I mean without fighting for the man you love. Not fighting with him. Fighting for him."

Eva opened her mouth, but once again, her mind was as blank as a new canvas.

Jessie wrapped her hands, warm and tenderly around Eva's still holding her cup. "There was a time when Kid thought he wanted to send to Europe for a wife. It's a long story, but he knew a rancher who had a wife from Europe and that's what he thought he needed in order to be a successful rancher. I almost accepted it. Thought if that's what would make him happy, that's what I would have to do."

Eva frowned. The thought of Kid wanting any

68

woman except Jessie was unfathomable. As was the image of Jessie stepping aside for another woman to lay claim on Kid.

"But then, I changed my mind. We can't change other people, we can only change how we react to them—make them see us in a different light." Jessie sat back in her chair, and her face took on a determined gleam. "I decided if Kid ordered a wife from Europe, I'd meet her at the dock and put her back on the ship she sailed in on."

"What? Surely—"

"No, he didn't actually order one. It was a mind set I created. I also became determined to become the wife he wanted." A smile lit her face, showing how absolutely beautiful she was. "It turned out, I didn't need to change. I was the wife he wanted. He just hadn't known it yet."

Eva grinned, happy for her friend that all turned out perfectly. "I'm sure it didn't take you long to convince him."

"No, it didn't," Jessie admitted with a long, contented sigh.

The sound stabbed Eva's heart like a red hot needle. "That's wonderful, Jessie. But I really don't see how it has anything to do with Bug and I. He hates me. He'll never forgive me for not telling him about Willamina."

"Well, that is serious. Bug loved her as much as the rest of us did, but, he loves you, too. And forgiveness only strengthens love."

Eva rose and walked over to dump out her once again cold coffee. She left the cup in the sink, her stomach was unsettled enough. "What if he never comes home, Jessie? Or if he does come home and brings a wife with him? I'll never have the chance for him to forgive me."

"You think the woman that was with him might be his wife?"

"I don't know. They seemed awfully familiar with each other."

Jessie had spun about in her chair, mouth gapped open. "And you didn't stick around long enough to find out?"

Frustration made Eva snap, "I couldn't."

"Like hell you couldn't!" Jessie stomped across the room and grabbed Eva's elbows. "I know you better than that. Some people may think you're shy and quiet. But I know the real you. You've come through every blow life has given you as a stronger, more determined person. There isn't anything you're afraid of tackling."

"That's only because I've had all of you to lean on. You, and Willamina, and Ma, even the men, you've all been there for me."

"And we still are. Always will be."

Eva broke free, moving across the room. Frustration churned inside her veins. She twirled around, facing Jessie again. "But this time is different. There's nothing I can do."

"Oh, yes there is."

"What?" She flayed her arms in the air, feeling completely helpless. "What is there I can do this time? Bug's in Pennsylvania. He has his oil! He has another woman!"

"But he doesn't have his family." Jessie took her hands. "We both know he'll be home. It's already been too long."

"But what if she's with him when he does come home? It'll be too late for me. Probably already is."

Jessie cupped Eva's cheeks, looking deep into her eyes. "Don't wish for trouble, Eva. Don't give it the opportunity to take hold, because then it will. Instead, focus on what you can do to welcome him home. Be here and be ready for him. Show him exactly what he left behind."

"What if he no longer wants what he left

behind?"

A deep growl emitted from Jessie, the sound completely out of place from someone so sweet and pretty. "Eva Robertson, you make me want to scream!"

"I want to scream, too!" she shouted back.

"Then do it!" Jessie yelled. "Scream until your chest burns and your throat is on fire!"

Jessie's shout made her irritation burst. Eva drew in a deep breath that built in her chest until her lungs were about to explode. Throwing her head back, she released the air and pent up frustration with a scream that must have driven the birds from their perches clear to Dodge. If any were left in the trees, the yell Jessie emitted would surely have sent the last ones flapping their wings.

Their joined howls softened as the last bits of air seeped over their lips. Eva glanced to Jessie, and their eyes spoke. As one they took another deep breath and opened their mouths.

This screech was interrupted as the back door flew open. Summer, waving a cocked pistol, flew into the house. "What? What did you see?" Flaying the gun in every direction, she hollered, "Where? Where is it?"

Coughing and sputtering, Eva waved her arms. Unable to speak with the flames still racing along her vocal cords, she shook her head. "Nothing," she squeaked, flinching at the pain in her throat.

Summer glanced at her anxiously, before spinning about to stare at Jessie who collapsed on a chair in a fit of giggles. Releasing the hammer carefully, Summer set the pistol on the table. "And what, Mrs. Quinter, do you find so funny?" The smile on her face denied the tone of her voice.

With one hand on her stomach, Jessie tipped her head back, looking up at Summer. "You, Mrs. Quinter, and the way you stormed through the door."

Both women laughed, and Eva, smiling at their antics, experienced another wave of regret building in her chest. She wanted to be Mrs. Quinter, too. More than anything else on earth, that's what she wanted.

"So," Summer said, resting both hands on her hips. "What's going on here? What was all the screaming about?"

"A tension releaser," Jessie offered off-handedly. "What are you doing here?"

Summer sat down, but her stare was on Eva. "I came to find out exactly what happened between you and Bug. And don't tell me you didn't see him. No matter what you said the other night, I know differently."

Eva took a breath. Whether it was due to the fact Summer was half Sioux, or because Jonas Quinter, the brothers' father, was her guardian angel, somehow Summer had the uncanny ability to know things others didn't—couldn't. Afraid of what Summer did know, Eva attempted to bring up a different topic. "Where's Drew?"

Summer gave Jessie a knowing look before her dark-eyed gaze met Eva's again. "Drew is two now, and lives his life planted on his father's hip, following in Snake's footsteps, or seated on the saddle in front of him. My baby is just fine, so don't try to change the subject."

"Bug has a girlfriend," Jessie stated so matter of fact that Eva's heart jolted.

"No!" Summer gushed. Her long black hair swished as she flipped her head to gawk at Jessie.

Jessie nodded, and as one, the other two turned to stare at Eva.

Her legs gave out. Grabbing the nearby chair, Eva planted her bottom on the seat and let her head fall onto the table top. "Yes," she moaned into the wood.

Someone smacked the table. Eva lifted to see who it was.

Summer's hand thumped the table again, and then she pointed at Eva. "Sit up, take a deep breath, and start at the beginning. I need to know everything. Every little detail."

Eva did as instructed, sat up and took a deep breath. As it exhaled, she flopped her head backwards, resting her neck on the top rung of the chair.

"I'll make a fresh pot of coffee," Jessie said, standing up.

"Make it tea, please." Summer patted her slightly rounded stomach.

Over a couple pots of tea, and the coffee cake Summer had carried in the basket she'd had looped over the arm not holding the gun when she burst through the door, Eva repeated her New York City adventure. This time with Summer's gentle ways, she didn't feel like screaming, instead a deep, enveloping gloom hovered around her shoulders.

Summer stared across the table. "Oh, no," she whispered.

"What?" Jessie asked.

A moment later, Summer was on her feet and pulling Eva from her chair. "Oh, no you don't."

"Don't what?" Eva asked. Drained of energy, she barely managed to stand.

"There was a time when I was so depressed I didn't want to get up in the mornings." She hooked her arm through Eva's. "Snake threw me in a tub of water."

"He didn't?" Jessie asked, eyes round.

"Yes, he did. Thank goodness. Something had to snap me out of it." She nodded to Jessie. "Let's go for a walk. The sunshine will do us all good."

They went out the back door and down the

steps, arms hooked at the elbows like three schoolgirls. They walked past the flower garden in full bloom, to the center of the yard where the wind twisted their skirts and the sun kissed their faces. Eva lifted her chin, and closing her eyes, soaked up the rays.

"I'm going to tell you what Buffalo Killer once told me," Summer said.

"Oh, what's that?" Eva asked without opening an eyelid.

"Don't let someone, anyone, dead or alive, steal your joy."

Eva lowered her face and opened her eyes. The words seeped in, but their meaning eluded her. She had no joy. Blinking at the brightness, she let her eyes readjust and gazed about, at the blue sky, the field of waving, golden brown grasses, and the still standing, still solid, sod house she and Willamina had called home.

She moved then, toward the tiny fence circling a single headstone. Right now she missed Willamina as badly as she had those first few days after her death. Jessie and Summer followed, and soon all three of them sat cross-legged beside the grave, plucking the weeds growing amongst the grass.

"Bug's not in love with that other woman," Summer said, snapping the head off a yellow dandelion.

"He's not?" Hope rose in Eva's chest. Quelling the optimism, she asked, "How do you know?"

Summer's smile was soft and sweet. "The same way you know." She patted her stomach. "That little part of all us that knows right from wrong. Good from bad. It tells me Bug loves you."

Eva tossed aside a weed and watched as it fought the wind to find a place to land. "The only thing I know is she was very beautiful and by the looks of her clothes, very rich."

"You're very rich, too," Jessie offered.

"Do you really think Bug cares that much about money?" Summer asked. "He loved you long before you were rich."

Eva let out a false laugh. "People change." Her gaze went to the waving field of summer grass. "The only thing about Bug that will never change is oil. He's loved it for years. Probably always will." She lifted a hand. "You can't see them, but that field is full of little markers he'd set out. Places he swore oil flowed deep beneath the ground."

An eerie feeling made Eva turn to the other two women. Jessie and Summer stared at each other, as if they were silently communicating. The eeriness grew. Eva was somewhat afraid, but still had to ask, "W-what are you two thinking?"

Jessie turned to Eva. "Did Bug ever say exactly how they get the oil out of the ground?"

Frowning, Eva answered, "Derricks and pipes."

Summer was chewing on her bottom lip. "Snake won't be starting wheat harvest for a month or more."

Nodding, Jessie added, "Kid must have a book on how to build a derrick."

Eva waved a finger between the two. "What are you thinking?"

"If Bug wants oil, give him oil," Summer said.

"Right here in your backyard," Jessie added.

"I don't know anything about oil," Eva admitted.

"This isn't about oil, Eva," Jessie assured. "It's about the man you love."

****

Bug followed the constable down the hall, never once letting his gaze bounce to the cells he passed. He didn't want to see the faces of the men he'd heard crying deep in the night. Their late night whimpers would stick with him long enough. There was no need for images to join the sounds.

At the end of the hall, the constable pulled open a door and gave Bug a shove toward the stairs. Pebbles poked through his socks as he climbed. At the top of the stairway, an alcove was littered with boots of every shape and size.

"Find a pair," the constable said.

Bug scanned, but the sheer number made finding the ones that one day had been his impossible—besides the fact that every boot was scuffed and worn. His had been fairly new, and as far as he could see, not included in the pile. He picked up two boots that might be a pair, then again, might not. They fit, and would serve their purpose until he could purchase a new pair.

The constable then led him to another door and threw it open. It was like going from night to day, not only did sunlight fill the room, but the dankness and dirt from the lower floor was replaced with polished marble and whitewashed walls.

Bug squared his shoulders, encouraging the change to wash over him as well, and strolled beside the constable across the room and down another hallway. The man opened a door and waved a hand.

"Jack!" Bug rushed forward. "Damn, it's good to see you."

Jack held his hand out, but Bug brushed it aside to give the man a good hug. Laughing, Jack hugged him back, but then said, "It's not over yet, Bug."

"I know, but..." He gave a low whistle. "It's bad down there."

"I'm sure it is. Come on, the Judge wants to see us in his chambers." Jack led the way across the room and pulled open yet another door.

The man sitting behind a big desk was dressed in black, completely bald, and frowning. All in all, he reminded Bug of a school teacher he once had. His stomach quivered as if it was full of grasshoppers.

"Gentlemen, please, take a seat," the Judge said,

slipping on a pair of round, wire-rimmed glasses.

Bug glanced around the room, taking in the wood-paneled walls and thick leather furniture. He stepped around a chair and lowered himself onto the cushion.

"Judge Holden, I see your painting arrived," Jack said.

Glancing up, Bug froze.

Hanging above the Judge's head was a painting of cowboys branding young stock. The men in the picture caught and held his attention. It was Kid and his foreman, old Joe.

The scene was so real, it was as if they were in the room with him. He could almost hear Joe's scratchy, gruff laugh, and an urge to wrap his arms around his oldest brother had his clenched hands throbbing.

"Yes, yes, it did," the Judge said. "It's magnificent, isn't it? You know I traveled across Kansas once. Took the train all the way to the coast and back. It's amazing how the round trip that took Lewis and Clark two and a half years, now takes nine days. Of course, I didn't take the same route they did, I went through Kansas and out to California. This picture reminds me of that trip every time I look at it."

Bug couldn't pull his eyes away. What had he been thinking? Staying out here, when he had all that back in Kansas. The sun, the wide open spaces, and most of all, his family.

"Well, let's see what we have here, shall we," Judge Holden continued. "Mr. Quinter, it says here you were arrested for thievery."

"Excuse me, Judge," Jack said. "But Mr. Quinter was set up. I assume you received the testimonials of the two young lads. If not, the boys are sitting out front in the waiting room, ready for questioning."

"Yes, I have them here. Was just reading them."

The Judge peered over the top rim of his glasses, eyeballing Bug. "This young woman who claims you stole her purse, had you ever seen her before, Mr. Quinter?"

"No, sir."

"And the pouch they found in your pocket, that wasn't familiar either?"

"No, sir."

The Judge nodded, and made a notation on the pad in front of him. He then turned to Jack. "Mr. Houston, it appears you have done a lot of work since Friday."

"Yes, sir, I have. Mr. Quinter is a close friend and is anxious to return to Kansas. Which is where he was on his way to, when he was arrested." Jack leaned back. "He's very good friends with Miss Reynolds."

Pulling his thick brows into a frown, Judge Holden asked, "Reynolds?"

Jack nodded to the painting.

The Judge turned wide eyes to Bug. "Eloisa Reynolds? You're friends with her?"

A soft, comforting smile rose from his heart and settled on his mouth. "Yes, sir. Matter of fact, as soon as I get home, I plan on marrying her."

"Were you at the show the other night?"

"Yes, sir."

"Her work is truly remarkable." The Judge turned around to gaze up at the painting for a few minutes. When he spun back around, he laid his pen on the desk, and met Bug's gaze eyeball to eyeball. "I can make this incident go away, Mr. Quinter. By this afternoon you could be on a westbound train."

Bug nodded, knowing there was more to come. He's was willing to do anything. "I'd be obliged, sir."

"There was a painting at the show the other night. My wife fell in love with it, but it was already purchased."

"Which one?" Jack asked. "Describe it."

"It was of an Indian..."

Bug quit listening while his heart tumbled to his stomach. The very painting he'd accused Eva of exploiting Buffalo Killer and his People was the painting he needed in order to be a free man.

Would she ever forgive him? She probably hated him so much right now she'd rather spit in his eye than speak to him.

Because of him, she'd not only left her art show, but ran back to Kansas.

His gaze went to the painting. When his brothers heard how he'd treated her, they'd probably take him out back and not stop until he had two black eyes and several broken ribs.

And then there would be Ma to contend with.

"Wonderful, my wife will be so pleased."

Bug snapped his attention to Judge Holden. The man stood now, and Bug rose as well. Holden held his hand out. "Mr. Quinter, I wish you the best of luck with your marriage."

"Thank you, sir."

"And, Mr. Houston, I look forward to receiving that painting." The Judge and Jack shook hands.

"I'll get it to you as soon as she completes it," Jack promised.

The Judge squirmed slightly. "Um, Jack, do you think you could have her personalize it? Maybe just sign the back with, to Fred and Emma?"

"I'm sure that won't be a problem, Judge. You should have it by Christmas time," Jack assured as he moved to the door. "And thanks again. I'm glad we were able to work this out."

As soon as the door shut, Bug turned to Jack, "I'll pay you back, Jack. Whatever it cost you to pull this off, all of it."

Jack walked across the other room, toward the hallway door. "I know how much you made working for Staples. In the past three years you haven't made enough to even begin to cover a portion of what this little episode cost." Jack pulled the door open, and as Bug walked over the threshold, he added, "And it's not over, Bug."

Chapter Seven

Bug couldn't catch a train leaving New York until the next day. He could have taken a freight rail or two, but a passenger train, with connections to Dodge and then Scott, didn't leave until Tuesday afternoon. Jack had said if he was willing to wait, there was a luxury liner leaving on Wednesday, but Bug couldn't wait. Wearing new boots, clothes, and hat, he handed over his ticket, took a seat, and let out the biggest sigh of relief a man ever exhaled.

There hadn't been a time in his life where he was happier to say good riddance to a city. What all these people found here, he'd yet to discover. No, he'd never discover it, because he'd never be back. Legs stretched out in front of him, and with the brim of his hat pulled over his eyes, he waited for the chugging and clanking to begin.

Half an hour later, he still waited. How many times would that conductor yell *'All aboard'*? He stuck his head out the window. There was still a stream of folks walking up the steps. This car was already full, he was scrunched up next to the window, due to the overly large woman who'd plopped down beside him, and across from him, three kids squirmed about on the tiny bench.

He liked kids, was looking forward to seeing all of his nieces and nephews. Would he even recognize them? The three across from him, two boys and a girl, must be siblings because all three had red hair and freckle covered faces. Their bright green eyes landed on him.

He grinned.

In unison, all three stuck their tongues out.

He turned back to the window. Whipper-snaps. His mother would have thumped all three of them on the back of the head if she'd seen that. A shiver ran up his spine. He spun from the window and surveyed the seats filling the car. Hell, every bench held kids—some of them still in nappers. There were only about four adults, including him and the fat lady next to him in the entire car. And the row outside the window, still boarding, were kids, too.

He shivered.

Three days later, Bug squeezed his temples. They'd crossed the Kansas state line this morning, and the stops there had him more frustrated than all the others. The occupants of the long train had dwindled, but the whimpering and crying remained. Bouncing off the dirty floors and soot covered walls like acorns falling off a tree.

He couldn't blame the children. It hurt to watch them go. All he could do was hope the folks who took them in were kind and would give the kids a good home. Every town they came to, the adults would parade a dozen or so children out onto the platform and auction them off like they were cattle in the stockyards.

Appalled at the first stop, he'd questioned the fat lady, who thankfully was now on a different car. He'd made her so mad she'd turned beat red— moments before she hit him over the head with her satchel.

A kinder, thinner, but older woman had explained it to him. Called it an Orphan Train. Mrs. King said she was part of a mission that rescued homeless children from the streets of New York and transported them west, offering folks along the way the opportunity to adopt them. It sounded a whole lot nicer than it actually was. Brothers and sisters were separated, and the rock in Bug's guts said the siblings would never see each other again.

Hell, he'd considered telling the train to drive straight to Scott were he'd beg his family to take the kids in. What was happening wasn't right. He'd told as much to the kinder woman, but Mrs. King made him see reason. His family couldn't possibly take in over a hundred children. But damn if it wasn't hard to watch them walk off the train on shaky little legs and with tear stained faces.

The three redheaded kids from the bench across from his were siblings. Tucker, Reed, and Heather. Tucker was a smart kid, knew his numbers and letters. He was seven, and the oldest. Reed, who was reed thin and coughed a lot, was five, and little Heather, who right now was tucked under Bug's arm, sound asleep, was only four.

A shrill whistle split the air, and her little body jumped.

"Shh," Bug said, patting her tiny arm. "It's all right."

She snuggled in a bit closer, but when the whistle blasted again, she sat straight up. "Are we stopping again?"

"Yes, darling, we are," he admitted. Her little face fell. His heart constricted. "Don't worry. You won't have to get off here."

"Are you sure, Bug?" Reed asked, covering a cough.

"Yes, I'm sure."

Screeching to a halt that tossed the passengers about in their seats, the train stopped as the whistle blew a final time. Tucker and Reed stuck their noses against the smeared window. It was a small crowd this time, nothing like those in Kansas City.

"Sit down, boys," he instructed. The auctions were hard to watch, yet at the same time, he'd fought with himself to pull his eyes away.

The click of heels stopped near the benches he

and the kids sat on. It felt as if fingers of steel wrapped around his spine. He glanced up. Shaking his head.

Mrs. King puckered her lips. "Mr. Quinter." Her voice had the school marm tone that could turn fire to ice.

"No," he insisted, tightening his arm around Heather.

"Mr. Quinter." Mrs. King curled one finger. "A word with you please."

He couldn't argue with her in front of the children, he knew that, so planting Heather between her brothers, he leaned close. "Don't move. All three of you stay put."

They nodded. "We will, Bug. I'll make sure." Tucker had a cowlick on top of his head that could make a tornado jealous.

"Good boy, Tucker." Bug ruffled the kid's hair, and then ran a hand threw his, smoothing it back before he put his hat on and followed Mrs. King to the back of the train car.

"Mr. Quinter. You have to stop this. You've refused to allow those children to leave the train since New York."

He folded his arms. He knew what he'd done. She didn't need to repeat it.

She let out a sigh. "All you're doing is getting their hopes up."

"I already told you. I'll take those three."

"And I told you, that's impossible. We have people in the field who have interviewed families and assure they meet all of the qualifications to adopt." She shook her head. "You haven't been qualified."

"That's because you won't give me the papers. I told you I'll fill them out. I got a Ma, and brothers, and sisters-in-law, and—"

She interrupted, "And you aren't married, nor

do you own a home and have regular income."

He took his hat off, wiped away the sweat on his forehead and plopped it back on. "I'll be taking care of that as soon as I arrive."

"And once you do," she said kindly, "if you are still interested in adopting, you can contact us and we'll send out a field worker to interview you. If it all works out, you might even be able to adopt children off the next train."

"I don't want kids off the next train, I want those three. Tucker, Reed, and Heather."

"Mr. Quinter," she said, sounding quite frustrated.

"Mrs. King," he reiterated, feeling as irritated as a trapped coyote.

They both turned when "Mrs. King!" was shouted from the back of the train.

"Oh, great," Bug said. "The fat lady's back."

"Mr. Quinter!" Mrs. King admonished, but she didn't hide the tiny smile tugging on the edges of her mouth.

Bug grinned back.

She let out a little huff and poked the tip of one finger against his chest. "Those children get off at the next stop."

He nodded.

As if she didn't believe him, she repeated, "The next stop, Mr. Quinter."

****

Eva packed up her paints, carefully stowing them in the basket. The painting of the derrick was coming along much better than the drilling. Kid and Snake, as well as some of Kid's ranch hands, had worked on it all week. The tall, A-framed scaffolding stood against the blue sky like an odd, hollow building as it held the long lengths of pipe that descended deep into the earth. Yesterday, they'd hooked it to Snake's thrashing machine. He'd said something about using the steam powered engine to drive the pole into the ground. Too busy capturing the event on canvas, she hadn't completely listened to his explanation, until last night that is.

Snake had said they'd hit rock that was too hard to drive through. Kid said he'd search his books and try to figure out what else they could try. They would, she knew that, but she also knew they were needed at home, especially Snake. The welcome home party he'd planned for September was tonight. When Eva and Jessie and Summer first came up with the drilling plan, the men had been skeptical, but since neither Snake nor Kid were willing to deny their wives practically anything, they'd soon agreed to the venture. Eva had financed it, and helped the first few days, but the men insisted she stay home and let them do the heavy work.

She glanced at the sky. It was past noon, time for her to get ready and go help with last minute preparations. Hog and Randi as well as Skeeter and Lila had arrived yesterday by train. Holding the painting with one hand, she folded up the easel, slipped it over her arm, and picked up the basket of paints. Balancing everything as the wind tossed and teased her skirt, she walked for home. It was sure to be a festive night—but a lonely one.

An hour later, dressed in a pale blue dress she'd bought in New York, she wondered if it was too fancy for the celebration. The chiffon was light and airy, and the matching shawl would ward off any chill that might happen once the sun set. Jack had told her to buy it, and he certainly had good taste. She patted the pleats at her waist one last time. Yes, she'd wear it, because if nothing else, it made her feel pretty. Lila, Randi, Jessie, and Summer were so beautiful, Eva always felt like a field mouse next to them. Not that any of them ever did anything to make her feel that way. Matter of fact, it was just the opposite, the women loved helping each other put up their hair and choose outfits for one another to wear.

She'd joined them more than once, dressing for different occasions, but like everything else, she made herself feel like an outsider. The only one who wasn't a Quinter. May never be one.

Her gaze went to the bedroom window, and she crossed the room to peer out. Far off, just grazing the tip of the horizon was the top of the derrick. The men had worked until sweat soaked their shirts. A few days ago, with Jessie and Summer's excitement, it seemed like a good plan. Now, it felt like a failure. She had nothing to draw Bug home.

Eva spun about and without a backward glance, strolled out of her bedroom. Summer would be disappointed to know Eva was once again wallowing in self pity. She couldn't do that to the woman. Squaring her shoulders, Eva marched down the stairs. Tonight, for everyone who looked on, she was going to be happy and gay, no matter how hard it was.

Her optimism helped, but more than that, the camaraderie at Snake and Summer's soon had her heart singing with happiness at the love flowing around her. The entire county had turned out for the event, as well as those from neighboring ones. Hog had his fiddle going long before the sun started to set, and anyone else who had a musical instrument took over whenever he needed a break.

Table upon table held an assortment of food and beverages, and children played games all afternoon. She'd even taken a turn in the three-legged race, partnering with August. Her pale blue dress now had a long streak of dirt down one side—proof they'd fallen over the finish line.

Elliott Hampton was in attendance, and Eva danced with the lawyer when he asked, enjoying the lively tune someone blew into their harmonica. It was a shuffle dance, where you switched partners continuously, and each time Elliott caught her hand, he'd smile so brightly lines crinkled around his eyes.

When the dance ended, Eva, breathless, allowed him to escort her to the row of benches.

"Mrs. Quinter," Elliott said, nodding at Ma.

"Mr. Hampton," Ma responded.

Eva took a seat beside the older woman. "Thank you for the dance, Elliott."

"You're very welcome." He gave a slight bow at the waist, and then moved along to join a group of men chatting nearby.

"He's a nice fella, that Mr. Hampton," Ma said, following Elliott's departure with a steady stare.

"Yes, he is," Eva admitted.

Ma let her gaze roam to the children playing hopscotch. "He's got a good business going, too, being a lawyer and all."

"Yes, he does," Eva answered, wondering if more was coming.

It was. Ma let out a deep sigh before she said, "Willamina would be proud of you Eva. I am, too. Going to New York City and all like you did. You're a strong girl. Got a good head on your shoulders, using the talent God gave you like you are."

"Thank you, Ma." Eva breathed through the pain that slipped in at the thought of Willamina not being there. "I miss her. Some days I miss her like it was just yesterday."

Ma laid a hand on her knee, patted it softly. "I know. We all do."

Twilight was settling, veiling the earth with a muted light that made everything look soft and gentle. A couple of men played a ballad on their guitars. The music matched the evening air with perfection.

"You know, Eva," Ma said, "I'd never make you

do something you didn't want to do."

Eva turned, and searched Ma's wrinkled face for more. Her pale green eyes held a unique sincerity. "I know, Ma."

"I promised Willamina. It would always be your choice." With that, Ma stood up and walked across the yard.

Eva sat, wondering exactly what Ma meant. She hadn't found a conclusion when Elliott stepped in front of her again. "Would you care for another dance?" he asked.

Surrounded by her grandchildren, Ma, as if she sensed Eva's stare, turned around. Ma smiled and gave a little nod. Eva looked up, found Elliott smiling down at her, and nodded, "Yes, Elliott, I'd like that."

****

Bug stepped off the train in Scott City. His shoulders dropped clear to his hips. The town was as dead as Dry Lake in July. The only thing moving was a dust devil stirred up by the wind. He hadn't wired anyone, so he shouldn't have expected someone to meet him, but would it have been too much to ask to at least see a familiar face? Hell, just a face.

The train whistle blew as it began to chug away from the station. Moving across the platform, he found a hint of joy in the fact the porter hadn't just tossed him out the window as the train rolled by.

He made his way down the empty street to the livery. A closed sign flapped in the wind. "What the hell?" Spinning around, he looked for any sign of life. The sun was still out, yes, it was falling fast, but the whole town couldn't be sleeping this early.

Maybe there was some kind of a plague. He pinpointed the first house and bore his stare on the door. Nope, there wasn't a red flag signaling quarantine. Picking out other doors, he searched them all for some type of sign from where he stood outside the livery.

A whinny sounded behind the door. He pushed, and though it creaked on its hinges, the door swung open. Several horses stood in their stalls, munching on oats and swishing their tales at pesky flies.

He searched, but couldn't find anything to write with. Scratching his head at the emptiness of the town, he located tack and saddled a horse. He only needed it overnight. Hopefully, Art Rockford still owned the livery. The old man wouldn't mind if he borrowed one.

Riding out of town, he couldn't help but glance over his shoulder, once again, probing for anything that might say someone lived behind the dark windows. He pulled the horse up short. Hell, it was Saturday night and even the Bull's Horn Saloon had a closed sign hanging on the door.

He kneed the animal. Something was definitely wrong. Eva's place was on the way to his. He'd stop there first. Besides wanting to see her, surely she'd know what was going on.

The horse was heaving, and they were both sweating when he wondered which fell first, the reins from his fingers or his jaw. Eva's little soddy had transformed itself into a two-story white-washed house with red trim on every window. A matching barn stood off on one side.

Something behind the house caught his attention. He reached down, gathered the reins, and made his way around the west end of the house that was covered with windows. There stood the soddy. He slipped from the saddle and looped the reins around a spindly tree. The big house looked as empty as those in Scott had, so he walked to the soddy.

He didn't go inside, not only because it, too, looked empty, but because the little fence beside it drew his attention. His heart thumped in his chest.

"Aw, Willamina," he whispered, opening the gate. Flowers, wilted and limp, lay near the base of the headstone. He knelt, and bowed his head.

There were a million things he wanted to say. A hundred apologizes and a thousand I love yous, but none of them came out his mouth. They didn't need to. The wind whistling over the prairie calmed, and Bug experienced a sweet peacefulness.

He stayed there until the sun's light mingled with the night sky falling to take its place. Wiping the backs of his hands over his eyes, he whispered, "I'll be back to visit you on a regular basis. I promise," before he made his way out of the little enclosure. Glancing at the empty house, wondering about how many other changes he'd encounter, he climbed on the borrowed horse.

Nothing ever stayed the same. He'd always known that, but had never understood it as profoundly as he did right now. Letting the animal set the pace, he traveled down the road to Snake's place, contemplating how he'd react to other changes that must have occurred.

The music hit his ears first, a soft lullaby type tune. The music was followed by the shouts and laughter of people. Lots of people. Bug brought the animal to a stop and stared at the party. That's why no one was in Scott. Every last one of them had to be at his brother's house.

His family didn't know he was coming, so it couldn't be a party for him. It sure didn't look like a funeral. He nudged the horse forward.

The crowd was so busy not a single person noticed him. Oh, some glanced his way, but not long enough to recognize him. He unsaddled the horse and let it loose in the corral with several dozen others, and then made his way to the yard. Another song had started up and couples, arms folded around each other, swayed to the soft tune emitting from the strings of a pair of guitars.

He picked out couples, Kid and Jessie, Skeeter and Lila, Hog and Randi, and Snake and Summer. There were a few others he knew, but more that he didn't.

Then, as if he'd been sucker punched, his gut hit his backbone. Eva hung onto a tall fella as he sashayed her slowly over the ground. Her face looked up at the man's, and was smiling, as was the fella's.

Bug balled the hands hanging at his side.

"Uncle Bug! Hey Pa! It's Uncle Bug!"

Eva dropped her hands from Elliott's shoulders, turning to where August's shout had come from. As if it would help to hold the sob at the back of her throat, she covered her mouth with one hand.

It *was* Bug. Standing not ten feet away. Her heart started and stopped a dozen times within a spilt second. She saw no one, heard nothing, except him. Starting at his boots, she followed the long lines of his legs, over his hips, up his chest, neck, and chin. When her eyes met his, she gasped again.

He glared at her just as he had back in New York, when she'd told him about Willamina. Her nose burnt as she inhaled, trying to hold the tears at bay. He'd never forgive her. Never.

His eyes never wavered as he walked forward. Every step brought him closer. She couldn't have moved even if she wanted to. Her hand did fall away from her mouth when he stopped in front of her.

"Bug," she muttered.

He grabbed her, one hand on each side of her head, and the next instant his mouth crushed against hers. The heat and fury of his lips took her even more by surprise than his appearance had, but it only lasted a second, for then her mouth pinned beneath his, leaped into life. Searching, wanting, needing, her lips mingled, tasted, and explored his mouth as feverishly as his did hers.

Her hands found his sides and dug into the leather of his vest. She stepped closer, pressing her breasts against his solid chest. His fingers dug into her hair, squeezing her scalp with divine pressure, and his tongue was in her mouth, hers in his. The action had her head swooning and her toes curling. She wrapped her arms around his back, holding on and begging him to never, ever stop.

She sucked in air every chance she had, knowing she needed it to live. But she wanted more. He was devouring her from the inside out, the outside in, and she responded, knowing she needed him more than she required air.

He was the one to finally break their connection. Trailing kisses along the side of her face, he pressed her head against his chest and laid his cheek on the top of her head. "Eva, oh, Eva girl," he moaned.

Kissing the skin left open by the v of his shirt, she said the only thing repeating itself in her head, "Bug, oh, Bug."

Chapter Eight

The world seemed so perfect with his arms holding her tight. Eva had no idea what went on around her, that is until Bug lifted his head. "August," he said, "Find the preacher."

"Uh?"

Eva didn't know if she said it, or if August had.

Bug grasped her face again, tugging and forcing her to look straight into his eyes. The grin on his face made his eyes glimmer in the pale light. "Find a preacher, August," he repeated. "Eva and I are getting married."

Her heart stopped mid-beat. "W-we are?" she stuttered.

"Yes, we are," he said, dipping his face to hers.

Cheers broke out, along with clapping and shouting.

His lips found hers again, and her heart leaped back into life. Thumping and jumping every direction. He kissed her long and hard, until the world around them ceased to exist.

She was somewhere lost in a brilliant, wonderful place when a sharp and thundering blast rattled her eardrums. Eva spun about, whether on her own or with Bug's help she had no idea. Blinking and shaking her head at the ringing in her ears, she attempted to focus on the crowd of men and women. Everyone stared at the house.

Ma Quinter stood on the front step. Her big shotgun was in her hands, and the barrel, pointed at the sky, had smoke swirling out the end.

"Dang it, Stephanie, put that blasted thing

away!" Sheriff Turley shouted.

Ma pointed the gun at the Sheriff. "Stay right there, Malcolm." The barrels swung to the edge of the crowd. "You, too, Reverend Kirkpatrick. There ain't gonna be no wedding tonight."

Eva froze.

Kid shouldered his way past the men, holding his arms out in front of him. "Give me the gun, Ma."

"There ain't gonna be no wedding, Kid." Ma repeated.

Kid walked up the stairs. "No, Ma, there won't be a wedding tonight."

"I mean it, Kid."

"Just give me the gun, Ma. I promise there won't be a wedding tonight," Kid repeated calmly.

Ma handed the gun over, and the look in her eyes pierced Eva's heart. She read the apology, but there were no answers for the zillion questions zipping through her mind.

"What the hell," Bug exclaimed, staring at the porch.

The girls, Jessie, Lila, Randi, and Summer, rushed past Kid. Still frozen, Eva watched as they escorted Ma into the house. Her mind couldn't comprehend it all. Bug being home, asking her to marry him...And Ma saying no.

"What's wrong with Ma?" Bug asked.

Eva had no answer, but even if she had, Snake, in his calm and understanding way, said, "She's just shocked, Bug. We all are. Why didn't you say you were coming home?"

"Yeah," Hog agreed. "We barely hear from you for three years, and then you show up, ready to marry little Eva, here." One of Hog's big arms wrapped around Eva's shoulders and pulled her away from Bug.

Bug snatched her elbow, tugging her back. "Everyone's always known Eva and I would get married."

Skeeter, tall and wiry, stepped in front of Bug. "Maybe three years ago. Things are different now."

Snake, Hog, and Skeeter were all big men, with blond wavy hair and pale gray-green eyes like Ma's. Eva had never doubted the brothers liked her, always knew they would stand up for her or protect her if the need ever arose, but she'd never dreamed they'd prevent her from obtaining the one thing she wanted more than anything else in this world—their little brother.

Bug, lips pursed, stared at each of his brothers. Tension sparked in the air.

Kid, the oldest, and the one Bug's dark hair and eyes resembled, stepped up to the gathering then. His gaze was controlled and even as it went from brother to brother. When his dark eyes landed on Bug, he shook his head. "What are you trying to do? Get us all killed."

"Hell no, Ki—"

"You waltz in here like you were just home yesterday, grab Eva, and tell August to get the preacher," Kid interrupted. "No, hello. No, good to see you. No, I'm home!" He exaggerated a shout by throwing his arms in the air. "Did you really think that wasn't going to set Ma off? Did you lose all your brains out east?"

"No, Kid, I-I," Bug stuttered, glancing between the brothers.

Kid looked at her. His brown eyes, softened. "You all right, Eva?"

She nodded, but for some reason, couldn't look at Bug.

Kid gestured toward the crowd of folks murmuring and shuffling about. "Snake, go tell your guests the ruckus is over." He glanced at Bug. "But the party's not." Grabbing Bug around the waist, Kid hoisted him in the air. "Our little brother is home!"

Skeeter was the voice she heard above the others. "Start the music, fellas! We got some celebrating to do!"

Eva took a step away, but as soon as Kid let him down, Bug's hand found her elbow again and tightened to spin her about.

"Eva, what I said, I meant. We're getting married." Bug nodded toward the house. "If not tonight, tomorrow then."

She bit her lip, glancing between him and the house.

"Don't you want to marry me?" he questioned. The perplexed look on his face made her step closer.

"Yes," she admitted, resting a hand on his chest. The solid thud of his heart ricocheted of her palm. "Yes, I do, Bug." Her gaze went to the house again. "But right now, I better go see to Ma. Make sure she's all right."

He looked at her perceptively, as if reading every pitter-patter of her heart. A tiny grin lifted the sides of his mouth before he nodded. "All right."

She started to walk away, but he still had a hold of her elbow and stopped her once again. "Eva, how do you feel about red-headed kids?"

Caught off guard and more than a little confused, she answered, "I think red-headed kids are just fine."

"So, you'd be okay if we had, say, three of them?"

Her cheeks flushed at the thought of the intimate act that produced children. She couldn't help but smile. The thought of having children with Bug was more than pleasurable. Attempting to downplay her delight, she warned, "Since we both have brown hair, I'd say it's highly unlikely we'd end up with one red-headed child, let alone three."

"But if we did, have three, you'd be okay with it?"

She'd agree to litter of puppies. Squelching a

giggle, she nodded. "Yes, I'd be okay with it."

"Good," he let out a loud sigh.

It was quite baffling. Her forehead tightened as she turned for the house again.

"Eva," Bug said, stopping her yet again. "What happened in New York, those things I said, I'm sorry. I don't think you're gullible. And you were right. There wasn't anything I could have done about Willamina."

"Oh, Bug." She fell back into his arms, overwhelmed by the guilt that roared up to slap her insides. "I'm so sorry about that."

"Shh," he whispered, kissing the top of her head. "It doesn't matter now at all." Rubbing his cheek against her head, he repeated, "Not at all."

The crowd moved in on them then, slapping Bug's back and offering greetings of hello. The actions forced Bug and Eva to separate, and with the men shouldering their way closer to him, he couldn't stop her as she slipped away. Making her way to the house, she did glance over her shoulder.

Standing a good half of a head taller than most of the other men, less his brothers, Bug's gaze met hers. His casual, yet, saucy wink sent her heart leaping about again. She grinned before turning around and bounding to the house.

Bug wanted to follow her, he didn't ever want Eva out of his sight again, but he hadn't forgotten the wrath of Ma. That would take a whole lot more than three years to forget. He wanted to see her, too. Ma was one of a kind, and she loved her family to no end. But he'd let the women calm her down a touch before making his way into the house. No matter what Kid thought, he hadn't lost one iota of his brain.

"Uncle Bug! Uncle Bug!" Something hit his chest so hard he had to lock his knees to keep from tumbling backwards. August wrapped both arms about his neck and created a choke hold on Bug that was almost life threatening. "I knew it was you. I just knew it!"

Bug caught the kid around the waist and hoisted him up, hugging and at the same time, keeping August from cutting off his air flow.

"I knew it was you as soon as you walked into the yard." August leaned back, eyeing Bug. "Where you been anyway?"

"You know I've been in Pennsylvania. You wrote me several times," Bug answered.

"Yeah, but you didn't write back much."

Bug set August on the ground. "Sorry. I'm not much of a letter writer." Rubbing the kid's mop of blond hair, he said, "Whoa, you've grown!" August stood nearly chest level.

"Yeah, well, I'm eleven now. If you'd been home, you'd know that."

Bug automatically turned toward the house. The women were still behind the closed door. "If I'd been home, there're a lot of things I'd know."

August started talking about all the things Bug had missed, from Snake and Summer's two-year-old son Drew, to how August's big yellow lab, Jerome was the best guard dog in the state. Bug didn't have a chance to answer. Someone slapped him on the back.

"Come on, little brother," Snake said, "Gerald hauled most of the Bull's Horn out and set it up behind the hayshed where Ma wouldn't see."

Hog, laughing his belly laugh, said, "Not that it did any good. She was back there before he served his first beer." He punched Bug in the arm, and then hooked his elbow around Bug's neck. While tucking Bug's head into his big shoulder, Hog knocked off Bug's hat and knuckled the top of his head.

Twisting and squirming, Bug finally got his head pulled out from Hog's grasp. Throwing a couple punches at Hog's gut, Bug dodged another head lock. "Come on, big brother, is that all you got?" he teased.

"I'll show you what I got," Hog insisted, attempting to snatch Bug's flaying fists.

"Hey, you two, I'm thirsty. Let's go," Kid said. Catching Bug off guard, Kid got him in a head lock.

Bug wrapped his arms around Kid and gave his oldest brother's back a couple good whacks. "It's good to be home, Kid. It's really good to be home."

Skeeter, standing nearby, planted Bug's hat back on his head when Kid let him loose. "It's good to have you home, baby brother."

By the time they rounded the hayshed, Bug had not only hugged all of his brothers, he'd stopped to greet, shake hands, or give bear hugs to several town folks. He caught sight of Art Rockford. "Hey Art!" he shouted. "I got one of your horses in the barn!"

Art waved. "Then were even! I still got the one you left at the livery three years ago. Maybe it's the same one!"

Laughter abounded, and the men crowded in around him as if he was novelty to ogle over. They all wanted to know how Pennsylvania was, and Bug, never one to back down from a good story, let loose a tale about a wildcatter who used nitro to frac a well.

"What the hell's a wildcatter, Bug?" someone yelled.

"We had a cat killing our calves last spring. Finally shot the thing. It had paws the size of horse hooves," someone else piped in.

"Nitro? As in nitroglycerin? That's some mighty stuff," another man offered.

Bug took a swig of his beer and relished the taste of good brew for a second before he swallowed. Then over the heads of those standing nearby, he shouted, "A wildcatter is someone who takes a chance and drills where his gut tells him." He spun to the other man. "Yup, nitro is. But I know how to use it. With one little bottle I could blow the devil out of hell if I could find a way to drop it on him."

The crowd roared, and Bug kept telling oil story after oil story. It was good to be home. Good to be Bug again instead of Brett. The crowd was full of his friends, good friends, and family. He considered his brothers some of his best friends.

Therefore, it was a good hour later when Bug had the courage to make his way to the house. The cups of beer he downed might have built his valor, but he believed he'd gained it himself, just somehow knew it was time to see Ma.

Jessie, Lila, Randi, and Summer had all been out to see him. Told him not to worry. Ma was fine, they'd said, she'd just been shocked at seeing him. He hoped that was the case. Eva hadn't come out yet. His heart, which had started to feel pretty normal again, slid down to his stomach to float in the beer he'd consumed. Life was full of ups and down and ins and outs, but dang it, he'd been put through a wringer the last two weeks. It was about time things settled down.

He stopped on the front porch, taking a deep breath and determining marrying Eva was the solution. Everything would fall into place when that happened.

Through the panes of glass beside him an image formed. Ma sat in the living room. Light from the lamp beside her chair reflected off the big window. Taking another deep breath to build up his reserves, Bug entered the house.

He wasn't even over the threshold when Ma asked, "So you finally came to say your how do's?"

A grin settled on his lips. The glint in her eyes said a whole lot more than her gruff tone. "Hey, Ma." He moved across the room and wrapped his arms around her as she hoisted herself from her chair.

His breath paused, she felt tinier and more fragile than he recalled. Stepping back, he looked down at her face. Wrinkles creased the skin, but a healthy glow sat on her cheeks, and her green eyes sparkled as bright as ever.

He hugged her again. "Aw, Ma, it's good to see you. Good to be home."

Her grasp was as firm as he remembered, and Bug held on tighter, let his mind wonder back through the years when her touch doctored his cuts and bruises, and her kisses healed his internal wounds.

"I've missed you, Buggie-boy," she said, lifting her face.

He planted a kiss on her wrinkled lips. "I missed you, too, Ma." Giving her one more hug, he added, "I love you."

She stepped out of his arms, and patted his cheek. "I love you, too. I love all you boys."

Bug waited until she'd sat back down in the rocking chair. He scooted the little stool she often propped her feet on closer in front of her, and sat on it. "I know," he admitted. "I've always known you loved us."

Ma started to rock. The slow, even motion gave him the impression she mulled over a few serious thoughts. "I love my girls, too." She kept rocking. "All of them. Jessie, Lila, Randi, Summer, and Eva." Her gaze met his for a moment. "Love them as much as I do you boys."

He nodded, knowing there was more. There always was with Ma, but besides that, he wanted to hear what she had to say.

"And those grandbabies, all of them, are nothing shy of angels. I didn't know I had that much love in my old heart. With every one, my heart just gets bigger and bigger."

Smiling, he agreed, "Yeah, they're good kids,

aren't they. There are a few new ones I see."

"Yup. Summer and Snake had Drew first. Then Hog and Randi had Josephine. Skeeter and Lila didn't wait long before having Steven, and then Kid and Jessie had baby Oscar."

He knew all this from their letters. Kid and Jessie now had three kids, as did Skeeter and Lila. If you added in September and August, Snake and Summer had three, too. The three he had to go fetch would catch him and Eva up to his brothers and their families. Only Hog would be left lagging behind in the kid department. Eva had said she wouldn't mind three kids, and the knowledge sent his heart skipping about. Tucker, Reed, and Heather would like Eva, and she'd make a wonderful mother.

"She's upstairs."

That snapped his attention. "Who?"

Ma laughed. "I could tell by the look on your face you were thinking of Eva."

Denying it was impossible, besides it would be stupid to try and lie to Ma. "Is she all right?"

"Yes, she's fine. She's reading the older ones a story. It's past their bedtime." Ma glanced to the window. "Though I don't know how they're gonna be able to sleep with all that ruckus going on out there."

"It's quite a party," Bug admitted.

"Well, the town hasn't had one for a long time. I suspect it'll carry on until it's time for morning milking."

Bug had figured as much. He nodded his agreement, and couldn't hold in his questions any longer. "Ma, I want to marry Eva."

The sigh that left her chest sent icy chills racing in his veins.

"I know you think you do," she said.

"I don't think—"

She held up a hand. "I promised Willamina that

Eva would marry whomever she chose."

"Well, she chose me."

Ma shook her head. "Years ago, maybe. But you've been gone a long time. You're not the same man you were when you left."

"Yes, I am."

"No, life does that to us." She pointed a finger at him. "The Bug who left here would never have treated a woman the way you did Eva tonight."

"What do yo—"

"I'm talking about the way you barreled in here. Grabbing her out of Elliott's arms and kissing her like she was a harlot." She continued as he started to protest, "And then shouting at August to get the preacher. That's no way to treat a woman. The Bug I used to know would never have done that."

"Ma, I—"

"Why even your clothes. Look at you. Dressed in black from head to toe, right down to those shining boots. The only folks around here that dress in black are preachers, and those peddlers who pass through now and again. Not even a gunslinger wears only black. He knows folks would run him out on a rail. But you..." She shook her head. "Strutting around in those new clothes like you got airs or something. That's not the Bug I know."

"Ma, it's me. I had to buy new clothes for the trip home." He didn't admit that Jack had picked out the pants, shirt, vest, and boots while Bug was at the hotel washing away the prison grime. They'd veered too far off the subject already.

As if she heard his thoughts, she sighed again. "Bug, I can't let you break that little girl's heart."

"Break her heart? I don't have any intention of breaking Eva's heart."

"I'm sure you don't." She leaned back in her chair. The rockers creaked as the chair swayed back and forth. "Eva's got a gentle soul, Bug. She's fragile."

Shivers rippled his face. "What's wrong? Is she ill?"

"No, I'm not talking about being sick. She's strong. A real hard worker. It's her soul I'm talking about. It's as gentle and pure as a newborn's. Always has been. Willamina and I both saw it. You used to know that." Her eyes met his with a serious gaze. "The old Bug saw it, too. He knew how to treat her."

His mind was a mixture of thoughts and viewpoints. Trouble was he wasn't sure if either were right. There was no doubt he'd changed a bit over the last few years, that happens when a man's out on his own, but Eva...she'd always been shy and soft spoken, still was. It was part of what he loved about her.

Ma didn't give him much time to sort things out. "You need to give her time to get to know you again. Let her decide if you are who she wants to marry," she said. "If in a few months she decides it is you, then we'll have a wedding."

"A few months?" he questioned. She couldn't possibly mean that long.

"Yes. You've been gone three years. A few more months ain't gonna matter."

"But, Ma." Bug bolted to his feet. His thoughts were once again tripping over themselves. The images of three little red-headed kids now were included.

She remained seated. "No, buts." Rocking back and forth, she said, "I won't change my mind on this, so don't try to make me."

"I don't have months. I have to get started drilling. I have to get a house. I have—"

"Why are you in such a hurry now?"

He rubbed at the throbbing in his temples.

The rockers plunked against the floor, coming to a stop. "If you were that much in love with her, you wouldn't have stayed away so long."

Bug's mind screeched to a stop, too. In the past three years, there had been one thing that had held strong in his mind. Eva. And how she was back here waiting for him. He then did something none of his brothers had ever dared to do—proclaim his mother was mistaken. "You're wrong, Ma."

He walked to the door where he stopped and spun around to face her. "I stayed away because of how much I love her."

Chapter Nine

Eva waited until Winifred's deep breaths said the child was sound asleep. Even though she was only three, Winifred had long blonde curls that hung to her waist. With her big blue eyes, the little angel looked identical to her mother, Jessie. Tucking the blanket beneath the child's chin, Eva dropped a feather-light kiss on the girl's forehead, and then did the same to six-year-old Kendra, who was sound asleep beside Winifred in the tiny bed. Kendra was Skeeter and Lila's oldest child, and she, too, resembled her mother to no end. She had Lila's red locks and spring-green eyes.

A smile fluttered across Eva's lips, recalling how Bug asked her about red-headed children. All three of Skeeter's kids had hair the color of a summer sunset. She'd never known Bug was so partial to it. But as she told him, since she had hair the color of a spring mud puddle and his was as dark as morning coffee, it was highly doubtful their children would have the beautiful locks that Kendra did.

Eva blew out the light and made her way to the door. September was just leaving the room across the hall. "Are the boys sleeping?" Eva asked.

"Yes. Joel fell asleep right away, but it took four stories for Charles to settle down. He's more like Skeeter."

"Yes," Eva agreed. "And Joel is more like his daddy." Kid and Jessie also had Oscar. He, along with the other two babies, Skeeter and Lila's son Steven, and Hog and Randi's daughter Josephine, were asleep in cradles in one of the other upstairs bedrooms.

September hovered over all of the children as if they were her own. "Thank you," the girl said, "for putting the girls down. I could tell how tired they were."

"You're welcome. I enjoy when I get to spend time with them. Children are so wonderful." Once again happiness settled in Eva's heart.

"Well, you and Uncle Bug could have your own by this time next year," September said with an impish grin.

Eva bowed her head, trying to hide the way her cheeks burned.

"Wasn't that romantic?" September asked.

"What?"

"The way he pulled you away from Elliott and then kissed you." September let out a big sigh. "I wish Grandma would have let the wedding happen tonight. That would have been perfect."

Eva wanted to admit she agreed, but didn't. She hooked her elbow with September's and led the girl down the hallway to the chair sitting outside the door where the babies slept. "Ma has her reasons. Don't say anything to her about it, okay."

"I won't. But, sheesh, she made Pa marry Summer while he was unconscious."

"I know."

"And she made Kid marry Jes—"

"I know." Eva interrupted. She knew all about how Ma had married off every one of the brothers. "She has her reasons this time. We'll just have to wait to see what they are."

"You really want to wait?"

No, Eva wanted to scream, but she couldn't release her frustration on September. "I've waited a long time. A bit longer won't matter."

"It sure would to me."

"September, is there someone you're sweet on?"

Eva changed the subject for two reasons. One she needed time to gather her own thoughts on Ma's reasons, and two, she was curious if September was fawning for someone.

"No," September assured. "I just know how much you love Uncle Bug."

"Yes, that I do."

September picked the book up off the chair seat, and then sat down. "Let me know if you want me to talk to Grandma. She listens to me." September was already opening the book to the page she'd marked with a slip of paper. When she wasn't watching the children, September was reading.

Eva kissed the top of the girl's head. "Thank you. I'll remember that." She turned to walk away, but then paused. "Have you said hello to Bug yet?"

"No. I figure I'll wait until morning, when we have time to talk. There are a few things I want to say to that young man."

September went from a child to an old woman and back again on a regular basis. Eva smiled. "All right. Feel free to come get me if you need help with the children."

The girl nodded, but her nose was already buried in the book. Eva made her way down the stairs. Ma sat in her rocking chair in the living room. Taking a fortifying breath, Eva walked across the room.

"How are the grandbabies?"

"Every last one of them is sound asleep, and being well looked after by September. Except for August of course."

"A team of wild horses couldn't pull him in here when his Pa and uncles are all out there." Ma patted the little stool near her feet. "Visit with me for a minute."

Eva sat, and folded her skirts around her knees. When she'd entered the house, the girls had Ma surrounded, and Eva had heard commotion coming from the kitchen. September had been herding the children upstairs, calming their fears caused by the gunfire. The women had soon followed, helping to dress the children for bed, and changing and caring for the babies who'd been awakened as well.

Her nerve endings pricked Eva's skin. She had to talk to Ma, but she didn't want to upset her all over again. Reaching out, she patted Ma's knees. "Are you doing all right?"

"I'm fine. How about you?"

"I'm fine."

Ma stuck her needle in the center of the cloth and then poked the embroidery hoop into the basket beside her chair. "Are you upset with me?"

"No." Eva shook her head, yet she had to be honest. "But I would like to know why you don't want Bug and I to get married."

"It's not that I don't want you two to get married. I can't let you marry."

"Why?"

"Well, Eva girl, that's kinda hard to explain, but I'll try. I was just like you, thought as soon as Bug got back from his oil searching tomfoolery, you and he'd marry up. I hoped he'd take up with Kid and his cows or Snake and his farming." Ma's weary gaze went to the window. Music still filled the air, as did happy shouts of people having a good time. "But, after a year went by, I figured that was no longer the plan." She turned and faced Eva again. "Willamina and I talked about it. We both agreed if Bug came back, there wouldn't be a wedding until you said you wanted one."

"But I do want one, Ma. I love Bug."

"I know you do, honey. I do, too. But we both love the Bug who used to be here. We don't know the man he's become." Ma patted Eva's hands. "I'll love him no matter what. I'm his, ma, I have to. But you…" she paused as if trying to find the right words. "Eva girl, it's one thing to find a man you gotta bed down with every night, but it's a whole other thing to find the one you want to bed down with every night for the rest of your life."

Eva let the words settle, trying to consider Ma's point of view, but there were too many other thoughts racing about. "I don't mean to sound disrespectful, Ma. But you didn't worry about that with the other boys. You forced each one of them into marriage."

"Yes, I did." Not an ounce of regret filtered Ma's words. "And I'll tell you why. 'Til my dying day I'll never forget riding up to that old sod house and finding little Jessie inside. That place wasn't fit for snakes to live in, let alone someone as sweet and innocent as her. I knew in an instant I was taking her home. There was no way I could let her live one more day in that place. I also knew Kid would know how to treat her. He already thought of himself as a king, he just needed a queen at his side. I knew Jessie would be his queen from the get go."

"And Lila and Skeeter?"

"Well, now that was a little different. Skeeter brought Lila home, and I thought she was a right fine girl. 'Til I discovered she was pregnant with little Kendra. I had to make those two get married on account of the baby. The good Lord would've struck me dead if I hadn't."

"And Hog and Randi?"

"Those two were in the same bed together in Dodge City." Ma's eyes grew stern. "You and I both know what happens to unmarried women in Dodge."

Eva swallowed the lump in her throat. If it hadn't been for Willamina rescuing her that night long ago, Eva would most likely be working as one of Danny J's girls yet today. Or dead. The options and mortality rate of women in Dodge City wasn't anything to argue about. "And Snake and Summer?"

"Land sakes, girl. I didn't marry those two off, Jonas did." Ma's gaze was on the painting Eva had made of Snake's family that hung over the fireplace. The faint image of Jonas Quinter, Ma's husband, hung in the air over Summer and Snake. Summer claimed Jonas was her guardian angel, and that he had been since the day he died in her arms when she was but a girl. The rest of the family believed it as well. Too many things had happened for them not to.

"He just did it through me," Ma whispered.

Thoughts flowed in and out of Eva's mind. They were a jumbled concoction of all the brothers, their wives, she and Bug, Ma, the children sleeping upstairs. She loved them all, every last Quinter as if she'd been born into the family. A sinking sensation happened in her stomach. Was she in love with Bug, or did she want to be a Quinter so badly, nothing else mattered? She glanced to Ma. "What does this all mean for me?"

Ma leaned forward and wrapped her tender, work-harden hands around the base of Eva's face. "First off, Eva girl. I love you like a daughter. I couldn't love you anymore if you'd been sprang from my womb, and no matter what, that will never change. Same with all the boys, girls, and babies. All I'm asking is that you and Bug take a couple of months to get to know each other. If after that time, you do love him, and want to spend the rest of your life loving him, then we'll have a wedding the likes this town's never seen."

Eva wanted to smile, she truly did at the thought of marrying Bug, but the other notions mingling about wouldn't let her. "A couple of months?" she asked, knowing Ma waited for her response.

"Yup, if by the time Snake's done harvesting his wheat, you and Bug are still convinced you want to get married then you shall." Ma stood and with one hand, encouraged Eva to do so as well. "Come on, I'll have Kid give you a ride home. I'm sure he and Jessie are ready to call it a night." Walking to the door, she added, "The rest of those fools will most likely keep on until morning milking. Trust my word, there ain't a one of them that's gonna be good for nothing come sunup."

"I have my horse and buggy, Ma. I can see myself home."

"Nope. Not tonight you can't. One of the other boys can drive you, but Kid'll follow." Ma's tone didn't promote a rebuttal.

Kid and Jessie were ready to leave. By the time Eva helped gather their children, Kid had the wagon ready and her horse, Bracket, hitched to her buggy. Eva carried baby Oscar while Jessie carried Winifred and Snake carried Joel to the wagon. After Kid settled the sleeping older children into the back, Eva handed Oscar to Jessie.

"There really isn't any need for you to follow me home. I'll be fine," Eva said.

"I think Ma wants to make sure you don't have a night time visitor." Jessie nodded her head toward Eva's wagon and horse.

Bug stood beside Bracket, running a hand along the liver-colored spots on the paint's stout neck. Ma, as well as Skeeter, Hog, and Kid stood near him. Their conversation was intense. Eva hitched up her skirt, and hurried to the buggy.

"I'll hitch up another wagon," Skeeter said as she arrived.

"Another wagon? What for?" Eva asked.

Bug had his arms folded across his chest. As did Ma. There was definitely a showdown happening. Ma was the one to break. Without taking her eyes off Bug, she said, "To give Bug a ride back here after he drives you home."

"That's not—"

"Just get in the buggy, Eva," Kid whispered near her shoulder.

Bug was at her side then, assisting her into the buggy. The seat bounced on its springs and had barely slowed before he jumped in from the other side and snatched up the reins. By now there were several other wagons and buggies hitched to teams or single horses, yet a large crowd still decorated the lawn. Greetings of farewells echoed as the wagons fell in line behind her and Bug.

She'd never been shy around Bug. He'd always been the one person she could talk to. Maybe the first day they'd met, she'd shied away from him, but later, after she and Willamina moved into the soddy, she and Bug had become friends. The kind that could talk and laugh together with no uneasiness, so why was her stomach flipping and flopping now?

"Nice rig you got here," he said.

The little black awning prevented the moonlight from landing on his face. She had no idea if he was smiling or frowning. "Thank you. Kid helped me pick it out."

"Good looking animal, too."

"His name is Bracket. Buffalo Killer gave him to me."

"Buffalo Killer?" His grunt wasn't very telling.

"Yes, you remember Buffalo Killer, don't you?"

He laughed. It was the clear, clean laugh of the old Bug, and it brightened her insides. "Yes, I remember him," he agreed. "How's he doing anyway?"

"Good. He shows up every now and again. Just out of the blue, but it's usually when something is happening and his help is needed." She watched Bracket's white mane flay in the wind as she added, "Chief Red Elk has even come out a couple times to see Summer."

"Really, that's a long trip for an old man."

"Not with the trains running daily. It's not a long ride at all. Just a few hours. And Chief Red Elk has gotten back some of his youth since finding his daughter. He really loves Summer. All of the family for that matter. I was a little surprised he wasn't here to welcome September home." The thought made her frown. "I hope nothing has happened." She shook off the ounce of dread trying to seep in. She already had enough to worry about. "I'm sure Summer would know if something had. Buffalo Killer would have contacted her."

"I'm sure you're right," he agreed.

The silence was back then, hovering between the two of them like thick soup. The jingles of harnesses, clomps of hooves, and rattles of the rigs behind them, as well as the happy shouts, and murmurs of other passengers, floated on the evening air, but none of it was conversation worthy in their buggy.

Stars twinkled, all the way down to where the sky met the earth in the far ahead horizon. Eva did have things to say, but where to start eluded her.

Bug broke the silence. "Ma said you talked to her."

"Yes," she admitted. "I did."

"And that you agreed we wouldn't get married until after wheat harvest."

"Yes." Her insides grew heavy.

"Why?"

It was a simple question, so why wasn't an answer available? The moonlight glistened off the gyp road they traversed along. The white glow laid a never ending path ahead of them. Staring at it didn't help her conjure up an answer.

"Don't you want to marry me, Eva?"

She grabbed his arm. It was solid and thick, and she relished the sense of having something to hold onto. "Yes, Bug, I want to marry you. That has never changed, and it never will. But we can wait a few months, can't we? If it'll make Ma happy?"

"What about us? What about making us happy?"

"I'm happy that you're home, Bug. So happy."

His arm slipped out from her hold and a second later it wrapped around her shoulders. He may have tugged her close, but she was already scooting across the seat, plastering her side against his.

"I'm happy, too, Eva girl, very happy." The little kiss he pressed to her temple was so soft and sweet it seeped all the way into her soul.

"Tell me, Eva, tell me everything I've missed the last couple of years. Start with the kids, how many of them are there now?" He sounded like the old Bug.

She giggled, and resting her cheek on his shoulder, she began to share all of the wonderful blessings that had bestowed the Quinter's since he'd left. He knew it all from the letters everyone had sent, she included, but she was happy to tell him about the little sweet and silly things that may have been missed. Like the birdhouse August made her for her birthday, as well as the way he'd been expelled from school for putting a snake in the teacher's desk drawer.

They were laughing by the time they pulled into her yard. Really laughing in a way she hadn't since he'd rode away for Pennsylvania. He brought the buggy to a halt. She sat up, and followed the trail of his gaze.

"Nice house, you got, too, Eva."

"Thank you."

The smile slipped from his face like melting snow falling off a roof. "You've done real well, for yourself, haven't you?"

There was more behind his statement. The quiver in her bones said so. "I've had help. Your brothers and Buffalo Killer and Jack."

"But not me." His solemn, almost lost gaze met hers. "You didn't need me at all, did you?"

The bone shivers spread to her nerves. "I needed you, Bug. I still do. I just had to keep busy while you were gone, or I'd…" He was gone, had jumped from the buggy and disappeared behind the leather side wall.

Eva spun, scooting to her side of the seat to climb down. Bug was already there, holding his arms out to help her down. She put her hands on his shoulders, and he grasped her waist on both sides.

When he lifted, he didn't set her down. Instead, he hoisted her clear of the wagon and held her suspended in the air. "Well, I'm here now, Eva girl, and I'm gonna find us enough oil to make old Rockefeller take notice."

His lips caught her open mouth. The way his tongue collided with hers sapped the strength from her system. She wrapped her arms around his neck and held on for dear life as the sensations carried her away.

The kiss may have lasted minutes, or hours, she had no way of knowing. All she understood was that she didn't want to quit kissing him—ever. He was the one to break the contact, and after a couple other small pecks to her throbbing lips, he lowered her to the ground.

She stumbled, and fell against his solid frame until her legs remembered they were needed to hold her upright. Lifting her head, she encountered the brothers, all of them except Hog. He'd stayed behind to control the crowd still at the farm.

"Come on, Eva, I'll walk you in while Bug puts away your horse and buggy." Kid took her arm.

"I can walk her in," Bug insisted, tightening the one arm still around her.

"After you put away Bracket," Snake said.

Skeeter slapped Bug's back. "I'll help you little brother. You easterners don't know how to handle good horse flesh."

Bug stiffened. "Like hell, I don't. I wasn't gone that long."

Laughing, Skeeter winked at her before he tugged Bug from her side. Kid and Snake, one on each side of her, walked her to the house. She couldn't deny she wanted Bug to walk her inside, but was thankful for the moment to talk to Kid and Snake. After they entered the house, and while Snake was lighting the lamp on desk near the door, she said, "Please don't tell Bug about the oil well."

"Why not?" Kid asked, closing the door behind him.

*Because he thinks I don't need him.* She shook her head, knowing she couldn't tell them that. "Because I don't want him to know right now."

"Eva, we did as you asked when it came to Willamina's death, but he's gonna see that derrick." Snake replaced the glass chimney and turned around.

"I know," she admitted. "But I want to be the one to tell him." *When the time is right,* she added to herself.

"All right," Kid agreed. "We won't say a thing. Don't worry about it."

"Thank you," she offered, sighing.

Snake patted her cheek. "We'll see you tomorrow."

Kid wrapped her in a solid hug. "Don't worry, it's all going to work out just fine."

She hugged him back. "I know. Thank you, for bringing me home."

"I thought I was the one that brought you home," Bug said before the door swung all the way open. He glared at his brothers. "I'll be out in a minute."

Snake and Kid shook their head, not in denial, but as if they'd just seen something they couldn't believe. They both said good-bye as they walked out the door, leaving it open in their wake.

Bug had both hands on her upper arms. "Why is it every time I see you, you're in another man's arms?"

"I—" She puckered her lips and folded her arms across her chest. "That was Kid. Your brother."

He cracked a smile. "I'm just teasing."

Her ire dissolved, leaving her more than willing to plummet into his embrace. He kissed her again, but the shouting from the yard cut it short.

"Hey, Bug!" Overly loud yells echoed into the house. "My beer is empty!"

"Mine, too!"

"Say good-bye, Buggie-boy!"

Eva had to smile. A good half dozen men filled the back of the wagon Snake and Skeeter drove.

"I'm coming!" Bug yelled.

"Will it be tonight?" one recanted.

"Go," Eva said. "Jessie needs to get the babies home, and Kid won't leave until you do. Ma made him promise."

"I know, but I gotta say something first."

The shouts came again.

"Then talk fast," she instructed.

"I don't want to wait until after wheat harvest. I don't want to wait long at all. We don't need Ma's approval. We can ride down to Garden City and get married tomorrow."

She was tempted, oh, so very tempted, but she couldn't. Not only had she promised Ma, she had some thinking to do. "We can't do that."

"Yes, we can," he insisted.

"Yoohoo, Bug? I'm coming to get you!" A thud followed the shout. She couldn't tell if someone jumped or fell out of the wagon.

119

"Don't answer me right now," Bug said, kissing her cheek. "Just think about it. I'll be by tomorrow morning." With that, he was gone. The glass in the front door rattled as the door snapped shut.

Eva didn't move. The click of his heals ended as he left the porch. Her heart plunged to her toes. His homecoming had a part of her reeling with delight, the other part wallowing in dread.

Bug leaped off the porch and bounded across the yard. He shouted a farewell to Kid and Jessie as he grabbed the sideboard of the wagon with both hands and leaped in the back.

"Let's go!" he shouted to Skeeter. "Gerald still has barrels of beer for us to sample."

He plopped down on the bed before being jostled out. The hoots and hollers were deafening, not that it mattered. Neither did Gerald's beer. He'd just pretended to drink the last few. The brew wasn't needed to create the good feelings making his insides dance. Why hadn't he thought of it earlier? He and Eva would elope. By this time tomorrow night, they'd be married.

Chapter Ten

Bug opened one eye, but quickly closed it, flinching at how the sunlight tried to blind him. His head was heavy, and his stomach woozy. He ran a hand through his hair and scratched his scalp. *What the hell?* He hadn't consumed enough beer to have a hangover, yet it sure felt like one—a bad one.

"Hey, are you going to sleep all day? You already missed breakfast." Skeeter sounded way too happy.

"Shut up," Bug grumbled.

The whistling was worse than the shouting had been.

Bug sat up, holding his head with both hands. The smell of hay and animals registered. Opening his eyes cautiously, he glanced about. Skeeter forked hay into the cow's feed bunk.

"What time is it?"

"Going on noon. You should be glad Ma did the milking. If I had, you'd have been up hours ago." Skeeter stabbed the pitchfork into the haystack and walked over to pick up a cup. "Here," he said, holding out the cup as he walked closer. "Summer sent this out to you."

Bug took the cup, and sniffed the contents. "What is it?"

"Don't know." Skeeter patted his belly. "But it'll cure what ails you."

Bug downed it. His stomach gurgled and rumbled, but stayed put. "Thanks." Setting the cup down, he gradually stood. "What the hell happened? I didn't drink that many beers."

"No, you switched to the punch."

121

"Yeah, I did. I didn't want to have a hang—"

"It was spiked."

Bug rubbed at the throb in his temples. "I'd say." He needed to be at his best today, it was his wedding day. His plan had been to be at Eva's long before now.

Skeeter dumped some oats beside the hay and put the can aside. "Elmer Burnett makes it from corn mash. It's as clear and tasteless as water, but boy, oh, boy, does it have a punch."

"I'd say," Bug repeated. "Is that outdoor bathing tub still usable?" Snake had built a big holding tank years ago, and the boys always used it for their baths. Of course, the new house had indoor plumbing. They'd been planning on putting it in even before a fire burnt the original house to the ground.

"Yup." Skeeter scooped up the cup. "I'll even loan you some clothes and stand guard so that no one comes around the shed."

"Thanks." Bug didn't care if anyone came around the shed or not, he just wanted to cleanse his body, and hoped the action would help his insides as well.

They left the barn, and Bug had to look twice at the front yard. It was as spic and span as Ma's kitchen. If he didn't feel so rotten, he'd wonder if there had been a party here last night.

Skeeter laughed. "The last of them rolled out an hour or so ago. You slept through it all."

Side by side, Bug and his brother walked around the wash shed. "I haven't slept since I left New York, not much anyway."

"How was it out there? You make a good deal with that Staples guy?"

The water sparkled invitingly in the sunlight. Bug smiled and ripped off the black leather vest. His boots were next. It wasn't until he started unbuttoning his shirt that he answered, "No. We parted as friends, not partners. Chester's refineries are too far from Kansas. It wouldn't be profitable to ship crude that far."

"Are you going to build a refinery here?" Skeeter sat down on the bench, ready to visit.

Bug didn't mind in the least. His life out east had been more solitary than he'd realized. "Maybe someday." He tossed aside his shirt and undid his britches. "But first I gotta get the oil out of the ground. I think I'll try old man Rockefeller again."

"Think he'll talk to you this time?"

Before he went to Pennsylvania, he'd written to Rockefeller at his Standard Oil Company, but the reply had said they weren't interested in the oil seeps Bug had found. That's when he'd decided to take a sample first hand to the oil companies out east. The increasing population of the west had amplified the need for kerosene and other petroleum products.

For as long as he could remember, Bug had been fascinated by the black tar around the area—and read everything he could find about the crude. Oil had been around since the beginning of time, some Indians thought the oil seeps had great healing power, and used it for medicinal purposes. Others, like Buffalo Killer, used it to water proof their moccasins and such. The major source of lamp oil had been sperm whales for years upon years, but the supply hadn't been able to keep up with the demand for the past several decades.

Now that he'd seen for himself just how huge the industry revolution was, he was even more positive his oil venture would pay off in no time. Not only did homes need the oil for light and heat, companies needed it to run their machinery.

Bug lowered himself into the large tub. Refreshing and welcome, the water, warmed by the sun, flowed over his skin. "I know he'll listen to me this time."

Holding his breath, he slipped beneath the surface. Life didn't get any better. Within no time he'd be a married, rich oil man, with three red-headed kids.

****

Doubled over by the pain, Eva wiped at the sweat dripping from her brows with the crook of her elbow. Her monthly flow had hit harder than ever. Since shortly after Willamina passed, her pattern fluctuated until it was as erratic as summer storms—flying in and out with great ferocity, and the cramping had become increasingly worse. She'd thought of talking to Ma about it, or even the new doctor in Scott, but her shyness had won out, and she'd held her silence. This morning, however, sitting on the chamber pot she'd pulled from beneath the bed, she wondered if she'd hemorrhage to death in the middle of her bedroom.

It had hit so forceful and quick she hadn't had time to make it to the water closet. Another fierce cramp knotted her insides and warmth trickled from beneath her bottom. She moaned, watching deep-red blood seep into the edges of her nightgown rippled across the floor around her.

Tightening her leg muscles, she tried to stand, but a new onset of cramping and gushing made her cry out. When it eased, her legs shook uncontrollably. She let them go lax, and leaned against the edge of the bed that kept her upright on the chamber pot.

The relief lasted only a second before the cramping brought her forward, grasping her stomach again.

Bracket whinnied. The sound floated in through the open window. She moaned again. The horse needed to be fed, the cow had to be milked, and the chickens probably wondered why she'd forgotten them. It had to be almost noon. She'd been sitting here, bleeding, for hours.

The entire trip to New York had been full of worries that her monthly would descend while she traveled. It had almost kept her from going. Almost. Not even that fear had been strong enough to stop a chance at seeing Bug.

She'd gone, and her time had stayed at bay. And, now Bug was home, but if the bleeding didn't stop, she'd die before ever becoming Mrs. Brett Quinter.

Another whinny blew in with the breeze.

She willed her ears to listen. That one hadn't sounded like Bracket. The buzzing in her head grew too loud to hear around. The blood soaked material of the gown covering her toes swirled before her eyes. If not cleaned up soon, the blood would permanently stain the wood floor. Eva lifted her face, trying to focus enough to build the strength to yell, hoping the other whinny was Ma or one of the girls.

Her neck wasn't strong enough to hold up her head. Moaning, she let her chin fall to her chest. Seconds later, she tried lifting it again. Blurred, a human shape filled her open doorway.

"Eva?"

"Buff—" She didn't have the strength to say his name. "Help."

Solid arms lifted her. She didn't have the gumption to protest or worry about the mattress as Buffalo Killer laid her down.

"Eva," he said urgently. "I've got to put a pillow between your legs."

She nodded. He swiftly lifted her gown and placed a pillow between her thighs, and pushed her knees together. "Keep that there."

Nodding again, she clutched her stomach as the

cramps continued, tearing at her insides with agonizing potency. A few minutes later, the foot of the bed lifted so high she thought she might slip off the other end. The wall behind her head would stop her. Thank goodness because she was too weak to do anything else about it.

A cloth covered her face. Cool and damp, it was heavenly.

"I'll be right back," he said.

She didn't have the wherewithal to answer. Eyes closed, she let her mind go blank. The pains gradually lessened. Exhausted, she welcomed the haziness engulfing her.

The next thing she knew, her heart began to race, in an excited way. She opened her eyes in answer to the voices. Bug stood beside the bed, his hand grasping hers. She returned the hold, grateful he was near. He bent over, and ran a hand along her cheek. "Eva, what happened?"

A wave rushed over her, bringing tears to her eyes. She couldn't decipher why the tears appeared. Perhaps because she loved Bug so much and his nearness filled her with comfort.

"Honey, tell me who did this. Tell me what happened." Worry filled his voice.

She shook her head, wanted to tell him not to fret. The words wouldn't form. It was too embarrassing to tell him it was just her time. Perhaps once they were married they could discuss such things, but not now.

Ma appeared over Bug's shoulder. "Go watch for the doctor, Bug. Let me talk to her."

"No," he said, never taking his eyes from hers.

Eva closed her eyes and waved a hand, gesturing for him to leave. He shouldn't see her like this. She didn't want him to think she was weak or feeble. No man wanted those qualities in a wife.

"You want me to leave?" he asked.

Without lifting a lid, she nodded.

His grumbles were too muffled to understand. The tears slipped faster from the corners of her eyes. They stung her cheeks and her heart as the click of the door closing declared he'd left. She missed him so much.

Ma asked then, "What happened, Eva?"

"M-my monthly." Another bout of cramps hit her stomach, but they'd softened, weren't nearly as bad as they had been earlier. "I'll be fine in a few hours." She let her head sink deep into the pillow again. The worst of it is over. "I don't need the doctor. I'll be fine. It's just the first day that's this bad," Eva assured.

"The first day? Is your monthly always this bad?" Ma asked.

"This was the worse one ever. But I'm already feeling better."

Ma's hand gently caressed her shoulder with comfort. "You just lie there until the doctor has a look see."

"I don't need a doctor. It's just—"

"Eva," Ma interrupted. "This isn't right. Not this much blood."

Eva snapped her eyes open.

Ma's hand, cool and soft, brushed Eva's hair from her forehead. "Why didn't you tell me about this?" Ma asked.

Eva's stomach tightened, it wasn't a cramp, but a cold knot of fear. "What do you mean, not right?"

Someone knocked on the door, and then a man, beanpole tall and with slouching shoulders, walked into the room. A single ring of dark hair circled his head from temple to temple. "Hello, Eva. I'm Doctor Weston. Let's see what's happening, shall we?"

Eva glanced to Ma, looking for aid. Ma, with a supportive yet fretful grimace, nodded.

Lila elbowed her way around the doctor. "I had

him wash already—with soap."

Summer, standing near the foot of the bed, added, "We're all right here, Eva. It'll be fine."

"Excuse me," Dr. Weston interjected, "I'll need you all to leave."

Eva reached for Ma's hand. The woman's grasp was firm as she glanced to the girls. "You girls go on, now." Her gaze then narrowed as it landed on the doctor. "I'll be staying."

"Mrs. Quinter, that's highly—"

"I'll be staying." Ma nodded again to Lila and Summer, who slipped from the room after tossing reassuring glances at Eva. "I won't get in your way, Doctor, but I'm not leaving."

He nodded then and made his way around the side of the bed. "Step aside then."

Ma walked to the other side of the bed. The hand she laid on Eva's shoulder relieved a touch of the anxiety rippling Eva's mind.

Doctor Weston started asking questions, beginning with how old she'd been when she started menstruating. She answered and he nodded, taking her pulse and listening to her heart while asking other questions about her flow and frequency.

He then suggested she remove her gown so he could further examine her. Eva looked to Ma for advice.

Downstairs, pacing the kitchen floor, obsessed by the fact Eva didn't want him upstairs, Bug spun around when the back door flew open. Jessie raced in like a hen flying the coop.

"Where is she?" Jessie asked of no one in particular, but glancing to everyone.

"She's upstairs with the doctor." Summer closed the door after Kid made his way in.

"What happened?" Jessie took Summer's arms by the elbows.

Summer shrugged. "She claims it's just her

monthly. But, Jessie, I've never seen so much blood. Buffalo Killer found her and then came and got us. That's all we know right now."

Jessie removed her bonnet, and after hanging it on the hook by the door, she walked toward the arched doorway that led into the front room and the staircase. Nobody tried to stop her, and since she didn't return, Bug figured she hadn't been asked to leave Eva's room. Not like he had.

He'd just stepped out of the bathing tub when Buffalo Killer rode into the yard. His happiness at seeing the brave quickly turned to alarm when the man said Eva was bleeding to death. Few waited for the wagon Hog started to hitch. Someone must have saddled a horse for Ma, or maybe she'd done it herself, for she arrived in Eva's yard moments after he leaped from the horse he'd ridden bareback.

Summer and Buffalo Killer had followed him up the stairs as well. There had been so much blood, he'd thought her dead. At that moment his heart had hit his heels, leaving him empty and hollow from tip to top. She'd moaned then, and he'd rushed to her side, begging her to stay alive.

Bug had no idea what had gone on around him, nor how long it had been until Eva opened her eyes. In that span of time that seemed to have stopped, he'd seen his life without her. It was awful and lonely and the last thing on earth he wanted.

Chasing the memories from his mind, he stomped to the stove and refilled the coffee cup he'd been holding for what seemed like hours. A kettle of chicken soup bubbled next to the coffee. Randi had set about making it shortly after she'd arrived. He gave the soup a stir and replaced the spoon to the plate Randi had it resting on. His brothers and their wives sat around the table, talking softly. Snake had gone for the doctor, and now mentioned how the man had just delivered Rodney Zimmerman's second child. While he'd been out east, Rodney had married a gal from Finney County.

So many things had changed during his absence. Evidentially it included him and Eva. How was he going to make it up to her? Make her see he was still the same person.

The sound of footsteps on the stairs had him rushing to the front room. Jessie paused on the staircase. "You need to come up here, Bug."

He bolted and arrived in Eva's bedroom mere seconds later. She wore a different gown. This one was pink with white stripes and a little red bow tied beneath her chin. The bedding had been changed, too. Crimson blood no longer dominated the room.

The foot of the bed was still propped up with two cast iron pots, making Eva lay downhill. Bug went to her side, kneeling next to the bed. Even pale and sickly, she was beautiful. So beautiful and so very precious it took his breath away.

"Hi," he whispered.

"Hi," she answered. A soft, but strained smile curled her lips as she wrapped her fingers around his.

"Mr. Quinter," the doctor shot a guarded look at Ma, "you'll want to hear what I have to say."

Bug's nerve endings exploded. He glanced to his mother standing on the other side of the bed. Staid, she stared back. Bug squeezed Eva's hand harder, and kissing the delicate hairs of her brows, whispered, "Whatever it is, we'll get through it together. I'll be here for you. Always."

Eva closed her eyes. The single tear slipping from one corner singed his heart. Taking a breath, preparing for what was to come, Bug turned to the doctor. "What's wrong with her?"

"My physical examination has revealed a tumor." The doctor's tone was gravely serious. "A large one. It's hard and smooth and slightly mobile within the uterus. I believe it will continue to grow rapidly. I recommend immediate removal."

Bug said the first thing that came to mind. "Well, then do it."

"I can't," the doctor said, shaking his bald head. "She needs an Obstetric Surgeon. They specialize in women's aliments. There's a very good one in Wichita. He's performed this type of surgery several times and has experienced excellent mortality rates."

"Mortality rates?" Bug gulped. His heart beat in his throat, plugging his airway.

"Yes. It's a very serious operation," the doctor confirmed.

"Isn't there something else you can do?" Bug grabbed the headboard with his spare hand, keeping himself from toppling.

The doctor rubbed his jaw. "No, I'm afraid not. She's going to continue to experience episodes like today, and there's nothing I can do about it." He pointed to the bed. "Whoever propped the bed up probably saved her from hemorrhaging to death today."

Bug went ice cold and started to sweat at the same time. "Well, then, get a hold of that doctor and get him out here."

"Eva will have to go to him. I can contact him to see when he can schedule her. She'll need to remain in Wichita for six to eight weeks, I would assume. But first she needs to recover from today's episode. She's extremely anemic. I've explained she needs to eat fresh, raw beef liver as often as possible to increase her iron levels."

Quivering at the thought of anyone having to eat raw liver, Bug patted the back of Eva's hand that was clenching his other one. "When can she travel? Get a hold of that doctor and tell him we're on our way as soon as possible."

The doctor glanced between Eva and Ma. Neither said anything for a few stilled seconds. "The surgery will include a hysterectomy," the doctor said.

"What's that?" Bug asked when everyone held their silence.

"The removal of all her reproductive organs. After the surgery, Eva will never be able to have children." The doctor glanced at Eva. "She wanted you to know before she makes her decision." His gaze then went to Ma. "Let's leave these two alone for a moment."

Bug watched them leave. He had no idea what to say. The wind blew in through the window, rustling the curtain beside the bed and tickling the back of his neck. It was easy to ignore. The doctor's news, however, was not easy to disregard. It weighted the air like a pending storm.

The click of the door closing seemed like hours ago, when Eva said, "Bug?"

He planted his knees on the floor, and still holding her hand, laid his arms on the edge of the mattress. Leaning forward, he brushed a kiss across her knuckles.

"Doctor Weston says there's a chance it won't keep growing. That I might have a baby if I don't have the surgery." The pain in her voice stabbed his heart.

His mind searched for an assuring answer. But only one thought remained on the forefront. "I'm sorry, darling. I'm sure not having a baby is hard for a woman, but I can't take the chance of losing you."

"You want me to have the surgery?"

He nodded. "As soon as possible."

"But last night you said you wanted children. Three of them."

Now was not the time to tell her about the orphans. "I want you more," he admitted. "I'll always want you more."

Tears fell from her eyes. "I'm so sorry," she sobbed.

His next actions came without thought. Careful, so he wouldn't jostle her too much, he crawled onto the bed and slid one arm beneath her neck and the other over her stomach. He aligned his body with hers and held her tight as she cried. Tears stung his eyes as well, whether for her or with her, he wasn't quite sure.

Chapter Eleven

By the next morning, the cramps were little more than slight nuisances, and though Eva felt better, besides stiff from lying around too long, her heart was direly heavy. The smell of coffee brewing lured her from the bedroom. She had no idea who might be in the kitchen, but had thoughts of who she wished it would be.

Before he'd left, Doctor Weston had given her some pain powder, insisting she swallow a dose. She'd slept then, but fretfully. A smile touched her lips. Every time she'd opened her eyes, Bug had been sitting beside her bed. They'd talked in small increments, before she'd doze again, but neither brought up the subject of children. It held too much pain.

Slipping her arms into a dressing gown, she stopped in the upstairs water closet. Her flow was much more manageable this morning, and after padding herself from the stack of ironed rags she kept in the room for that purpose, she made her way down the stairs.

Ma sat at the table of the otherwise empty room. "Good morning," she greeted. "Have a seat. I'll get you some coffee." Ma paused then. "Or maybe you should be back in bed. I can bring it up to you."

"No. I'm fine today. The coffee smells good." Eva walked across the room. "I can get it."

"No, you sit down. I'll get it." Ma took her arm, and shy of wrestling the woman, Eva knew there was no arguing with her.

"I'm not an invalid, Ma." Eva had to say it, if for

no other reason than to convince herself.

"I know you're not. But I'm here to take care of you." Ma turned to retrieve a cup and saucer from the cupboard. "I had Snake bring me some things. I'll stay here with you until you leave for Wichita."

Eva glanced around.

"Bug went to get you some beef liver from Kid," Ma stated before Eva had a chance to ask.

Eva took a sip of coffee, and then ran a finger over the rim of the fragile bone china, contemplating how long it would be before Bug returned.

"Not long," Ma said, reading Eva's mind.

A rattle in the yard made Ma stand up again and move toward the front room. "Not even Bug is that quick."

Eva followed, but hung back as Ma opened the front door. "Hello, Doctor."

"Mrs. Quinter," Doctor Weston greeted. "Aw, Eva, you look much better today. How are you feeling?"

"Fine."

"I doubt that, but better I'm sure," he insisted. "I'd like to examine you again. I sent a telegram to Dr. Robb yesterday afternoon, and he replied with some questions."

"When can he see her in Wichita?" Ma asked.

"As soon as she can get there. That's another reason I need to examine her again. Dr. Robb is afraid the hemorrhaging could renew itself." Dr. Weston nodded toward Eva. "If the examination is good, as I suspect it will be judging from how healthy you appear this morning, then we could see about passage on the afternoon train. It would put you in Wichita early tomorrow morning."

"Tomorrow morning?" Eva asked. She'd thought there would be more time to get used to the idea of— of all of it.

"Get to examining then," Ma said. "I'll pack us a

couple of bags."

Dr. Weston's examine was thorough, and Eva had just slipped her nightgown back over her head, when the door to her room flew open. Dr. Weston, with his back to her while he replaced his instruments in his black bag, spun to the door, catching it as it swung wide.

Bug glanced between her and the Doctor. "What happened?"

"Nothing—" she started, wanting to erase the concern covering his face.

"I needed to examine her again," Dr. Weston explained. "I'm going to secure passage for her and Mrs. Quinter on the afternoon train."

Eva flinched at how Bug exclaimed, "The afternoon train?"

"Yes, Dr. Robb wants her there immediately." Dr. Weston snapped his bag shut. "My examination proves she can travel."

Bug bolted into the room, putting himself between her and Dr. Weston. "I'll be traveling with her."

Dr. Weston moved to the doorway. "Well, then, young man, I suggest you go pack."

Eva held her breath. Bug shrugged. "I'm ready." He held up a package and a basket. "I even got her beef liver."

The doctor chuckled. "Fine, she can eat it before you leave. What else do you have there?"

Shrugging again, Bug set both packages on the bed. "Strawberries. Lila says Eva has to eat them with the liver. Something about the vitamins in the berries will help her absorb the iron in the beef."

The doctor lifted his fuzzy eyebrows. "That's correct. Who is this Lila? Is she aspiring to join the medical field?"

"No, Bug said. "She's just Lila, my brother Skeeter's wife."

Eva agreed with a nod. Lila had probably read more medical journals than Dr. Weston. She was always reading them. Last night Lila had assured everyone that she'd heard of Dr. Robb in Wichita, and from what she'd read, was thoroughly impressed with what she called his track record.

"Hmm," Dr. Weston said thoughtfully. "Is Lila the tall red-head? The one that made me wash my hands before I entered the bedroom yesterday?"

Eva and Bug nodded.

"Smart woman." He winked at Eva as he picked the package and basket off the bed. "I'll go prepare the liver, and see you downstairs."

She peeked around Bug's shoulder, resting a hand on it as she said, "Thank you, Dr. Weston."

Before the door had shut, Bug turned around and gathered her into his arms. She went willingly, thankful for his presence. The thinness of her gown offered the slightest barrier. Her breasts flattened against his hard chest, and the heat of his body quickly penetrated the cotton. His wonderful hands rubbed her back, making big circles that soothed her inside and out. The fantastic scents of outdoors, leather, and him, all breathtakingly superb, filled her nose pressed near the hollow of his neck. Eva closed her eyes, snuggled in, and reeled at the encompassing sensations.

He rested his cheek on the top of her head, and sighed as heavily as she. "It'll all be fine, Eva girl," he whispered. "As long as we've got each other, everything else will fall into place."

Eva held her silence, praying he was right, that the day he'd regret loving her would never come.

****

There wasn't a private car on the afternoon train, so the three of them, Eva, Bug, and Ma, sat in the coach with the couple dozen other folks. A crying baby couldn't be hushed near the back of the car, and though the baby's squalls didn't bother him, Bug could see the agony rippling Eva's fine features. He racked his brain, trying to remember what Mrs. King had done to quiet the babies on the orphan train.

He snapped his fingers, and then dug in his shirt pocket for the peppermint sticks Dr. Weston suggested he purchase for Eva. The doctor said it would settle her stomach if needed. Perhaps it would help the babe as well.

"I'll be right back." Bug patted Eva's shoulder and rose.

The rocking of the train had him holding onto the backs of the seats as he made his way to the far end of the car. The Atchison-Topeka-Santa Fe Line was an offshoot of the Santa Fe Railroad. Therefore the cars were smaller and rough. In Great Bend most of the passengers would catch a Santa Fe passenger train that would go to Kansas City. The ride would be much smoother and quicker, but he, Eva, and Ma, would stay on this one. Which meant, their ride all the way to Wichita, would be on this bone jarring, loud, and sooty train.

When he stopped, catching his swaying by grabbing the seat in front of the woman holding the baby, he nodded a greeting.

She gave an apologetic smile. "I'm sorry for the disturbance. He's teething."

"Maybe this will help." Bug held out one of the peppermint sticks.

"Oh, my." She glanced at the candy and back up at him.

"It might help," Bug repeated. The little tyke's face was scrunched up and beet red. Bug brushed the tip of the candy stick across the babe's mouth. Instantly, the baby stopped crying and smacked his lips together. "I think he likes it."

"I think he does, too." The woman took the stick

and let the baby suck on one end. Little arms and legs started going at once. "Yes, I'd say he likes it for sure." She glanced up, smiling. "Thank you. Thank you very much."

Bug patted the baby's soft head. "You're welcome." Turning around to make his way back to the front, he froze.

Eva, looking at him quite quizzically, bit her lip, and spun to gaze out the window beside her. His heart might as well start living in his boots, since that's where it ended up more often than not lately. Grabbing the backs of the seats again, he practically pulled himself all the way back to his seat since each step got to be a bit harder to make. He'd only wanted to calm her anxiety, not add to it.

The rattle and clank of the wheels rolling along the iron tracks made talking a useless feat unless you wanted to yell, so after sitting down, he tugged his hat over his eyes, and continued to scold himself for his behavior. It was just like him to point out someone else's baby while she was fretting about never having any.

With the whistle screaming and the wheels screeching, the train arrived in Great Bend with a jolt that uprooted some of the passengers. Bug set his feet hard against the floor, and prepared for the thrusting, uneven bump. He stretched an arm in front of Eva, bracing for when she jerked forward. She caught his arm with both hands, and smiled her thanks.

Passengers, carrying bags, boxes, and other traveling gear, crowded the narrow center aisle, waiting for the porter to open the front gate. The woman, with her infant tucked safely in her arms, paused near Bug's seat. "Thank you, again."

"Sure," Bug said. The babe peeked his way, and Bug swore the kid grinned at him.

"You're a lucky lady," the woman directed at

Eva. "You husband is very kind."

Eva's smile was bright and friendly. "Thank you. And yes, he is."

Bug's insides swelled, he arched his back, giving the warmth more room. Then he glanced at Ma, wondering if she was going to set the woman straight on him and Eva not being married. She just stared back, with one brow slightly arched.

"Good day," the woman offered in farewell. Moments later, she and the babe disappeared through the door.

"What did you give her?" Eva asked in her quiet and gentle tone.

Bug dug in his pocket to show her. "A peppermint stick. Doctor Weston said they'd settle your stomach if need be. Do you want one?"

"No. Thank you, though. That was very kind of you."

"I figured the trip would be shorter without a baby wailing the whole time." He gulped. The lump in his throat felt as if it was made of glass shards. "I thought it was upsetting you." Aw, hell, nothing came out sounding right.

"It wasn't upsetting me. I just felt sorry for him."

"Me, too," he admitted, tugging his hat back down.

The delay in Great Bend wasn't long. Soon the train was chugging its way toward Wichita, and Ma dug out the basket of foodstuff. They ate, commenting on how good Randi's cooking was. Bug found himself wondering about Eva's cooking. Ma's wasn't anything to brag about. Not that he was one for complaining, he'd never gone hungry. But it really hadn't been until Kid married Jessie that he'd tasted food. Before that he'd simply ate whatever Ma put on the table. When Jessie first moved into Kid's house, she made the best cookies he'd ever eaten.

Not even Randi, who made food taste so good you wanted to hug her after every meal, could make cookies like the ones Jessie had.

He'd eaten over at Eva and Willamina's before heading out east, but he'd never wondered if Eva had cooked or if Willamina had. The food must have been all right, since he didn't remember it being awful. Maybe Jessie would teach Eva how to make those cookies—if she hadn't already.

He handed his napkin to Ma, so she could stuff it in with the others. It was an odd thing to sit here worrying about. Then again, eating was something he did quite regularly, and liked when the food was palatable. Besides, it kept his mind off other—not so good—concerns.

"Eva." Ma's voice interrupted his musing. "You should try to sleep again, keep your strength up."

Eva nodded, smiling, but didn't make a move to settle in for a nap. Bug had an urge to wrap his arm around her and let her rest her head on his shoulder, but with Ma here...Frowning, he changed the route of his thought. Who cared if Ma was here? Eva would soon be his wife, and then his mother wouldn't have the right to say a peep about anything.

He ran his hand along the back of the seat and let it fall onto Eva's opposite shoulder. Tugging her closer while he scooted nearer to her side, he leaned back against the seat, giving her as much space as possible to rest her head on him. Grinning up at him, she cuddled in like Jerome—when he was a pup—had done to August.

With his other hand, Bug tipped the brim of his hat over his eyes, blocking out the stare he assumed Ma was giving him.

Their arrival in Wichita happened in the wee hours of the morning. A night sky, still hosting a million twinkling stars met them as Bug aided first

Eva and then Ma off the metal steps. He kept them on the platform for a moment, gathering his bearings. The depot was in the center of a spider web of train tracks. The clanking and banging echoed loudly in the dark. Damn, not even New York had been this congested with trains.

"Mr. Quinter? Mr. Quinter?"

Bug spun about, looking for where the sound came from. A man, with a shirt so white it caught every angle of the moon, jogged closer.

"Mr. Quinter? You are him, aren't you?"

"Yes."

"I got a wagon ready. Right this way." The man snatched up two of their traveling bags and started jogging off again.

Bug lifted his bag, the one the man had left, and herded the woman, one on each side, in the direction of the fading white shirt. They arrived at a two-seated buggy as the man stuffed the bags in the cargo hold. Bug plopped his bag in with the others, and then assisted Eva in while the man helped Ma into the back. With the women settled in the rear seat, Bug climbed in next to the driver.

Snatching up the reins, the man explained, "We'll take Miss Reynolds to the hospital, and then you to your hotel."

"Miss Reynolds?" The name raked Bug's nerves. "Who are you?"

"Buddy Murphy. Mr. Houston hired me. I'll be at your service as long as you need."

"Is Jack here?" Eva asked. The hope in her voice didn't do Bug's nerves any good, either.

"He told me to tell you he's on his way, ma'am. He'll be here as soon as he can. He's arranged everything at the hospital as well," the driver explained as he released the brake.

Bug grabbed the awning brace as the buggy surged forward. He hadn't wired Jack, and wondered who had. He liked the man, a lot, he'd still be rotting in jail in New York if not for Jack, but he wanted to be the one to take care of Eva. Not everyone else.

The buggy jerked to a stop. Men carrying red-globed lanterns littered the train tracks like cow chips in a pasture. They waved for buggies and wagons to cross some tracks, while they made others stop as trains barreled along the iron rails. When one of the men waved them forward, the driver instructed, "Hold on, the tracks are rough."

Bug had ridden broncos that hadn't bucked as violently as the buggy did when the wheels bounced over the uneven rails. They crossed several sets, and while the springs were still jostling everyone around, the driver flayed a whip in-between the two ponies hitched in front. They picked up their hooves, and thankfully, as their gait evened out, so did the bouncing.

"It's not far to the hospital, and your hotel is only a block away from there." Buddy flashed a grin that showed a gap between his front teeth the size of a dime.

"Dr. Weston didn't say she'd go to the hospital tonight. We have an appointment with Dr. Robb tomorrow. You can take us all to the hotel," Bug instructed.

"No." The driver weaved around a slower moving rig, making the buggy swing unevenly as it swayed back over before colliding with an oncoming one. The traffic could rival that in New York.

"Slow down, would ya?" Bug asked before he added, "And what do you mean, no?"

"Mr. Houston arranged for her to be admitted tonight. The surgery will happen first thing in the morning."

Bug had chomped his teeth together so long his jaw ached by the time Buddy pulled up in front of a big brick building. Two women wearing funny hats rushed out the front door. "Is this Miss Reynolds?"

"Yeah," Buddy said, leaping from his seat.

The women were at Eva's side before Bug had crawled out.

"Right this way, ma'am, we'll get you all settled," one of them said.

Still clenching his jaw, Bug reached over the woman's arm, and grabbed Eva's hand. "Excuse me," he said, shouldering his way in. "I'll help her down."

"That's not necessary. We got her. Are you Mr. Houston?" The second one wanted to know.

"No, I'm Mr. Quinter, her hus—" Bug cut himself off short. He already thought of himself as her husband, wished he was, but he couldn't flat out lie. Eva laid a hand on his shoulder, and he nudged himself between the women and the buggy to lift her down.

She trembled beneath his fingers, and he wrapped his arm around her shoulder as soon as her feet touched the street. He turned to the women. "Excuse us for a moment."

The women looked at one another before they stepped back up on the boardwalk, giving him and Eva a touch of privacy.

"There's nothing to fear. I'll be right here the whole time." He kissed her forehead.

She sighed, leaning against his touch. "I know. It's just happening so quickly."

"Do you want to wait a day or so? I'm sure we could arrange that." *Or Jack could,* he added silently.

She shook her head, but her hands wrapped around his waist. "No, it's better this way. I'd only fret if we waited."

He'd fret no matter what, already was, but couldn't let her know that. "Then let's get you inside and settled for the night."

The driver was back up in the buggy, and Ma

stood with the two women by the door. Bug kept Eva enveloped in his arms as they stepped onto the boardwalk and then walked toward the door.

One woman held Eva's bag while the other stepped forward. "We'll take her from here."

"No," Bug nodded toward Ma, "we'll see her inside."

"You can't, sir. Visiting hours are over. You can come see her in a day or two." The woman was shorter than Ma, and just as stout, but much younger.

Eva's hold tightened on his waist. She sucked air in so hard he heard the wheeze. He wished he could have the surgery for her. This was too much for her. She's was too fragile.

"Excuse us," he said, spinning Eva about. Near the brick wall, where the shadows provided them an ounce of privacy, he stopped and took a hold of her face. Looking deep into her sweet, big eyes, he offered, "We can leave."

"No." She shook her head. "We've came all this way."

His mind attempted to conjure up solutions, as it had a million times today. "I wish there was something else we could do, but we both know that's not the case." He kissed her brow. "I'll be here in the morning. They won't be able to keep me out."

A tiny smile curled her lips. "That I believe."

"Believe it forever, Eva. I love you. I have for years, and while I was gone, it grew stronger and stronger." He was putting his heart on his sleeve, but he didn't care. It was the truth, and he wanted her to know it.

"I love you, too, Bug. I always, always will."

He kissed her, a soft tender kiss that left him bleeding inside. He loved her so much. The thought of going on without her was unimaginable. As soon as he got to the hotel he'd wire Jack if that's what it took for little miss haughty to let him through those doors in the morning.

Eva wished the taste of his lips could stay on hers forever. Pressing her face into his shirt, willing the tears to remain behind her closed lids, she clung to him with all her might. The hardest thing about this whole surgery escapade was the affect it had on others. She was causing Bug more worries than he deserved. All of the Quinter's for that matter. There wasn't a way she'd be able to make it up to them.

Straightening her shoulders, searching for an ounce of bravery, she released her hold on him. "You and Ma have to be tired. You go to the hotel, and I'll see you tomorrow." She hoped her assurance didn't sound as weak as it felt.

"Bright and early," he said, before he brushed his lips to hers again. The love she felt in the merger made her want to beg him to take her home.

She broke away from the kiss. "Bye, Bug," she whispered and then bolted for the door before she couldn't.

Chapter Twelve

Her stomach was on fire, as was her head. Her limbs shook, and the sweat beading on her skin made her shiver with chill. A moan slipped over her vocal cords. The vibration stung. Eva attempted to swallow and sooth the burning, but her tongue and throat were swollen and wouldn't work. Her heart fluttered, fearful the fire would consume her.

"Here, sip this," an unknown voice said. Pressure formed against her lips.

She opened her mouth, and something tepid and pungent flowed over her tongue. It dripped into her throat, and made her cringe at the pain it caused.

"A little more," the voice insisted.

There was no stopping the bitter drops. Eva willed herself not to gag. It was no use. A convulsion ripped across her throat at the same time a spasm revolted in her stomach. The pain was intense as her body expelled the small amount she'd consumed. Thankfully the reaction was short lived.

Afterwards, she fought to stay awake. Bug? She needed Bug.

His voice came then, soft and caring it filtered into her ears, gently vibrating into her consciousness. Trying to stay alert, she lifted a hand. Warm fingers wrapped around hers. The comfort was so great she let the darkness surrounding her come closer.

She had several such episodes, where she tried to wake, but an overbearing force was too strong for her to break through. Each time, there was a hand holding hers, and she'd accept the comfort and flutter back down the tunnel as soft whispers sounded in her ears.

When at last she had the strength to break through the barrier, pain sat on her stomach like a heavy bucket. The dull, steady ache was a relief compared to the earlier fire. Eva drew in a breath, and let it out slowly.

"Hey."

Bug's soft voice filled her heart with sunshine. His hand tightened around hers as she tugged her eyes open.

"Hi," she greeted. He was as handsome as ever, sitting beside her bed as if he didn't have anywhere else to be.

The smile on his face revealed nothing of the worry that his eyes couldn't hide. "Here, let me get you some water."

She shook her head, squeezing his fingers and not wanting him to leave for even a second. His hair was mussed and his shirt wrinkled. "You've been here for awhile."

"I told you I'd be here."

A sheet covered her stomach and she carefully touched the area with her free hand. The heavy weight was invisible, and her touch didn't increase the pain. "The surgery?"

"Went well," he said, laying his other hand on top of hers. "But you spiked a fever, you've been very sick for the past few days."

"The past few days?" Time held no memory for her. "Didn't I just have the surgery this morning?"

"No," his whisper was very soft. "It's been four days, honey."

The darkness of the room registered, and the window revealed the lazy glow of the moon. "You've been here the whole time?"

"Of course." The simple statement held conviction. "How do you feel? Should I get someone?"

She shook her head. "You're here."

"Yes, I am." He brushed a gentle kiss on her forehead. "You sound sleepy."

"I am."

"Then rest. We can talk later." His chin sat softly on her shoulder as his forehead rested against her temple. The soothing, calm touch encouraged her to close her eyes. Knowing he'd be there when she woke, she drifted into a healing sleep.

Hours later she awoke again. Sunlight sparkled against the white ceiling, but it was the pressure on her stomach that had roused her out of the deep sleep. Two hands were settled on her stomach, she followed the arms connected to them until her gaze met those of a tall blond haired man.

"Hello, Miss Reynolds. I'm Doctor Robb." The man straightened, removing his hands from her stomach. "How are you feeling?"

"Much better." Her mind tossed about and she added, "I think. It's all kind of a blur." She took in the rest of the room. A woman with a long, white apron stood on her other side, but otherwise the room was empty. Her heart beat increased.

The woman patted Eva's hand. "Don't worry. Your friends are right outside the door. They had to leave while Dr. Robb performs his examination."

"Oh, thank you," Eva answered. Her eyes then landed on a small table near the window. Several bouquets of flowers, in all colors, shapes and sizes, filled the top.

"Miss Reynolds," Dr. Robb said. "I'm going to remove your drain tubes. It shouldn't hurt overly much, but you will feel a sting. Hold on to Mrs. French's hand tightly, and try not to flinch, all right?"

The woman took a hold of Eva's hand as she answered, "All right."

The sting was strong, and she sucked in air,

absorbing it as it raced across her stomach.

"That's it. Lie still. There's one more," the doctor instructed.

Eva kept her eyes on the flowers. Studying the big red roses as she would a scene she wanted to paint. She imagined how to roll her brush to make the petals appear velvety, and the colors she'd need to mix to create the tiny paler thorns on the thick green stems.

"Good girl," the doctor praised. "Just a bit longer. I need to examine the wound."

Focusing on the flowers, she felt his hands on her bare midriff, but didn't allow her mind to veer from the plants. Daisies sat amongst the roses, as did carnations and mums. Pinks and yellows and pale lavenders, the flowers spoke to her, telling her which ones needed to be painted first to allow the others to be spotlighted in the final picture she created to be painted someday when she returned home.

"All done," Dr. Robb said.

The woman let go of Eva's hand and tugged her gown down and the sheet up.

Eva turned from the flowers then, to glance at the doctor. His blue eyes twinkled, and he winked before he walked across the room. There he splashed his hands in a basin and wiped them on a towel before he came back to stand beside her bed. "You can tell Mrs. Quinter I washed thoroughly, before and after."

He sat on the chair then. "Let me tell you what's happened."

She nodded.

"I had to perform a complete hysterectomy. The tumor was larger than either Dr. Weston or I imagined. You must have been in terrible pain lately."

"Some," she admitted.

"Well, I removed everything, so there's nothing left for it to grow back. I've found that to be most effective. The surgery went remarkably well. You did spike a fever afterwards, which isn't unusual, and that's also why I wanted to remove the drain tubes as soon as possible. We don't want to worry about infection setting in. We're going to keep you here for a few more days, and then we'll transfer you to the convalescence hall. I'd like to see you remain there for at least another week before we release you to a home."

"A home?" The way he said it made her question the term.

"Yes, Mr. Houston says he'll arrange for you to be taken to one of the recovery homes. You'll have private care until you are fully recuperated."

"How long will that be?"

"No more than six weeks would be my guess at this time. But some of it is a waiting game. Some patients make complete recoveries. Other's need a second surgery."

"What for?"

He shrugged. "Different things. Usually it's infection. But I've discovered the faster we remove the drain tubes, the less chance there is of infection."

She settled her hands lightly on her stomach.

Dr. Robb gently patted her fingers. "You're going to be stiff and sore. The incision is quite large and will take some time to heal. But you're young and very healthy. Actually, you are the youngest patient I've performed this surgery on, so I'm carefully monitoring your recovery for my medical journal."

"So it's all gone?" she asked in a whisper. "I'll never have children?"

He took a hold of one hand. "I thought that was explained to you before you arrived."

"It was," she admitted. "I was just wondering if..."

"I'm sorry, Miss Reynolds. But there really wasn't an option in your case. What Dr. Weston said is true. You'll never bear children."

An overwhelming, emptiness filled her so quickly her eyes and nose stung. The tears she cried at home, with Bug lying on the bed beside her, renewed themselves. Deep down there had been a little ounce of hope that had said things might turn out differently. That little bit was gone now, leaving her hollow inside and out.

"I'm sorry, Miss Reynolds. Do you have any other questions I can answer for you?"

She shook her head.

"I'll be back to see you tomorrow then." He stood, and patted her hand one more time before he removed his hand from hers. "I'll send your family in."

"No," she choked.

"No? They're right outside the door."

She shook her head. "I'd like to be alone for a few minutes."

He rubbed his jaw and looked at the other woman, Mrs. French. The woman patted Eva's shoulder. "I'll stay with her for a few minutes, Doctor. You can tell the family I'll let them in when she's ready."

"All right, Mrs. French, thank you." The doctor's exit was finalized by the click of the door.

Eva wanted to tell Mrs. French she could leave, too, but something told her the woman wouldn't go. She turned back to the flowers, begging them to absorb her attention again. It was to no avail. Painting the flowers no longer appealed to her.

Outside Eva's door, Bug paced the hall. The doctor had been in her room for over an hour. When the man strolled into the room earlier, Bug had refused to leave, as he had every day since the morning of her surgery. Today, Dr. Robb had insisted. He said he couldn't remove the drain tubes with others in the room, and after the man had explained that if he didn't remove them soon, infection might set in, Bug had no choice but to comply.

The past four days had been agonizing. He'd been afraid to close his eyes, let alone leave her room. The chance of her slipping away, never waking, was too real of an issue. He'd sat beside her bed, afraid he might miss something even in the blink of an eye lid. So he'd watched. Watched her sleep, watched her breathe, and knew he'd spend the rest of his life watching her, for he didn't want to miss another moment.

And now he was. He had no idea what was going on in that room. He stomped to the door, and reached for the knob. Before he clutched the glass handle, the door swung open. Stepping forward, Bug caught a glimpse of Eva lying on the bed. He stalled for a moment, which was long enough for Dr. Robb to step into the hallway and push the door shut behind him.

"How'd it go?" Jack Houston asked, jumping from the chair he'd taken a few feet away from the door.

Dr. Robb braced an arm on the door jamb, preventing anyone from entering the room. "Good," he said. "Real, real good. No infection. Everything is healing. I'm confident her recovery will be complete and quick."

"Is she awake?" Bug asked, wanting to shove the man aside.

"Yes, but she's asked for a few minutes alone." Dr. Robb shifted, but didn't move away from the door. "She's upset in learning she won't bear children, which is to be expected. You need to give her some time to get used to the idea. It's mentally challenging. Women have an inner sense that their purpose on earth is solely to procreate. I've never seen it, but I've heard women have gone mad after hysterectomies, believing their lives are over, and others who have refused to have the surgery for that same reason."

"That's crazy," Bug said. "I don't care if she can't have babies."

"It's not for you to care, young man," Dr. Robb said, not unkindly, but to the point. "It's Eva who cares. And it's Eva who needs to accept it."

Bug bowed his head, awash with guilt at putting his feelings before Eva's. The doctor patted his shoulder. "Don't blame yourself. That won't help her either." He turned to Jack then. "I've explained that once she's well enough, you've arranged for her care to happen in a care home."

That made Bug snap his head up. "I'll care for her."

"Once she's back at her place maybe, but while she's in Wichita she'll have the best care I can find, Bug." Jack's demand held no room for argument.

Once again Bug realized how insignificant he was to Eva. Would there ever come a day when she needed him? Would he ever have something he could offer or provide her that no one else could?

Bug turned back to the doctor. "She's healing though? There's no complications or infection or anything else we need to worry about?"

Dr. Robb offered an assuring grin. "No, nothing else. She's doing remarkably well. She's young and healthy. I don't foresee her having any other issues in the near future." The doctor patted his shoulder again. "I knew you'd be upset when you couldn't go right back in, but be patient. Give her a little time, and all will be fine."

Bug nodded, since there was nothing else he could do.

"Where's your mother?" Dr Robb asked,

somewhat cautiously.

"She went back to the hotel for a bit," Jack answered.

"Good. Be sure to tell her I washed with soap and water, before and after the examination."

Jack grinned. "We will, Dr. Robb, and thank you."

"Yes, thank you," Bug repeated, shameful of being remiss. He offered his hand. "Thank you very much."

The doctor shook both his and Jack's hands as he said, "You're welcome. I'm sure I'll see you both tomorrow." Laughing he added, "And every day Miss Reynolds is here."

The man made his way down the hall then, and Bug stared at the door, wishing he could push it open, but knowing he couldn't. After a few minutes, Jack slapped him on the back. "I'm going to go take your mother out to lunch. I'd ask you to join us, but I know you won't go. I know you're the one she'll want to see when she's ready, so give Eva my love and tell her I'll see her this afternoon."

Bug spun about. "Do you think so?"

"Yes, I'll be back this afternoon."

"No." Bug shook his head. "Do you think I'm the one she'll want to see?"

Jack looked thunderstruck. "Are you still questioning how much she loves you?"

"I... Aw hell, Jack, I don't know what to think," he admitted.

"Welcome to the world of love, Buggie-boy." Jack slapped his back again. "And get used to it my good man."

The hall grew so empty it threatened to close in on Bug within seconds of Jack's leaving. He walked over, plopped down on the chair, and hung his head over his chest. He was used to loving Eva, it was getting used to life that didn't make rhyme or reason that had his mind, heart, and stomach doe-see-doeing around each other.

He was lost in a world where he'd never left for Pennsylvania when something touched his shoulder. Bolting from the chair, he asked, "What? What's happened?"

"Nothing, Mr. Quinter," Mrs. French said. She'd been taking care of Eva during the days lately, and was a nice woman. It was the smart talking woman that tried to kick him out every night that he didn't like. "Miss Reynolds is ready to see you now. I'm going to get her something to eat. Would you like something?"

"Eat? She's up to eating?"

The woman smiled. "Yes. Would you like something?"

"No." He turned to the door. "Can I go in?"

"Yes, you can go in."

Bug didn't wait to hear what else she said. Something about returning shortly may have touched his ears as he pushed open the door. Eva was propped up on the bed, not really sitting, but not lying flat on her back anymore either. He tiptoed, not wanting his boot heals to click on the floor as he pulled the door shut and made his way across the room.

She turned, and though her eyes were red and somewhat swollen, she smiled at him.

"Hi," he said, unable to come up with anything else.

"Hello."

He stopped near the bed. She lifted a hand. A rush of relief, he wasn't sure from what, floated down his body. He took a hold of her hand and lowering himself onto the chair beside her bed, he brushed a kiss to her knuckles.

"Thank you for the flowers."

"You're welcome, but they aren't all from me.

Jack brought some in, so did Ma."

"I know. Mrs. French told me." She swallowed and leaned back against the pillows. "You used to bring me flowers all the time. Do you remember that?"

"Yes." He wrapped his other hand around the one he still held. "But I can't take credit for all of them. Snake was forever telling me to take a bunch to you and Willamina every time he pruned." He pinched his lips together, wondering why he always felt the need to explain things to death.

"I know, but you were the one who handed them to me." She closed her eyes.

"I'll bring you flowers every day for the rest of your life if it will make you feel better," he vowed.

"You make me feel better. Even right now, just having you sit beside me makes me feel better."

"Then I'll stay right here, forever." Her fingers threaded between his and she squeezed. "I love you, Eva. And I wish with all my soul there was something I could do right now."

"You are doing something, Bug. You're here for me." A single tear slipped from beneath her closed lid. "I love you, Bug," she whispered.

He leaned forward and kissed the tear away. "Tell me what else I can do, there has to be something you need, something I can do."

She opened her eyes and met his gaze. "Will you sit beside me, and hold me like you did that morning back at the house?" A little sob slipped over her lips. "Will you just hold me, Bug?"

The bed was narrow, but that didn't matter to him. He eased himself onto the mattress and leaned against the pillow, sharing the space with her. Once again he slipped one arm under her neck and the other around her front, and held her tight. "I'll always be here to hold you, honey, always," he whispered.

\*\*\*\*

The next two weeks flew by, with Eva feeling better every day, Bug found himself outside the hospital more and more. Not because he wanted to be away from her side, but because Eva had small errands she'd ask him to run. The fresh air and sunshine did him good she said, but for him, it was the smile on her face when he returned that had his spirits soaring. He brought her another bunch of flowers most every time he returned, and she'd thank him with sweet tender kisses.

A train whistle split the air, and he pulled his attention back to the depot. Ma sat near a front window in the first passenger car, she gave him another wave. He returned it. She'd agreed to go home after seeing Eva settled into the private care home yesterday.

Bug wouldn't necessarily call it a home, but more of a mansion. Built of bricks and hosting more than a dozen beds, it was where those who could afford it went to be pampered and catered to for a variety of issues. It was most certainly where Eva needed to be, but he questioned some of the other residents—who seemed to not be ill in any shape or form. The workers were excellent, and held pride in their abilities to see to their customer's every comfort. The only issue he had with the Westmaster Care Facility was the fact he couldn't stay there.

Eva told him not to fret, the weeks would go by quickly, but he feared they'd drag on. She could now walk around, and rarely slept during the day, but Dr. Robb wanted her in Wichita until the last of her incision was completely healed. Bug agreed, but the want to be home had been growing deeper and deeper within him.

"See you in a few weeks!" Ma shouted from the train as it started to roll away.

"Snake will be at the station when you arrive!"

Bug assured one last time.

Ma waved and then pulled her arm in. Bug watched as the train chugged along, until the last car had rolled past. He turned around then and jogged to where Buddy Murphy sat in the buggy. The driver had been at their beck and call the past weeks, and from the looks of him, he didn't mind it in the least. A smile was permanently pasted on his young face, along with a few freckles and blond peach fuzz. He couldn't be more than sixteen or so, but from the way he knew the city streets, had been wheeling a wagon about for years.

"All set, sir?" Buddy asked as Bug settled in.

"Yes."

"Then hold on." Buddy cracked the whip above the horse's ears.

"I always do," Bug replied, with a death grip on the canopy brace. "I always do."

Buddy laughed, guiding the horses through the traffic with a precision Bug had grown to respect. "Anywhere else you need to stop?"

Bug glanced in the back seat. A bouquet of flowers wrapped with twine bounced on the leather. He snatched up the flowers before they slid onto the floor. "Nope, just the care facility."

"All right, then, sir."

Bug set the flowers between him and the driver. Buddy had told him where to buy them the first day, and most days since if Bug didn't make it to the store on the corner, Buddy did for him. Today it was a bunch of lilies—sparkling white with little hints of yellow. Eva would like them.

After Buddy dropped him off, Bug spent the rest of the afternoon visiting with Eva in the sunny garden. They talked of minor things as they did every day. Neither of them brought up her surgery, or the outcome of it, other than when he'd asked how she felt and she said fine. However, this particular evening after they had dinner together in a private suite off the small downstairs dining room, Jack arrived. The paints, brushes, canvases, and easels Jack, along with Buddy's help, carried in, made Bug once again wish he'd done it for her.

Eva was so happy she was almost jumping up and down with excitement. It wasn't that Bug wasn't happy, but somehow Jack's gifts made his flowers extremely insignificant. Pasting a grin on his face, Bug kissed Eva's cheek. "I see you're ready to start painting again."

"Oh, yes," she said. "I've felt so useless lying around." She hugged him. "The first things I'm going to paint are the roses you gave me at the hospital. The images have been dancing in my head for weeks."

Bug had to let her slip away, since she practically bolted out of his arms to hug Jack. "Thank you, Jack. You always seem to know exactly what I need."

Jack gave her a hug, and then he slapped Bug's back. "When you're up to it, there's someone in New York waiting for a picture of Buffalo Killer. Just like the one we sold at the art show."

His back teeth ached, forcing Bug to lessen the way he clenched his jaw. He also let the smile fall from his face. He'd forgotten about the Judge's request. It all seemed so long ago.

"What do you say, Bug?"

"Sorry," he offered. His mind had been back in New York.

"I said we'd carry this all up to the sun room off her bedroom, the light will be perfect for Eva to paint there," Jack said.

"Sure." Bug picked up the easel and canvas frames Buddy had carried in earlier, and followed Jack and Eva, who talked nonstop, out of the room. Crossing the large foyer, he glanced around as an eerie feeling tickled his shoulders. The elegant and stylish foyer reminded him of the Staples home back in Pennsylvania. His gaze landed back on Eva. She seemed comfortable with the classy ambiance, whereas it always made him uneasy—like he was walking in someone else's shoes.

## Chapter Thirteen

Eva looked at Dr. Robb. "Really?"

"Yes, really." The grin on his face said even more than his words.

Elation zipped through her. "When? How soon?"

"I'd say you're ready to travel today." He snapped his bag shut. "But it looks like it will take you a day or two to pack up."

Eva followed his gaze around the room. Paintings sat everywhere. Since Jack had brought her the paints two weeks ago, she'd spent every moment she could find in the sun room creating the visions dancing in her head. "I'm a little obsessive when it comes to painting," she admitted. "Would you be interested in helping me get rid of one or two?"

"How so?" Dr. Robb asked, moving to examine a painting she'd created of Mrs. French assisting a small child in an overly large hospital bed. His eyes returned to her. "This is remarkable, Eva."

"Thank you." She moved to the far side of the room and turned another canvas around. "This is the one I made of you." Eva held her breath, hoping Dr. Robb liked it. He'd done so much for her. She sincerely wanted to offer him a gift. The painting was of him listening to a child's heart with his stethoscope. It was a picture she'd seen at the hospital, when a mother had carried the young child into the hospital that first night, right after Bug and Ma had left. Of course, at the time, she hadn't known it was Dr. Robb who rushed to the child's aid. But later, upon receiving his excellent treatment herself, she'd recognized him. The supplies Jack had brought were everything she'd needed to create her thank you.

"Oh, my." Dr Robb stood next to the painting. "I don't know what to say, Eva. It's…it's, well, remarkable."

"Thank you. Would you care to take it off my hands? And the one of Mrs. French?"

He glanced her way. "Off your hands?"

"Yes. I painted them for you and Mrs. French, as a token of my appreciation."

"Eva, I know how sought after your paintings are, I couldn't possibly accept it without offering payment." His gaze never left the painting, as if it mesmerized him.

"I'll refuse your offer, so you might as well just take it." He spun around to gape at her. She giggled with happiness that he liked the picture so much, and held it up. "Please accept this token of my appreciation, Dr. Robb."

"I really am speechless." He relieved her of the painting. "Thank you, Eva. I will cherish it always."

"As I will the excellent care you provided me." She gave a respectful bow. "Thank you, Dr. Robb."

He bowed his head in return. When he lifted it, he said, "I shall miss you Eva. Not only have you been an excellent patient, you're a delight to be around. I've really enjoyed our time together."

A blush rose into her cheeks. "I shall miss you, too, but I'm extremely happy to go home." The news he'd provided her with made her laugh with glee. "I've missed my friends so much, and my home."

"I'm sure you have, my dear." He set the painting down near the door and then returned to the sun room to gather the one for Mrs. French. "I'll ask the staff to wrap these and have them delivered to the hospital. I have more patients to see before I leave." After he'd set it down with the other one, and as if it was an afterthought, he walked back across the room and gave her a gentle hug. "Though I know it's very unlikely, if you ever decide Bug isn't the man for you, look me up." He winked one of his blue eyes.

She giggled. "That's a tempting offer, but I've loved Bug for so long, there's no chance I'll change my mind now."

"That's what I imagined, but I had to try." His teasing was so sincere she almost thought he was serious for a moment. He held her gaze for a moment longer, and then he turned and walked to the door. "Speaking of Bug. I met his older brother earlier today."

"You did? Which one?" She followed him to the door.

"How many does he have?"

"Four. There's Hog, Snake, Skeeter, and Kid."

"Ah, are they all as unique as Bug?"

She nodded, grinning from ear to ear.

"Kid," Dr. Robb said, pulling the door open. "He's downstairs. He arrived at the same time I did today."

"Really? No one mentioned he was traveling to Wichita. I hope nothing has happened at home."

"I'm sure everything is fine. I've told you before that you worry too much, about others that is." He pulled the door open. "They're waiting for you in the library. I said I'd send you down there as soon as I completed my exam."

She stepped into the hall. "Then I shall go say hello. And tell them the wonderful news. I know Bug is anxious to get home." Hitching her skirt, she rushed to the stairs, knowing Bug would be as happy as she to hear she was healed.

The hem of her yellow sateen dress swished around her ankles at each step. She held it a touch higher, to assure she wouldn't trip as she hurried downward. At the bottom, she turned left to make her way across the foyer and down the hall to the library. The soft soles of her kid slippers slid silently across the floor, until heated male voices made her skid to a halt.

Listening, she leaned near the door that was slightly opened.

"What the hell all happened when you were out East?" Kid's voice was raised to a level Eva had never heard. "First Sheriff Turley brought me out a wire from some Judge in New York claiming new evidence came forward about your arrest and that he needs to speak to you about it. Then some young blond girl shows up at Ma's claiming you promised to marry her. And after that a family of seven arrives, telling us you adopted three of their kids."

Eva's hands began to tremble.

"Three little red-headed kids?" Bug asked. "Are they okay? How about Reed, how's his cough?" Eva cringed at how worried he sounded. "Is little Heather all right? She's shy, and needs a little coaxing to tell you when she's hungry. Tucker's taking good care of them isn't he? He's only seven, but he's been taking care of Reed and Heather for over a year now."

Eva leaned closer. He'd never mentioned...Her mind snapped, as if she'd just been slapped. Bug didn't want three red headed kids. He already had them. And he had his girlfriend waiting for him back in Scott. No wonder he didn't care if she couldn't have children, he had no intention of marrying her.

"Bug," Kid growled, sounding exasperated.

"Are they all right, Kid?" Bug asked again.

"Yes, they look fine." Kid said. "Ma settled the whole family in Eva's soddy since someone needed to care for her stock every day. That's not the point. What the hell happened? How did you end up adopting three kids? And what's this about being arrested? And who's the blonde that says you promised to marry her? Why didn't you mention any of this?"

"Aw, hell, Kid. It all happened so fast. My arrest, the kids, Eva's illness. Everything. I never had time to tell you about it. I've been out here for the past month. Have you forgotten that?" He moaned as if in pain. "Shit, Kid, I feel like I'm caught in the middle of a tornado."

"What about the woman?" Kid asked. "She's got Ma pulling her hair out. The woman has your wedding planned out. Invitations and all. She claims it will happen as soon as you arrive in Scott. Who the hell is she?"

Eva held her breath, hoping it would dull the pain ripping her heart into tiny pieces.

"A short, pretty blonde?" Bug asked.

She knew it. The woman from the art show. Why hadn't he told her? Then again, why hadn't she asked?

"Yes," Kid answered.

"Shit," Bug growled. Eva could imagine he was running his hands through his hair, that's what he did when he was frustrated and trying to think. "That would be Jenny Staples."

The softness in his voice was unmistakable.

"Staples? The man you worked for out east?"

"Yes, Jenny and I—"

The sound of footsteps made Eva spin about.

Jack waved. "There you are."

She rushed forward, stopping him at the edge of the hallway.

"I just ran into Dr. Robb. He told me the good news."

"I'm not leaving," she said abruptly.

"What?" Jack asked, shocked.

"I'm not leaving. So don't say anything about what Dr. Robb just said." The door down the hall had opened, and Bug now stood in the hallway.

"Come on," Eva said, pulling Jack in her wake. "And if you ever want to sell another one of my paintings, you won't utter a word."

Kid stepped into the hall beside Bug. Eva took a fortifying breath, and exclaimed, "Kid! It's wonderful to see you!" She rushed forward to wrap her arms around his middle and gave him a long hug. "What on earth are you doing here?" She didn't wait for him to answer. "Let me guess. You finally came to take your little brother home. And it's a good thing, too. He's been driving me crazy."

"What? Driving you crazy?" Bug asked, shaking his head.

She forced a giggle to trickle over her lips, and patted his cheeks. "Yes, driving me crazy. Along with yourself. I know how much you dislike the city, and I've said several times you should go home for a few days." It was true, she had, but he hadn't listened, and she hadn't wanted him to.

"I'm not going anywhere, not without you," he insisted.

She spun back to Kid. "I hope you're here to convince him differently." Hooking Bug's arm with one hand, and Kid's with the other, she led them back into the library. "I just spoke with Dr. Robb, and he says I'm healing quickly, but that I need to stay here for at least two more weeks." She hated lying, but turned to Bug and said, "It appears I'm not getting enough rest. He insists I have no visitors for the next two weeks."

"When did he say that?" Bug asked. "I saw him this morning, and he didn't mention anything close to that."

"He just left my room." She turned and met Jack's confused gaze. Begging for his aid, she said, "Jack just spoke with him, didn't you Jack?"

He frowned, staring at her deeply. Her teeth dug

into her bottom lip. Silently, she pleaded for Jack to support her story.

Ultimately, he did, "Yes, I just spoke with Dr. Robb. What Eva says is true. He'd like all of us to leave her alone for the next couple of weeks."

"No," Bug said. "I'm not—"

"Bug, please," she said, not turning around. She couldn't face him. Couldn't lie to him again.

"Where is he? I want to talk to him," Bug insisted.

"He's left already, Bug." Jack stepped forward, between her and Bug. "Come on. I'll tell you everything he said. Let's leave Kid and Eva alone for a minute. I'm sure she wants to hear how everyone back home is doing."

Bug hesitated, but finally gave in and allowed Jack to lead him out of the room. When the door clicked shut, she spun around. "Take him home, Kid. Please take him home."

Kid laid his hands on her shoulders. His knowing eyes bore into hers. "How much did you hear?"

She shook her head. "Just take him home. I don't ever want to see him again."

"Eva, I'm sorry. I shouldn't have spouted off like I did. I'm sure Bug can explain everything."

"I'm sure he can," she said. "But I don't want to hear it."

"Eva—"

"Just take him home, Kid." Tears fell now, she couldn't stop them. "Please, promise you'll take him home."

"I'll take him home, Eva. But what about you? What's happened?"

"Don't worry about me. Jack's here. I'll be fine." She wiped at the tears. "I'll write Jessie and tell her everything, but right now, I have to go lie down." She spun about and ran from the room, stumbling and crying all the way up the stairs.

She was lying on her bed, but her heart was still downstairs, splattered across the hallway in a million pieces when a knock sounded on the door. Before she had a chance to respond, the door opened and Jack came strolling in. She sat up, staring at the space behind him.

"He's left. For now," Jack said, closing the door. "But we both know he'll be back. And he'll have talked to Dr. Robb, know you're lying."

She twirled her thumbs, staring at how the tips could circle around one another.

The bed sank as Jack sat down beside her. "What happened?"

"You tell me," she said, not looking up. "Why was Bug arrested in New York?"

"That's not my story to tell. It's Bug's. Ask him."

She tugged her hands apart and folded her arms. "When did he adopt three kids?"

Jack remained silent.

"Are you going to tell me anything?" If not it was useless to ask about Jenny Staples and the impending wedding waiting for Bug.

Jack didn't even glance her way.

She bounced off the bed. "Fine. I thought you were my friend."

"I am. And because I am, I'm going to tell you the truth." He let out an exaggerated sigh. "I'm tired of this game you're playing."

Eva spun around to stare at him. "What are you talking about? What game?"

Jack met her gaze. "No wonder Bug left three years ago. You go from hot to cold faster than a north wind."

Flabbergasted, she could barely breathe, let alone speak.

"Don't try to deny it." He folded his arms, as if he was ready to wait her out.

"I don't know what you're talking about."

"Like hell you don't."

She turned around and walked to the window. "I sent Bug home because that's where he belongs. His fiancée' is there. His children are there."

"Oh, shut up." A second later he was at her side. "Or better yet, listen to yourself. Poor Eva, she has a conflict with Bug, so what does she do? Runs, or sends him away."

"I don't do that."

"Yes, you do. And I want to know why." He spun her about. "I've seen the other side of you. I've seen the Eva who doesn't flee. The one who stands up and fights for what she wants. Why don't you let that girl come out when Bug's around?"

"I…"

"You what? Think he wants a weak girl who runs as soon as the road gets a little bumpy?"

Her defenses where shattering. "Jack, I don't understand why you're being so mean about all this."

"Mean?"

She nodded.

"I'm not being mean, Eva. I'm being honest. You turn into some kind of little lost girl when Bug's around. Don't you think he'll get tired of catering to your whims someday? Don't you think he wants to know you can stand on your own?"

A chill rippled her spine. It was true. She was so afraid Bug wouldn't like the person she'd become the last few years. "I—" She swallowed. "Is it that bad?"

"Yes." He patted her cheek. "And no." Taking her hand he led her back to the bed and set her down. He sat beside her. "We all face rough patches in relationships. You've faced a really bad one with your surgery and all. And Bug's been here the whole time. Never once has he even complained about any of it. Yet, you, as soon as you learn something about him you don't like, you run or hide. I don't understand it. I've seen what you're made of. Bug told me you wouldn't let anyone contact him about Willamina or your art show. Why?"

"I had to do that."

"Why? Why are you so unfair to him?"

"I'm not unfair. It was because I didn't want Bug to find out about Willamina that way, or to come home until he was ready."

Jack took her hands in his. "In other words, you wanted Bug to come home for you, not because of something else."

"Yes," she admitted. That is exactly what she'd always wanted.

"Then why don't you tell Bug that?"

Eva's mind tumbled about, and her stomach plummeted. "I can't. Bug fell in love with the girl I was. If I've changed, maybe he won't love me."

He shook her hands sternly. "Eva!" After a disgust-filled sigh, he said, "Haven't you wondered why Stephanie Quinter refused to allow you two to get married that night?"

She frowned.

"Yes, I know all about it," he assured. "There's very little I don't know about."

"Because she wanted us to wait..." She plucked her mind for Ma's reasoning.

"Did the thought that perhaps she was giving you the chance to stand up to her, and show Bug just how much you love him enter your mind?"

Her spine grew stiff, like it does when the truth hits you smack dab in the stomach.

"If you had stood up to her that night, you and Bug would already be married." He sighed. "He wouldn't be pulling his hair out, and we wouldn't be sitting here having this discussion."

Eva bolted off the bed, needing to move and give her mind time to sort through the thoughts flying in and out like birds in a storm. She paced the floor, catching memories one at a time.

Jack sat, watching her. When she stopped and turned to stare at him, he said, "I don't know anything about Bug adopting three kids, he'll have to tell you about that. I do know about his arrest, and I believe I know what the new findings are, but again, that's his business. The one thing I can tell you is Jenny Staples is a woman who knows what she wants, and is willing to do about anything to get it. Including traveling across the country. When she heard about you, she didn't send Bug home, she tried to find a way to make him stay in New York, and when that didn't work, she followed him to Kansas. I'm shocked it took her this long."

Eva's mind had already been made up before he said his last piece, but now that he had, she became more determined. "Book me a seat on the next train heading west." She moved to the wardrobe and pulled her bag from the bottom.

"I'll have to check the schedules," he said.

"Jack." She pointed to the door. "There are four railroads rolling in and out of Scott City every day. I don't care if it's a cattle hauler. You find a train that will drop me off in Scott. Today!"

"What about Bug? He probably hasn't left yet. Don't you want to talk to him?"

"Why?" She set the bag on the bed and returned to the wardrobe.

"So he can explain—"

"I don't give a damn about his explanations. And I hope he hasn't left for home yet."

Jack looked dumbfounded.

She grabbed several gowns from their hooks and thrust them into his arms. "When Bug does arrive home, Jenny Staples will already be on her way back to Pennsylvania and the preacher will be ready to perform our wedding ceremony." She spun back to grab more clothes from the wardrobe. The easel holding the picture of a bouquet of roses stood beside the cupboard. "Oh, and Jack." She pointed to the painting. "My name is Eva Robertson, soon to be Eva Quinter, and that's how my paintings will be signed from now on. If you can't agree with that, I'll have to find myself another agent."

He opened his mouth. She shook her finger, stopping whatever he'd been about to say and pointed to the clothes in his hands. "Put those on the bed. You have a ticket to go purchase. I'll be at the station within half an hour."

****

Chasing down Dr. Robb was harder than catching a free range rooster. Bug tapped his toe on the floor, staring down the hospital hall, and waiting for the man's familiar shape to appear. He'd been ten steps behind the man all day yesterday and truly wondered if the doctor ever slept. Bug had been kicked out of the hospital close to midnight last night, so this morning, figuring it was the only way to see the man, he'd made himself an appointment to be seen. Dr. Robb had been in surgery all morning, and his first chance to see someone, was now, at three in the afternoon.

The click of heels on the wood floor had Bug leaping from his chair.

"Bug," Dr. Robb said. "What are you doing here? Has something happened to Eva? Why wasn't I informed?"

"How could I inform you when I couldn't catch up to you?" Bug replied.

Dr. Robb shook his head. "I'm sorry, there was a carriage accident that kept me in surgery all night and morning." The man rubbed his hands over his face. "What's happened to Eva? I'll get my bag."

Bug followed the man into his office, feeling a touch of empathy for how tired the doctor looked.

"You don't need your bag. At least I don't think you do."

"Then why are you here?"

"I want to know why you said she can't have any visitors."

Dr. Robb shut the door, and frowning he stared at Bug as if gathering his thoughts. "Visitors? I didn't say she couldn't have visitors. I released her."

"Released her?"

"Yes. She was ecstatic. I figured you'd already left for home." Dr. Robb walked across the room to where a large package sat. He tore the paper from the frame. "She gave me this as a token of her appreciation."

Bug moved closer to examine the painting. It was of the doctor and a little girl, but it was the signature down at the bottom that caught his attention. "She signed it Eva Robertson."

"So she did." The doctor looked up from the painting. "Who told you she couldn't have any visitors?"

"She did." Bug sighed.

Dr Robb shook his head. "I really don't know why she would have said that. Is she still at Westmaster?"

"I assume so. I haven't been back there since yesterday when she said she couldn't have visitors. I've been tracking you down the whole time."

The doctor moved to his desk and fluttered through some papers. "I should have a report here. They delivered the painting so I'd assume they would have sent her paperwork as well. Aw, here it is." He frowned as he read the sheet he picked up. "It says she left yesterday before noon."

"Left? Before noon?"

"Yes. I would have finished my visits there by ten or so. She must have left shortly after I'd seen her."

"Where'd she go?"

Dr. Robb set the paper back on his desk. "Home."

"Shit." Bug plopped onto the chair behind him. The way his mind ran circles around itself was downright exhausting.

"What's going on between you and Eva, Bug?"

He didn't know what the doctor asked. Shrugging, he shook his head, unable to answer.

Dr. Robb sat down in his chair. "You've told me some, Eva's said some, so has your mother and Jack Houston, but I'm still confused."

"Try being in my shoes," Bug muttered.

"Well, I have to tell you, if I hadn't seen with my own eyes how deeply in love the two of you are, I might not offer the bit of advice I'm about to offer."

"Oh." Bug was downright tired of the advice others offered on a continuous basis. All he wanted was for him and Eva to get married and live their lives. It might not look like a perfect life to others, but it would be for the two of them—that is if everyone else would back off and let it happen.

"If I were you," the doctor started, "I'd go home, and not give a damn what others want. I'd marry her in a heartbeat, no matter what your mother says. You're both adults and know what you want. Quit trying to please everyone else and please yourselves."

Bug stared at the doctor for a moment. A smile twisted his lips, gushing up from his chest like oil shooting out of a new well. He stood. "You know what, doc? I think that's the best piece of advice I've heard in years."

Dr. Robb stood and held out one hand. "Then get the hell out of here."

Bug, laughing, grasped the man's hand and shook it firmly. "Thanks, Dr. Robb. Thanks for all you've done."

"My pleasure. And I wish you and Eva the best of luck."

Bug nodded and then shot out the door. He found Kid pacing the boardwalk in front of the hospital. "So, what did you find out?" Kid asked.

Slapping his brother's back, he announced, "That it's time for a wedding."

Kid laughed. "Well, it's about time." He stopped then, as if startled and asked, "Whose?"

"Mine and Eva's," Bug declared solidly—and damn if it didn't feel good. "Let's go, big brother." He started walking. "We got a train to catch."

"Where's Eva?" Kid asked, marching down the street beside him.

"Probably at her house by now."

Kid shook his head. "Damn it's hard keeping up with you two."

Chapter Fourteen

The train arrived late in the night, so Eva didn't have a chance to put the plan she created in place until now—early this morning. Stepping out on her porch, she was a bit surprised to see several children running across the front yard. A thin woman with light brown hair followed them.

"Good morning," Eva greeted.

"Oh, goodness. Did we wake you? I'm so sorry," the woman said, moving toward the porch. "I'm Joanna Porter. Mrs. Quinter hired us to take care of your place until you got home. We heard you arrive late last night but didn't think we should disturb you by making our introductions."

"No, you didn't wake me," Eva assured as she moved down the steps. "I'm Eva Robertson, and thank you for taking care of everything." She nodded toward the children. "Who do we have here?"

"Oh, this is Adam, our oldest, and Anna." Joanna Porter pointed to the two children hiding behind her skirt. They looked about four or five. "And these three, are Tucker, Reed, and Heather." The woman pointed to the red-headed children standing a short distance behind her. Their little faces were sparkling clean and their hair freshly combed. Their clothes were new and neatly pressed.

Eva's heart skipped about. The children were adorable. The thought of the three of them being hers made her shiver with excitement. She knelt down. "Hello, Adam and Anna," she started, smiling at the first two. "And hello to you, Tucker, Reed, and Heather."

Tiny greetings murmured in the air. She kept her gaze on the three red-headed children. "Bug should be home soon." Their little eyes lit up. Eva could relate. "I know he's going to be very excited to see you."

Tucker stepped forward and handed Eva a basket. "We gathered these eggs for you, ma'am."

"Oh, well, thank you, sir," she answered. "My, the basket is full. You must be very good at gathering eggs. I think I might have to ask you to help me every morning."

Tucker twisted his foot in the dirt. "I could do that ma'am. Reed and Heather know how to do chores, too."

"I'm sure they do." The arrival of a man had Eva looking up.

The man bowed his head. "Ma'am. I'm Jonathan Porter."

She stood. "Hello. I'm Eva Robertson. It's nice to meet you, Mr. Porter. It's nice to meet all of you." Her first impression of the entire family filled her with warmth. She smiled. "I'd like a chance to talk with you, Mr. and Mrs. Porter. Would you have a few minutes?"

"Of course, ma'am," Jonathan readily agreed. Eva caught a sense of wariness in the look he gave his wife.

Joanna turned to the children, but before she said anything, Tucker spoke up. "I'll keep an eye on them, ma'am. We'll wait right here."

"Thank you, Tucker," Joanna said. Jonathan then cupped his wife's elbow and led her up the stairs.

"We can sit here on the porch, where we can see the children," Eva offered, waving a hand toward the set of wicker furniture on the corner of the porch.

Jonathan waited until Eva sat in one of the chairs and his wife on the small cushioned settee before he sat down beside Joanna.

Eva wasn't sure how to start. She didn't know the story behind their arrival, but sincerely wanted to find out all they were willing to share. "First off, please accept my gratitude for your willingness to take care of my place while I was absent. I do appreciate it."

"You're welcome, ma'am. It was our pleasure," Jonathan assured.

"May I ask what your plans are? I'm assuming you made the trip here..." she let her voice trail off as she glanced to the children sitting in a circle on the front lawn.

"Our house was hit by a twister three weeks ago. It wiped out everything. We didn't have the finances to rebuild." Jonathan took a hold of his wife's hand. "We decided it would be best to go back to Nebraska. We have family there."

"Nebraska? Where was your home?" Eva asked.

"Over past Great Bend." He swallowed. "We thought we better come explain what happened to Mr. Quinter."

"I see," Eva said, even though she didn't.

Husband and wife glanced at each other before he continued, "Mr. Quinter paid us to take care of the children until he could come for them. We're willing to give him back his money and keep the children."

A tight band squeezed Eva's heart. "Oh?"

"Yes, we weren't planning on adopting any children off the orphan train, but we had completed the paperwork just in case there was one or two we felt needed a good home. At the time we thought we could provide that." Jonathan shook his head as if shamed. "We still can. Once we get on our feet again."

Eva leaned closer. An orphan train? She had no idea that was where the children came from. The poor little angels. She and September had read a pamphlet about the trains while in New York, and had had a long conversation about them. The fact made her want to adopt the children all the more.

Joanna patted her husband's knee. "Mr. Quinter had been on the train with the children, and he asked us to take Tucker, Reed, and Heather, just until he could get everything settled here at home. He said he'd be back in a week or so to get them. Then he sent a telegram that said an illness prevented him from coming for the children and asked us to keep them a little longer. They're good kids, and we'd like to keep them—" Joanna stopped and put a hand over her mouth. Tears glistened in her eyes.

"I think I'm a little confused," Eva admitted.

"We're sorry, ma'am," Jonathan offered. "It's just that we really can't afford the children right now. The storm took everything."

"We do have most of Mr. Quinter's money," Joanna said, controlling the whimpers Eva knew the woman hid.

"Mr. Porter, are you set on moving to Nebraska, or would you be willing to stay around here for awhile?" Eva could almost hear Willamina whispering in her ear, encouraging the thoughts building in her head.

"Well, ma'am, to be honest, there's not a lot waiting for us in Nebraska. Just my brother. I'm hoping we can stay with him and his family until I find some work." A shimmer of hope appeared in the man's eyes.

It brightened Eva's outlook and encouraged her to continue, "You see, I live here by myself, for now, anyway, and I count on my neighbors for a lot of assistance. I could really use a hired hand, to take care of the animals and such. I have forty acres and would like to find someone to share crop it. You could stay in the soddy until we can build something a bit more permanent."

Jonathan's gaze had gone to his wife. Eva continued, "And Mrs. Porter, I'm a painter, and could use assistance with the house. Especially once Bug—Mr. Quinter, and I marry. I have no experience being a mother and would sincerely appreciate your help."

They both turned to her. Eva wasn't sure if they gaped or if their smiles made their mouths fall open. She crossed her fingers and asked, "Does this sound like something you might be interested in?"

"Yes, ma'am, it does." Jonathan nodded his head. "It does."

"Good. I have to go to town this morning. But when I return, we can discuss your wages and such." A sound inside the house made her add, "Oh, and my agent, Mr. Houston is here right now. But he'll be returning to New York shortly."

The couple looked at each other again, and then back to her. "All right," Jonathan said hesitantly.

Eva laughed. "Jack can be a little overbearing. I just wanted to warn you, there's nothing to worry about."

"All right, ma'am." He still sounded unsure, but Eva let it go.

"Now, as far as the children. I feel confident that I can speak for Bug—Mr. Quinter—I know he still wants to adopt the children. There's a lawyer in town that I will discuss the matter with. As far as the money, what he's given you was for the care of the children in his absence, which you have done. From their looks, you've done very well by them, so it is yours to keep. From today forward, I will be responsible for their needs, so if there is something, clothes or shoes, they need, please let me know so I can order them. I would however, appreciate your assistance in taking care of them, at least until I feel

I'm better prepared. They've already been through a lot of changes, and I don't want this one to be too disruptive for them."

Joanna looked deeply at Eva, glanced to the children, and then back to Eva. "You already love those children, don't you?"

"Yes, I do," Eva admitted. "From the moment I heard their names, I've loved them." She didn't admit she'd heard their names while eavesdropping, but some things should never be shared. "Well, if that's settled." She stood up. The Porters did as well. "I have to get to town. There are several things I need to see to."

"Is there anything you'd like me to see to today, Miss Robertson?" Jonathan asked.

"No, just the chores and..." She mulled the thought for a moment before asking, "Mr. Porter, do you know anything about drilling oil?"

"No, ma'am, I can't say I do, but I can learn."

"I plan on hiring some men in town today to work on the well I started a few weeks ago." This time she wasn't going to depend on the kindness of the brothers to help her. She had resources and it was past time she used them.

"I've seen the derrick ma'am, while hunting."

She liked the man, and her first instincts were rarely wrong. "Perhaps you wouldn't mind overseeing the other men I hire?"

"I could do that."

"Good." She glanced to the children, still patiently sitting on the front yard. "Could you hitch up my buggy then?"

"Right away, ma'am." Jonathan Porter nodded a departing greeting and walked across the porch.

"Oh, and Mr. Porter?"

"Yes, ma'am?" He paused near the stairs.

"There's a spool of rope in the barn and some wood. Perhaps you could build the children a swing, in that elm right there." She pointed to the tall tree beside the edge of the house, the one in front of her studio windows.

"That looks like a good place for a swing. I'll do it this morning." Jonathan Porter's smile was as large as hers.

"Miss Robertson?"

Eva turned back to Joanna Porter. "Yes?"

"Is there anything specific I can do for you today?" The woman stepped forward. "We sincerely appreciate this opportunity."

Eva took the woman's hands. "It's a wonderful opportunity for both of us." Her gaze once again went to the children. She really wanted to go sit with them and get to know each one of them, but there were a few other things she had to take care of first. The children, the Porters, the sunshine, everything around her made her want to smile. This was her life, she was in control of it, and would be from now on. She turned back to Joanna Porter. "Please call me Eva, and if I may, I'd like to address you as Joanna."

The woman gave a slight nod.

Eva grinned. "Do you know much about planning weddings?"

"Yes," the woman giggled. "I had three younger sisters."

"Wonderful. Mr. Quinter and I will be wed as soon as possible, and I have no experience in such things."

"Don't worry. You are in good hands with me." Joanna's face held a happy, healthy glow.

Eva wanted to hug her but thought that might be a bit much for the woman, considering they'd just met.

"You know," Joanna said, looking at the children. "We've come to love those kids, and we'd be willing to keep them, but both Jonathan and I could tell how much Mr. Quinter cared for those children as soon as we met him. It practically broke his heart to leave them with us, strangers and all."

Eva blinked at the tears. "That's Bug. He loves with all his heart."

"So do you. He's a lucky man." Joanna squeezed Eva's hand.

"No," Eva whispered, choking on the lump in her throat. "I'm the lucky one, and I'm just sorry it took me so long to do something about it." She squeezed Joanna's fingers. "There's my buggy. Please tell Mr. Houston I'll be back as soon as I can."

Eva skipped down the steps, loving the confidence that bloomed in her chest. She paused near the children. "I have to go to town, and I believe the store there has peppermints sticks. Do any of you like them?"

"Yes, ma'am, we do," Tucker said. "We all do."

"Then I shall buy all the store has and bring them home for you." Holding back the urge to hug each one of them, including the Porter children, she ruffled Tucker's hair. "I'll see you later." She winked and then rushed to the buggy.

The trip to town, though she had a lot to do, was fairly quick. By mid-afternoon, she was home, with a bag full of peppermint sticks and a buggy full of anything else she thought five children may need. The children barely had a chance to say thank you before Jack was tugging her into the house.

Once he had her in the front room, he set her down on the sofa and glared downward as if she had just insulted him. "What the hell have you been up to?"

"What do you mean?"

He waved one arm around frantically. "A dozen men showed up here while you were gone."

"I know. I hired them."

"What for?"

"To drill oil."

"What?"

"I started drilling an oil well a few weeks ago, but we hit rock. Wheat harvest is about to start, so Snake and Kid are too busy to help with it, so I hired men to do it." She folded her arms. "You were the one that said I had to show Bug how capable I am."

He opened his mouth, but she was faster, "And you were right. I have money. I can hire men to work for me. Just as I hired the Porters to help around here. I'll need the help even more once the adoption goes through."

"Adoption?"

"Yes, Bug and I will be adopting Tucker, Reed, and Heather as soon as we are married. Which by the way will happen this Saturday."

"That's the day after tomorrow."

"I know."

"Does Bug?"

She shrugged. "I don't believe so. He wasn't on the noon train, so I'm assuming he'll arrive on the late train tonight."

A tiny smile formed on Jack's lips. "What else did you do while you were in town?"

"I didn't see Miss Staples if that's what you're implying." She may be bold, but she wasn't stupid.

"That's exactly what I'm implying. Why didn't you see her?"

"Because I want to be in charge when I meet her."

"In charge?"

"Yes. I invited her to tea tomorrow morning at ten. I'd like to say you're welcome to join us, but I'd prefer our meeting to be private." A touch of uneasiness made her fingers tremble. She folded them together, but Jack had already noticed.

He leaned down and kissed her forehead. "I'm proud of you. And you have nothing to fret about. It's

Miss Staples who needs to worry. She's about to meet the one woman she'll never forget crossing."

\*\*\*\*

The train stopped long enough for him and Kid to jump off before it started chugging west again. It was a repeat for Bug, the quiet and still town, but this time it was because of the lateness. Moonlight bounced off the buildings, and Bug could almost hear the snores of those sleeping behind the dark windows. A slip of paper was nailed to the side of the depot. He walked over to read the message.

"What the hell?"

"What is it?" Kid asked, sticking his head next to Bug's shoulder. "Well, I'll be damned."

Bug ripped the paper from the wall, reading it again. *The marriage of Miss Eva Robertson and Mr. Brett (Bug) Quinter will take place on Saturday, June 2, 1888 at 3:00 PM at Eva Robertson's property. All are welcome to attend.*

"Looks like you *are* getting married, little brother." Kid slapped his back hard enough to dislodge the lump forming in Bug's throat.

Happiness started in his toes and by the time it hit his face, he was smiling brighter than the moon.

"Looks like I am." Bubbling with joy, he spun around and hugged Kid. "I'm getting married, Kid. I'm getting married."

"I take it your happy about it." Kid laughed, hugging him back.

"Damn right I am. It's about time." Bug let go and started walking for the livery. His steps were feather light and carefree. He never remembered being so downright happy.

Slips of paper were nailed on buildings and awning posts all the way through town. Each one made him smile brighter. Kid snatched one along the way, and Bug plucked a couple extras, reading each one over and over again.

At the livery they gathered their horses, the ones they'd both left behind when they'd left for Wichita. They talked some along the way, but mostly Bug thought. His mind was full of the changes that were about to befall upon him, wonderful changes that he could barely wait to happen. In no time they came to Eva's property. Without a word they both stopped to stare at the big, quiet, and dark house.

"You can see her tomorrow," Kid whispered.

"I know," Bug said, "But I—"

"Tomorrow," Kid interrupted. "You two have a lot to talk about. Let her sleep tonight." Kid leaned closer and sniffed. "Besides, you could use a bath. That cattle train has you smelling like a pasture."

Bug chuckled. "You don't smell so wonderful yourself."

"I know. Let's go so I can get a bath before climbing into bed with my wife. I love Jessie's homecomings."

Bug stared at the house for a moment longer, envisioning a time when he'd have such a homecoming.

Kid grabbed the loop of Bug's horse's rein. "Come on, little brother, the sooner you get home, the sooner tomorrow will come."

****

Kid was right. Bug felt as if his head had barely hit the pillow before someone was hitting him in the face with something. He batted it away, sitting up.

"What is this?" Ma asked, waving a piece of paper.

Bug grabbed it. Seeing the familiar post, he grinned. "What's it look like?"

"It says you and Eva are getting married on Saturday." She planted her hands on her hips. "No one asked me about it."

He read the paper again, smiling. "No one told me about it either."

187

"What?" She tried to take the paper back, but he held it over his head.

Grinning, he shrugged. "Eva must have planned it."

"Where is she?"

"Home."

"Home? No one told me that."

"Imagine that. Something you don't know about." He was so happy he couldn't even pretend to sound grumpy. Reading the paper again, he asked, "Where'd you get this?"

"You left it on the kitchen table when you snuck in last night." This time she got the paper.

He let it go before she tore it. "I guess I did."

"Why didn't you wire and tell us you were on your way home? Tell us Eva was on her way? Is Kid home, too?"

"Yes, Kid's home, too." Bug spun his legs off the bed. "We got in after midnight last night. But Eva got home the day before yesterday. You haven't seen her yet?"

"No, I haven't seen her yet. Why didn't anyone tell me?"

"I can't answer that, Ma. You'll have to ask her."

"I guess I will." A loud humph sounded as she marched out of the room.

He grabbed his clothes and hopped to the door while sticking his legs into his britches. "You're not going over there until after I do."

"What? You can't tell me what to do." Her green eyes snapped as she glared at him.

"Yes, Ma, I can. This is between Eva and me." He pulled another note from his pocket, identical to the one she held. "I had no idea about this until I got off the train last night. Eva must have planned it herself."

Ma studied her paper. A grin formed on her face. "I knew she had it in her."

"What?"

Ma spun around. "Nothing. You hungry?"

"Yeah, I am," he admitted. "And then I gotta take a bath before I head over to Eva's."

"I'll fix you some breakfast while you tell me about those kids and that other woman."

Bug sucked in air. *Shit!* He'd forgotten all about the kids and Jenny. Had Eva already seen them?

"Ma, I don't have time for breakfast."

"Oh, yes, you do," she insisted. "If Eva's posted those all over town, she's already met the kids and that other woman. You taking the time to explain it all to me won't make a difference to her, but it might just save your hide. You still aren't too old for a hickory stick."

"Who's getting a hickory stick?" Snake asked, rubbing his eyes as he walked into the kitchen.

"No one, yet," Ma said.

"Bug! When did you get home?" Snake crossed the room to whack him on the back. "How's Eva?"

Ma shoved the paper at Snake before Bug had a chance to say anything. "Well, I'll be damned," Snake said. "It's about time, little brother."

"What's about time?" Summer asked as she walked over to give Bug a hug. "Besides you finally coming home," she added as she kissed his cheek.

Bug gave Summer an extra long hug. Not just because he'd missed her, but also because he was happy she was awake. Her cooking was wonderful, Ma's—not so much.

"Look at this," Snake said, handing Summer the note.

"Oh, Bug, this is wonderful! Why didn't you wire us so we could have started planning things?" she asked.

Bug shrugged. "Because I didn't know."

"What?" Snake and Summer asked in unison.

It was an hour later before he had it all

explained and his stomach was full of Summer's fine cooking. Whistling, he carried cleaned clothes to the big tub behind the shed. It was sure to be a good day. Probably the best day of his life.

Chapter Fifteen

Palms sweating, Eva watched the buggy roll into the yard. She ran her hands over the pleats of her skirt. It was her favorite dress. Made of pale-orange lightweight cotton and edged with delicate ivory lace. Ma had made it for her last year, and Eva saved it for special occasions. Like today, when she wanted to look her very best. She'd even taken the time to wrap rags in her hair before bed to create the tiny curls dangling from her temples.

Eyes glued on the buggy that had now stopped in her front yard, Eva took a fortifying breath. Jenny Staples was just as beautiful, if not more, than Eva remembered. A hand fell on her shoulder.

"Don't worry, I'll be right here the whole time."

She spun around and gave Jack a steady stare. "No, you won't be."

"Oh, yes I will."

"I told you, this is something I have to do myself."

"I know," he said. "I won't be in the room, but I'll be listening to every word."

"No, you won't. You go see how the men are doing on the oil well."

"Eva—"

"I mean it Jack."

"Fine." Despite his disgusted sigh, he gave her a wink. "But I want to hear everything that happens when I return."

She couldn't stop the giggle that rippled up her chest. "Go!"

He tipped his hat and walked into the kitchen

191

moments before a knock sounded on the front door. Eva waited until she heard the back door close and then took a deep breath and turned the knob on the front door.

"Miss Staples," she greeted.

The woman eyed her up and down. "Miss Robertson," Jenny Staples said, and then with her nose in the air, she marched into the house.

Eva closed the door, whispering soft enough so the other woman didn't hear, "Won't you come in." She waved a hand toward the front parlor. The room was full of fresh cut flowers that Joanna had placed in decorative vases. Once again, Eva found herself thanking the dear Lord for sending the Porters when he had.

Joanna appeared just then, wheeling a cart. She smiled discreetly at Eva before she rolled the cart filled with tea and mini cakes into the parlor. Once she had everything arranged perfectly, she turned to Eva, "If there's anything else you need, ma'am, I'll be in the kitchen."

"Thank you, Mrs. Porter," Eva said, meaning it with all her heart. She then turned to her guest. "Miss Staples, please, make yourself comfortable."

There wasn't an ounce of friendliness in Jenny Staples's light blue eyes. The young woman had a perfect complexion, like that of a porcelain doll sitting in a store window, complete with rosy-pink cheeks. For a moment, Eva thought how it would be to paint Jenny. It would be difficult, because there wasn't anything that could be used to make the woman unique, other than her beauty. Eva tossed her perspective aside.

"Please, Miss Staples." She once again pointed to the chair behind Jenny.

Keeping her lips tight and her spine straight, the woman lowered herself onto the cushioned seat. Eva poured two cups of tea and handed one to Jenny before she sat in her chair.

Jenny set the cup down, not caring how the cup clattered against the saucer. "Where's Brett? I demand to see him this instant."

Eva took another deep breath, refusing to be riled by the woman's rudeness. "Bug isn't here right now."

"Where is he?" Jenny commanded curtly.

"Miss Staples. I invited you here so we could speak. I—"

"I don't want to talk to you. I want to talk to Brett."

The boorish behavior had Eva's spine tightening. "Miss Staples, if Bug wanted you to know where he is, he would have contacted you."

"Oh, and did you know where he was every minute of the last three years?"

Eva couldn't stop the gasp before it slipped out.

"I thought not," Jenny huffed. "Furthermore," the woman started as she dug in the small pouch hanging off her wrist which matched her mint-green striped dress. "What's the meaning of this?" Jenny tossed one of the posters Eva had had printed in town yesterday. She'd paid two boys to hang the announcement of her and Bug's wedding all over town.

Eva lifted the paper before the edge sank to the bottom of her tea cup and set it aside, smoothing the wrinkles from it. "Bug and I will be married on Saturday. You're welcome to attend if you're still in town."

"Attend!" Jenny leaped to her feet. "Still in town?" She leaned over the small table, putting her face as close to Eva's as possible. "If there's a wedding on Saturday, it will be mine and Brett's."

Eva folded her hands in her lap, willing her reaction to appear calm. She'd like to grab the woman by her blond curls, but that wouldn't be appropriate. "Miss Staples, throwing a fit isn't going to do you any good. Please sit down."

"Do you have any idea who I am? Do you know who my father is?" The girl all but screeched.

Eva stood. Her height, though only an inch or two more than the girl's, gave her a sense of authority. "Yes, I know who your father is. I also know he's on his way here. Most likely on the morning train."

Jenny's eyes grew round.

"It appears there's a judge in New York who'd like to speak to you about a magically appearing money pouch."

Jenny slumped, slowly lowering onto the chair behind her. Empathy for the girl blossomed in Eva's chest. It was very apparent how unexpected the news was.

Eva sat down. "Miss Staples, believe me, I know how irresistible Bug is. I've been in love with him for years. But the truth is, he's been in love with me for just as long. Neither of us will allow someone to come between us."

"You seem awfully confident." Jenny stiffened in her chair. "Especially since Brett never mentioned you to me. Not before your art show."

"I am confident. That's what love gives you. And Bug didn't need to mention me to you because your relationship with him was of no consequence." Eva leaned back, recalling the insight Jack gave her back in New York. "You see, Jenny, when a man first falls in love, it's all he can think of, all he can talk about. To the point others get tired of listening. But later, when that love has settled deep inside him, he protects it like the treasure it is. Oh, it's still all he thinks about, but it's so precious, he keeps it to himself, unwilling to share."

Jenny's face scrunched with a confused frown. "You're telling me Bug kept you a secret because he loved you so much?" She started to laugh. "Oh, that's about the best one I've heard."

Calmly, or at least appearing to be calm, Eva waited for the girl's outburst to end. She had harder ammunition, and now looked like a good time to use it. "I know all about the girl you hired to frame Bug. And so does Judge Holden in New York. Did you really think having Bug arrested would make him love you?" She stood and moved to the window. "A man doesn't want a woman who will just stand beside him. They want one who will stand up for them."

"I've been the one with him the last three years," Jenny said defiantly.

Eva spun around. "Only because your father asked him to be your escort."

Jenny huffed. Eva continued before the girl could speak, "I'm the one he came home to Miss Staples. I'll always be the one he'll come home to." Taking slow and steady steps, she didn't stop until she was directly in front of Jenny. "And I'll be here with open arms. Let me be perfectly clear. You are no threat to me. Never have been and never will be."

****

Bug slipped his arms into his clean shirt as he walked around the shed. The sound of traffic had been occurring since he'd climbed in the tub. Not that he'd taken an overly long bath this morning. He was in too much of a hurry to get to Eva's.

Two buggies and a wagon sat in the front yard, and from the swirl of dust hanging over the road, another one was on its way down the driveway. He was curious, but not interested enough to waylay his plans. It was already past nine. Even if Eva slept through the rooster's call, she surely was up by now.

He finished buttoning his shirt and tucked it into his britches as he made a beeline for the barn and the horse he'd collected from the livery last night. His steps were as light as his heart, fluttering with excitement. For a moment, he recalled the day he'd left home. It had been a hard decision. He'd known he had to go learn more about the oil business, but at the same time he'd wanted to ask Eva to marry him, and start their lives together.

A few months before he'd left the entire family had all been in Dodge, helping Hog build the Majestic. He and Eva had been friends, good friends for years, but it had been at the grand opening party in Dodge that Bug had realized he was in love with Eva. She'd been so fetching that night, he almost hadn't recognized her—and keeping his hands off her since that night had gotten excruciating.

He'd talked to Willamina about it, him leaving, and she'd said it was best. That when he returned, he and Eva would know for certain if they were in love or not. Of course, at the time, he'd only planned on being gone six months, not three years. As long as he was being honest with himself, he admitted the reason he hadn't returned wasn't Chester Staples and his job offer. It had become an oddity of sorts, one of those things that the longer you're away, the harder it is to go back. As much as he wanted to see Eva, and his family, the fear things had changed caused an undeniable fear within him. It had been crazy, he knew that now, but back East the thought of coming home to Eva being with someone else had been what made him get up and delay his return yet another day.

The day he'd left, he'd stopped at the soddy. He and Eva had walked through the back field. Things had changed between them. It had happened the night of Hog's big party in Dodge. Bug no longer looked at Eva as his best friend—the person he could tell his dreams to and talk about his fears with. She'd become something more—a woman. The one he wanted to spend the rest of his life with, and that alone had been enough to scare him.

Then he kissed her. Not a little peck to say good-bye, but a real, deep down kiss. She'd come to life in his arms and the want to lay her down had grown until his loins had been screaming with need. The ache had stayed with him all the way to New York. And back. He'd been branded from that moment on. Not once since had a woman created even the tiniest flicker in him.

He wasn't experienced in the mating between a man and woman, but he knew that wasn't a concern. Both he and Eva would know what to do when the time came.

Bug grinned and glanced at the morning sun filling his outside world with the same light he held inside. The years of waiting were almost over. He grasped the half-moon shaped handle on the barn door, but a shout made him turn around.

"Bug Quinter! What's the meaning of this?"

Of all the people he could ignore, Jessie wasn't one of them. His fingers slipped off the handle as he waited for Kid to stop the wagon beside the barn.

"Morning, Bug."

The grin on his brother's face made him smile just as bright. "Morning, Kid." He then glanced to his brother's wife. "Morning, Jessie."

She waved the handbill. "What's the meaning of this? Why didn't you let us know so we could start planning?"

"I already asked him that."

Bug recognized Summer's voice and turned around. A crowd of people followed behind she and Snake—Ma and September and August, his other brothers, their wives and kids, and Buffalo Killer and Chief Red Elk, and Chester Staples. Bug blinked. *Chester Staples?* What was he doing here?

"Did you know about this?" Jessie asked Lila who moved away from the crowd to give Bug a hug.

"Nope," Lila said. After kissing his cheek, she added, "Not until we got the telegram from Eva."

"She sent you a telegram?" Jessie asked at the same time he did.

"She sent us one, too," Randi supplied. "It arrived yesterday."

"Ours, too," Lila said.

"Mine, too." Buffalo Killer held a slip of paper in the air. Bug shook his head at the thought of a message carrier taking a telegram all the way out to the tribe's camp. More so, Buffalo Killer and his father, as well as Skeeter's family must have caught the midnight freight train to be here already.

The girls all started talking at once, and Bug pressed his back against the barn door. Their cackling was worse than a hen house. Thank goodness Eva wasn't like them. She was calm and rational, and sweet and kind. Not that his sisters-in-law weren't as well. But his brother's wives could be a bit unpredictable. There wasn't a one of them who'd think twice about pulling out a gun, including Ma—and they all knew how to use them. He'd seen it himself. Eva wasn't like that. She was thoughtful and contemplated her actions before making decisions. Always had. His life wouldn't be this chaotic. Nope, Eva would consult him, and together they'd mull over and plan things.

He sighed at the knowledge, watching the commotion. A chill waved down his spine. Actually, Eva had caused this pandemonium. The women were up in arms because she hadn't notified them, and they were blaming him for it. Hell, he hadn't known. How could he have told them something he didn't know?

When Eva had entered the library back in Wichita and said he needed to leave and let her rest, he'd been shocked, but after talking with Dr. Robb, and then after seeing the posters about their wedding, he assumed it was because she wanted to surprise him with the wedding. But that wasn't like her. Neither was it like her to not consult the rest of his family. Especially Jessie—and Ma.

He whirled around and pulled open the door.

"Where do you think you're going?" Ma shouted above the rest.

Bug ignored her yell and grabbed a saddle from the tack corner. Where'd she think he was going? He was going where he should have hours ago, instead of sticking around here trying to placate everyone else—going to Eva's.

He hooked the saddle with one hand, flipped it over his shoulder, and walked to the back paddock. The horse was saddled, and he was tightening the cinch when someone spoke, causing his fingers to stall.

"Brett, I would like a moment to speak with you before you leave," Chester Staples stopped beside the horse.

Bug tied off the cinch, and turned, waiting for the man to continue.

Chester shifted his feet. Bug frowned. The man gave the impression of insecurity. That was a characteristic Bug had never witness in Chester.

"I-I apologize for any trouble Jenny has caused." Chester glanced around. "And I hope we can come to an agreement about it all."

Bug's frown deepened, tugging on his brows until his forehead ached. He rubbed a hand against the twinge. "What are you talking about?" A thought hit him then. "I already told you I can't marry her."

"I understand that." Chester gave a respectful nod of his head. "I'm talking about the um-incident in New York."

"What incident in New York?" A twisting in his guts said Chester knew about his arrest, but what did that have to do with Chester or Jenny?

"Your arrest."

"What about it?"

Chester squinted, as if deeply inspecting him. Bug lifted a brow. It really was none of Chester's business, and Bug would just as soon put it all behind him.

"Hasn't Judge Holden contacted you?" Chester asked.

"Yes," Bug admitted. Kid had told him about the wire Sheriff Turley brought out to the ranch, but with everything else going on, Bug hadn't really given it a second thought. There hadn't been time with chasing down Dr. Robb and traveling home. "I'll get back to him and see what he needs, when I have time."

The man sighed heavily. "So you don't know about Jenny's part in your arrest?"

The hairs on the back of his neck stood up. "No," he admitted.

"She hired the girl who planted the purse on you."

Bug bit the inside of his cheek to keep his temper under control. It didn't help much. "Why the hell would she do that?"

"Well," the man now sounded as frustrated as Bug felt. "I haven't talked to her, yet, but I believe it was because she didn't want you to leave. She did have her heart set on marrying you." The man glanced around. "Still does evidently."

*Shit!* Kid had also said Jenny was here—and planning a wedding. He'd forgotten that as well. His mind had been on Eva and nothing else. "Where is she?" An instinct said he knew. Bug stuck a foot in the stirrup.

Chester grabbed his arm. "I was hoping to come to an agreement with you before I collect her."

Bug shook off his hold and hoisted himself into the saddle. "An agreement?"

Chester wrapped his fingers around the reins looping from the bit to the Bug's hands. "Yes. What will it take to keep you from pressing charges against her?"

"Where is she, Chester?"

Chester bowed his head. "The man at the hotel said she hired a driver to take her to Miss Reynolds's place this morning."

Bug tugged on the reins, forcing the horse to rip the leather out of Chester's hands. It was hard, but Bug walked the horse through the barn, knowing his family still stood near the door, he didn't want to run anyone over, but damn it, when had his life gotten so out of control?

"Where you headed?" Skeeter asked.

"To Eva's," Bug answered, steering the bay around the crowd.

"Hold up, I'll ride with you."

"Me, too."

"We'll all go."

Bug pulled the animal to a stop. He couldn't decipher who'd said what, but it really didn't matter. "No, you won't. None of you." He included Chester Staples in his glare. "You'll all stay here. I've had all the meddling I can take."

Ma let out a huff. "You listen here! I—"

"No," he interrupted. "You listen here. Eva and I are getting married. And no one is going to interfere." He settled his gaze on Chester. "No one." Bug kneed the animal, but after one quick leap he tugged on the reins and found Snake in the crowd. "Hide her damn shotgun!" Then he flayed the reins over the horse's rump and took off.

Chapter Sixteen

Art Rockford's son Louie stood in the shade of the barn door, beside a little black buggy. Bug returned his wave—briefly. Louie's attendance meant Jenny was here. Hell, he just couldn't catch a break. Since he'd spotted Eva outside the art show in New York it had been one blow after another. He was ready for it all to end.

Bug jumped out of the saddle and jogged toward the front steps. The ride over had given him time to think—somewhat. He had no idea what Jenny had told Eva, but knew Jenny could be a snit to contend with when her dander was up.

His foot was about to hit the first step when an earth shattering blast rattled every window in the house. "What the hell?" Bug spun around. Birds in the trees screeched and took to flight, as did his horse and the one tied to Louie's buggy. The kid ran after the buggy while Bug took off to the side of the house—the direction the blast had come from.

Eva barreled out the back door.

"What was that?" he yelled, coming around the corner.

Her skirt was hitched past her knees, and she ran toward the back field. Without glancing toward him, she shouted. "It must be the oil well!"

He caught up to her. "Oil well? There're no oil wells around here."

She didn't answer, just kept running. He sprinted beside her. "Eva, there's no oil well around here."

They topped the little hill behind her place and

Bug stumbled. He didn't go down, but should have. It was a ways away yet, but the unmistakable frame of a derrick stood in her back field. Moreover, a stream of black spouted out of the top and rained back down on the earth. Gallons upon gallons of oil.

"What the hell!" He caught his footing and increased his speed. In no time, he was running beside Eva again, but his mind was outpacing both of them. Had Chester Staples already started drilling out here? There was no one else who could have. Had the man been here the whole time he was in Wichita?

Eva was shouting something. Bug had to clear his mind so his ears could work—beyond the ringing the blast had caused.

"Mr. Porter! Is everyone all right?" Eva waved both hands over her head. "Mr. Porter!"

A man, one of many dripping oil from head to toe, ran towards her.

"Yes, ma'am. Everyone's accounted for."

Oil ran down the man's face, but Bug recognized him as the one he'd paid to take Tucker, Reed, and Heather. Mr. Porter met them several yards from where the geyser of oil continued to rain down.

Bug, unable to gather the dozen thoughts beating paths in his head, turned back to the commotion. Sunlight struck the puddles quickly forming and rainbows of colors burst forth in the long rivers trailing away from the derrick in all directions. The bitter, pungent smell of crude filled the air.

"Where's Jack?" Eva shouted above the roar. "Where's Mr. Houston?" Frantically, she glanced in all directions at once.

"Right here!" Jack Houston crawled out from beneath a nearby wagon. He leaped over some of the smaller rivers as he jogged in toward them.

Bug rubbed his eyes. Was this for real?

"What happened?" Eva asked.

Bug, still speechless, spun to the man she spoke to.

"Mr. Quinter"—Mr. Porter gave a nod in acknowledgement—"good to see you." He turned back to Eva. "One of the men you hired blasted the well with blasting oil."

"Blasting oil!" Bug quivered from head to toe. His gaze went to the stream of oil still shooting out of the earth. "How much did you use?"

"Just one bottle," Jack said, arriving at his side.

Bug's knowledge of how to frac a well—and the accidents he'd heard of crowded inside his head. "A whole bottle?"

Jack and Mr. Porter nodded.

Bug shuddered at the thought. Nitro was nothing to mess around with. Years ago a crate of it had blown up the Wells Fargo Building—the entire building—out in California and the state outlawed the transportation of it. Only those in the oil business, railroad, or mining were allowed to use it, and only after they had manufactured it on site. Dynamite had a small amount of nitro in it, and was easy to come by, but not pure nitro. If someone had found some, it had to be highly unstable and extremely dangerous.

"Hell, you could have been blown into Oklahoma."

"You mean we aren't in Oklahoma?" Jack looked serious for a moment, but then laughed and slapped Bug on the back.

Bug shook his head. Not in the laughing mood. "Is there any more around here?" As soon as he asked the question, he knew the answer. If there had been any more nitro, the blast would have set it off. They all would have been in Oklahoma.

"No," Mr. Porter said. "We just had the one bottle."

"Thank God," Bug muttered. His nerves settled down a mite.

All eyes went to the derrick. Bug knew he should tell them to cap it, but there was something about watching the black gold spewing into the air that was downright breathtaking and mesmerizing. He didn't have the wherewithal to interrupt the others from experiencing it firsthand.

A hand slid along the lower part of his back. He glanced down as Eva, eyes glued to the geyser, sidled up to him. He wrapped an arm around her shoulders and tugged her closer. She glanced up, and her big, brown eyes, glittering brighter than the rainbow rivers, captured his gaze. Mindless of the crowd, Bug twisted her within his arms and lowered his face to seize her lips.

Her arms wound around his waist, and her fingernails penetrated the thinness of his shirt as she grabbed fistfuls. Bug pulled her closer, growing lightheaded from the intensity of their merger, and then her lips parted.

He almost blew higher than the oil geyser. Sweet and playful, the tiny tip of her tongue slid across his lips, and then entered his mouth to tease and taste. A moan filled the back of his throat, and he twisted his tongue with hers.

"Brett! Brett!"

The name slightly penetrated, but it wasn't until someone touched his shoulder that he lifted his head, breaking the delightful connection. He paused and kissed Eva's sweet, moist lips once more before he turned around.

Jack had a hand on his shoulder, but the man looked back toward the house. Bug flipped his head the other way.

"Brett! You need to get a power head on that well. You're losing barrels by the minute!" Chester Staples ran down the hill, and behind him was every single member of Bug's family.

Bug waited until they came to a stop. "I see you all listened real well."

His brothers simply shrugged their shoulders as they turned to gaze at the oil falling from the sky.

"You've got to get that well capped!" Chester exclaimed again, his eyes full of excitement.

Another blast ripped through the air. Bug grabbed Eva's head and bent his body to protect her from whatever might fall from the sky. He glanced about. Everyone else was cowering as well, except for Ma, who had her smoking gun aimed at something out of sight. Bug straightened and found his brothers in the crowd. "I told you—"

"Put the gun down, girlie!" Ma's shout interrupted him.

Bug turned and looked over Eva's head. Jenny stood several yards away. The little pistol she held was pointed at Eva's back.

His heart landed in his throat. "Jenny," he started.

"Don't move!" Jenny steadied the gun with her other hand. "Don't move or she gets it."

Bug barely had time to contemplate his response when a blur flew by. Chester Staples snatched the gun from his daughter. "Good grief, Jenny. We don't have time for your foolishness now. We've got to get this well capped."

"Daddy!" she screeched.

"Don't Daddy me, young lady. I've had all I can take from you right now!" Chester grabbed her arm. "Do you have any idea how much trouble you're already in? I have half a mind to take you over my knee. And I might, yet. As soon as we get this well capped."

Bug glanced back to his family. Chief Red Elk, shaking his head, reached over and grabbed the shotgun out of Ma's hand. Ma glanced at the Indian and Bug flinched. The Chief had no idea what he'd just done.

An extremely remarkable thing happened then. Ma blushed and grinned at Red Elk. The Chief gave her one swift head nod, and Bug could have sworn he saw the man's cheeks darken as well.

"Brett! Come on, we gotta get this well capped!" Chester yelled again.

Bug turned to Mr. Porter. "You better get the power head on that geyser."

"A power head?" The man looked confused.

"Yes, the coupler and casing head. You know, to stop the gushing so you can pump it into the barrels." Bug glanced about. Other than a couple wagons, there weren't any tools or gear needed to complete the job. He pondered the sight. "You do have a power head, don't you?"

"No, sir. We didn't think beyond getting the pipe into the oil." Mr. Porter looked at the other men gathered around. "Anyone know what he's talking about?"

Half a dozen men shook their heads.

Bug's mind, which had been playing havoc on trying to decide which direction to go, stopped short. He glanced down at Eva. "What's going on here? Who's drilling this well? Who's in charge?"

Her cheeks turned bright red. "I'm in charge. I'm drilling the well."

"You?" Exhausted, his mind quit working.

She nodded.

"Why?"

Her hands ran up and down his arms from his elbows to shoulders. The movement made his knees quake. "Because," she said softly, "I want you to have everything you need, right here at home."

He squeezed her hips beneath his palms. "*You* are everything I need," he admitted without hesitation.

She smiled. "And you are everything I need." Her eyes twinkled. "I suppose I should tell you about something else, too."

"Oh?" The teasing grin on her face held his complete attention. "What's that?"

"As soon as we get married on Saturday, we will become parents to Tucker, Reed, and Heather. Elliot Hampton is on his way to Garden City to have the circuit judge sign the papers today."

"He is? We will be?"

She nodded, nibbling on her lip. Excitement shot up his spine. His quiet, sweet little Eva wasn't quite as quiet and shy as he remembered, and he loved her all the more for it. He picked her up by the waist and lifted her into the air.

She grabbed on to his shoulder. "Bug? Bug what are you doing?" Staring up into the sweetest, most adorable face on earth, he spun his heels, and laughing with delight, twirled around several times.

The way Bug spun them about made Eva feel like she was flying with the clouds. Giggling, she held on to his broad shoulders and never took her eyes off his glistening ones. The world surrounding them, the oil flooding the earth, the family members gathered around, and the men she'd hired, grew insignificant. All that mattered was Bug was here, and they'd never be separated again. She'd been working toward this moment for years.

She dipped her head and found his lips. He responded by pulling her closer. As her body slid down his and her toes touched the ground, her arms wrapped around his neck and his kiss continued to make her head whirl in the clouds.

Not until she was completely breathless, and clinging to him to even stay upright, did he lift his mouth from hers. Gasping for air, she laid her head on his chest and simply relished being in his arms. Their hearts beat in unison, erratic, yet everlastingly perfect.

"I love you, Eva girl," he whispered in her ear. His tone was serious and reverent.

She lifted her head to gaze into his handsome face. The way he made her feel was indescribable. "And I love you, Bug Quinter. So very, very much."

He grinned and tugged her back into his embrace. She sighed and then realized silence filled her ears. Lifting her head, she turned to where the oil had been spewing out of the ground. The geyser was no more. A crowd filled the base of the derrick. Still holding her, Bug turned so they both faced the area.

"I suppose," Bug said heavily, "I should go help them."

The unexpected melancholy in his voice made her ask, "Are you upset? I'm sorr—"

He spun her about and pressed a finger to her lips. "No, I'm not upset." He nodded toward the derrick. "Not about the oil. I'm just sorry we can't go on kissing each other. That's what I really want to do."

Tickled, she grinned. "Me, too." She glanced then toward the group of women who stood several yards behind her and Bug. Guilt made it hard to swallow. "But we have a yard full of company. I should go talk to the girls. I'm sure they are wondering why I didn't tell them about the wedding."

"Yes," he agreed. "They are." He kissed the tip of her nose. The sensation made her giggle. "I heard all about it."

"You did?"

He nodded.

"Are they angry with me?"

"Who could ever be angry with you?"

Love bubbled in her chest. "You are so wonderful. Always have been."

He nodded toward the women. "Do you want me to go with you?"

"As much as I love you, no. This is something I have to do myself." It was. She'd been the one who'd decided to take matters in her own hands, and she couldn't expect him to step in and rescue her. Not that she needed to be saved. She was in no danger from the Quinter women, but she did owe them all an explanation.

"I tell you what. You go with the women back to the house, and as soon as we get the well capped, I'll be down." He cupped her cheeks. "We still have a few other things to discuss."

"Like what?" she asked.

"Like how sorry I am about Jenny Staples showing up here. Like how I came to have three red-headed kids. Like how much I want to get married today instead of Saturday."

She giggled. "I already know Jenny's story. And I can relate to the girl. You are so easy to fall in love with. I know all about the orphan train, and I'm so excited to have three children." She placed a small kiss on the tip of his chin. "And I love you very much, but we are getting married on Saturday, and not a moment before."

He brushed his lips over hers in a teasing way. "Maybe I can convince you differently."

She ran her hands over his chest, caressing the hard mounds beneath his shirt. "I'm sure I'll enjoy your attempts, but Bug, there's something you need to know."

As if startled, he jerked his head up. "What? What's wrong?" Concern glistened in his eyes.

"Nothing is wrong," she whispered, breathing against the side of his neck. "But you should know I'm not the shy girl I used to be. I'm a determined woman who knows what she wants, when she wants it. When I say Saturday, I mean Saturday."

He tugged her hips forward, plastering her stomach against his harden groin. "Oh, Eva girl," he said, nibbling on her ear. "I knew that as soon as you smacked me in New York."

She flinched at the memory.

He laughed. "I'd say our life together is going to be an adventure. An extremely fun and exciting adventure."

****

Eva sat at the kitchen table, contemplating how well her conversation went with the women. Their happiness at the wedding was evident, but it was all of their support of how she took charge of the situation that surprised her a bit. Every one of the women, right down to Ma applauded her for her actions. They had left sometime ago with Ma announcing she'd have a wedding dress sewn before nightfall, and Randi insisting she and Hog would prepare the wedding supper.

Mrs. Porter had left with the Quinter women, upon Ma's insistence. She wanted to take measurements of the children for wedding outfits. Eva hadn't protested, she'd decided long ago which battles to fight, and which to let lie. Most with Ma were better left to lie until they died. In most instances, they didn't matter anyway. And the absence of everyone else would mean some alone time for her and Bug.

Jack had returned earlier, along with Jenny Staples. He'd loaded her in the buggy, and gone to town. Eva had no doubt Jack had told Chester Staples he'd make sure Jenny was at the hotel when her father was ready to talk with her.

Letting out a sigh, Eva picked up her cup and was half way to the sink when Bug opened the door a crack and stuck his head in. His water splashed face demonstrated he'd cleaned up some, but oil spotted his shirt collar and clung to his hair.

"Eva, I gotta go home and get washed up. I'll be back as soon as I can."

She rushed to the door, ready to say he couldn't possibly be that dirty, however the words stuck in her throat when she opened the door all the way. He was black from his boots to his neck. "Oh," she gasped. "Yes, you do need a bath." A giggle then tickled her throat. "Did you go swimming in the crude?"

He gave her a teasing look. "No, your hired hands didn't have anything to cap the well with. I rigged up a cap and sent some men with Chester to get the things needed to cap the well off properly, and to order a power cap and other supplies."

"I guess I didn't think about what to do once we struck oil." The temptation to touch him was too great. Eva reached out and wiped a drip of water from his temple. Her finger slid across his oil coated skin. "I'm sorry."

His grin was delightfully charming. "You're quite the wildcatter, Eva girl. That's a hell of a well."

"Really?"

"Yes, I won't know until we get the supplies we need, but I'd say we got a well that's going to give us a couple thousand barrels a day."

"Is that good?"

"Yes, darling, that's very good. The Empire well out in Pennsylvania was drilled back in sixty-one and produced thirty-three hundred barrels a day. It still remains one of the big ones."

She smiled, not only happy by the success of their oil well, but by the shine in his eyes. He did love his oil. And she did love him. "You could get cleaned up here. I'm sure Jack has something you could wear."

He looked down. "I don't know."

She took his hand, oil and all. "I do. Come on, I'll find you something to wear."

"I shouldn't go inside. I'm practically dripping."

"Don't worry. I'll clean it up." She tugged on his hand. He didn't move. "Bug, please? We need to talk and might not have another chance while everyone's gone."

"Everyone's gone?"

She glanced toward the backyard. "Are your brothers still here?"

"No, they left a while ago, along with Buffalo Killer and Chief Red Elk."

"Then everyone's gone," she whispered. A sweet heat swelled inside her. Dr. Robb had proclaimed her completely healthy, in every way. There was no telling how soon everyone may start to return, so therefore, there was no time to waste. "Come on," she insisted, tugging him through the door.

After leading him into the washroom upstairs, she left to gather a pair of pants and a shirt from Jack's room. Halfway back down the hall, she paused. They had a lot to talk about, but this chance really was too tempting to overlook. Biting her tongue to hold in an excited squeal, she flipped around and raced to her room.

Ten minutes later, dressed in nothing more than her night coat, she padded down the hallway and knocked on the door.

"Yeah?" His question was muffled by the sound of water splashing.

"I have some clothes for you," she said through the door.

"Just leave them in the hall. I'll grab them in a second."

She tried the knob, and smiled when it turned beneath her hold. "Bug?"

"Just leave them in the hall," he said louder. "I'll get them in a min—"

She closed the door behind her, grinning at his opened mouth gape. Soap ran down his forehead. He pushed it away with both hands, blinking.

"Eva—"

"Are you ready to start that adventure?" she whispered as she undid the loop of the belt holding her night coat closed.

Chapter Seventeen

Bug tried to pull his eyes away, but he'd never encountered something more difficult. Eva's fingers grasped the edges of her night coat near her throat. The slender slope of her shoulder came into view, and his breath locked in his chest. She pulled the front lower, exposing the upper swells of her breasts.

Bug, coughing, emptied his lungs and shot to his feet. Sloshing and dripping water, he bounded over the edge of the tub and pulled the material from her fingers, covering the heavenly globes.

"Eva..." he had no idea what he should say. His body was saying one thing, loud and strong, but his mind plunked honorable thoughts down one by one.

"Bug." Her breath tickled his neck, and her fingers ran up and down his sides as she stepped closer. The thin material of her coat was worse than if she didn't have anything on. "We are getting married tomorrow."

"I know, Eva darling," he wanted to bite his tongue, but didn't. "We can't do this. Not right now."

She swayed her body against his, branding him at every point. "Yes, we can."

He pressed his lips against her hairline, and drew in a deep, fortifying breath. "Believe me when I say there's nothing I want more than to carry you down the hall and make you mine forever more."

"Then—"

"Shh..." Digging deep into his reserves, he quieted her. "Shh..." He couldn't very well set her away from him. She'd see just how aroused he was— as if she couldn't already feel his excitement pressing against her flat stomach.

Her face tilted up. Those glorious eyes pleaded with him.

"Eva. I love you, and I won't have our first time rushed or covert. We've waited our whole lives for this. Tomorrow night we'll be married." He glanced to the door. "And there won't be any chance of someone coming along and interrupting our union."

The corners of her eyes dropped, and a red tint grew on her high cheeks.

"Oh, no," he whispered, "none of that." Her eyes met his again. "No embarrassment, Eva girl. I want it as bad as you do, and it's nothing to be ashamed of. I just want it to be perfect. I've been dreaming about it for years."

"You have?"

He nodded, and unabashed, admitted, "I've waited for you, Eva. You're the only woman for me."

"I am?" Her eyes grew wide. "You've never..."

"Nope. I've never wanted to be with anyone but you." He already knew, but he asked just the same. "Have you?"

Her spine stiffened. "Of course not."

He chuckled and kissed her nose. "I know."

She frowned. "You haven't even with Jenny?"

"No." He couldn't believe he was standing naked as a jay bird and having this conversation. "There has never been a woman, including Jenny, who could erase you from my mind or heart, and there never will be."

She leaned forward, pressing her forehead to his chin. "Oh, Bug. I love you so much. I've dreamt about us...I just want..."

"Shh. I know. I want the same thing. And we'll have it." He cupped her face and held it in front of his. "Tomorrow night."

Her little grin made his body groan with need all over again. "All right," she agreed. "Tomorrow night."

"Good girl." He planted a soft and gentle kiss on her lips, knowing his body couldn't take much more than that, and then turned her about face. Whispering in her ear, he pushed her toward the door. "Now be a good girl, and let me finish my bath."

\*\*\*\*

It turned out to be a very good thing Bug hadn't taken her up on her offer. He was still in the bathroom and she'd just gotten dressed and was only half way down the stairs, when the front door opened.

"That girl is maddening," Jack declared as he tossed his hat on the side table. "Where's Bug? His horse is still here."

Eva walked down the remaining steps. "He's in the bathing room, washing off the oil. I gave him a pair of your pants and a shirt to wear."

He glanced around, and then looked at her with a raised eyebrow. "And everyone else?"

"Mrs. Porter took the children over to Ma's so she could measure them for outfits for the wedding." Eva, much calmer than she should have been, or at least that's what she thought considering how on fire her body had been moments ago, walked toward the kitchen.

He followed. "The wedding is tomorrow."

"I'm not likely to forget that," Eva assured.

"She can't possibly sew outfits for three kids in one day. Half a day actually." He sat down at the table and smoothed back his hat-flattened hair.

"Yes, she can. Trust me. She also plans on making me a wedding dress." Eva filled the tea pot, and then the coffee pot with water and set them both on the stove.

"That's impossible."

"Then you don't know Ma Quinter." She scooped

the bits of beans Joanna had left in the grinder into the larger pot and replaced the lid. "I'll bet you your shares of my next two paintings the kids and I'll be boasting new outfits by this time tomorrow."

He chuckled. "I may be a gambling man when it comes to some things, but even I don't like the odds on that one. I'd never bet against Stephanie Quinter."

"What's Ma want to bet on?" Bug asked, strolling through the doorway. He set the basket down that held his oil crusted clothes and boots.

Eva walked across the room, and raised her chin for a kiss. Bug grinned and planted one on her lips. A solid kiss that had her head whirling all over again. Settling an arm around her shoulders, he asked again, "What's Ma betting?"

"Nothing," Jack said, eyeing Bug up and down. "Those clothes look pretty good on you. You should wear black more often."

Bug shook his head. "I'll give you a pointer. Don't wear black around Ma."

Jack frowned. "Maybe that's why she's never been overly fond of me."

Eva laughed and eased from under Bug's arm to gather cups and saucers. The opening of the back door stopped her.

Mrs. Porter peeked in. "The children wanted to see Mr. Quinter, is that all right?"

"It sure is!" Bug exclaimed. He crouched down, and as soon as the woman pushed the door open wide, Tucker, Reed, and Heather rushed forward. Bug wrapped them all three in his arms. "I've missed you. All three of you."

Eva's heart swelled at the sight. Bug looked up and reached for her hand. She wrapped her fingers around his, and he tugged her down beside him. Crouched on her knees, eye level with the children, a wave of love filled her. Three sets of green eyes stared at Bug with child-innocent devotion.

"How you feeling, Reed?" Bug asked, patting the boy's tiny face.

"Good, Bug, I ain't been coughing at all," the child answered. He turned and looked at Mrs. Porter. "Isn't that right, ma'am?"

"Yes, that's right," Joanna Porter assured. Her smile was bright and sincere.

"How about you, Heather, you been eating?" Bug asked.

The little girl nodded her head, making her pigtails jiggle about. "Yes. Every bite." She, too, turned to Joanna.

"That's right, Mr. Quinter. She's not shy about eating anymore. Not at all."

Bug ruffled the cowlick on Tucker's head. "You've done a good job, Tucker. I'm right proud of how you've taken care of your brother and sister."

Tucker puffed out his little chest. "I promised I would, Bug. I never go back on my word."

Joanna readily agreed. "That's true. He's a real good boy. A real good helper."

Bug put an arm around Eva. "You've all met, Eva?"

The children nodded. Reed grinned. "She bought us peppermints sticks."

"She did?" Bug asked as if it was quite a feat.

The children nodded again.

"Did she tell you that she and I are getting married?"

Eva held her breath. She hadn't told the children, and had asked Joanna not to either. She wanted to wait until Bug was here, so there was no chance the children would have any doubt they'd experience disappointment again.

Tucker was the first to comment. "No, Bug, she didn't. But we heard as much over at your mother's house." He scanned her up and down with a cautious appraisal. "I suspect the two of you will be having your own kids then."

A chill made her cheeks quiver. Bug squeezed her shoulder. "Well," he said, "I don't think we'll be looking to have any more kids, least not right away. You three are going to be plenty for us to start off with."

"Us three?" Tucker asked suspiciously.

Bug nodded. "Yes. I told you on the train that I'd adopt you. That we'd all live together some day."

Tucker still looked distrustful. Eva couldn't blame him. She could only imagine the number of times these children had been let down. Joanna knew very little about their past, only what the Children's Society worker, Mrs. King, had told her— that their parents had died and the children had been at the orphanage for the last three years.

Eva leaned forward and laid a hand on Tucker's little shoulder. "Tucker, you're a lot like, Bug. He never goes back on his word either."

Tucker's cheeks flushed, and he looked at his shuffling feet.

Reed, on the other hand, grinned openly. His eyes twinkled as he stared at her and Bug. He turned to his sister. "I told you, Heather. I told you we were gonna have a ma and pa."

The girl had her head on Bug's shoulder, tucked up to his far side as close as she could get. Heather gazed at Eva. Eva nodded, smiling at the child. Shyly, Heather slipped between her brothers and Bug and then wrapped her little arms around Eva's neck.

The emotions flooding into Eva's chest made her wobble. Bug's hold tightened on her shoulder. She wrapped Heather's tiny frame into a deep embrace and smiled at Bug over the little girl's bright red pigtails. The wondrous smell of the child, like sunshine and spring flowers, filled her nose, and Eva drew in a deeper breath. Contentment filled her.

Sniffle sounds made her turn her gaze to the others in the room. Joanna dabbed at her eyes, but it was Jack who pulled a handkerchief out of his back pocket and blew his nose.

"I'm gonna go check on the men. I think I heard a wagon," Jack said, moving toward the back door.

Bug sat down and crossed his legs. His movements encouraged Eva to copy his actions. She situated Heather onto her lap as Bug patted the floor, indicating the boys should sit down as well. While they were getting comfortable, Eva noticed Bug's bare feet under his folded knees. His toes were long, and made a perfect curve from the largest to the smallest. Did she love him so much she even thought his feet were handsome? For they were, and the sight of them had her stomach fluttering.

Eva, smiling due to the bliss filling her insides from her hair to her not so perfect toes—her second ones were longer than her big toes, felt an inkling of doubt. She closed her eyes, wondering for a second if Bug would think her feet were ugly. The thought fluttered away. He wouldn't care if her toes were long or short. He loved her, as she did him, and they both loved the children. Opening her eyes, she gazed his way. Not only was she marrying the most amazing man on earth, he'd already provided her with three wonderful children.

"I'm sorry," Bug was saying, "that it took so long for us to be together. And I'm proud of all three of you for being so good for Mr. and Mrs. Porter."

Reed crawled onto Bug's lap and hooked an arm around Bug's neck. Bug winked at him. Eva knew Bug had become acquainted with the children on the train, but she hadn't realized how deep the affection had grown. Then again, Bug was easy to fall in love with, as were the children.

"I have one more favor to ask of you kids," Bug

said.

"Whatever it is, we'll do it, Bug," Tucker said seriously. He sat directly in front of Bug. "I'll make sure Reed and Heather behave, too."

"I'm sure you will, Tucker. But," Bug paused to chuck Heather beneath the chin and touch the tip of Reed's nose. "Heather and Reed aren't your responsibility. You're a good big brother, and it's important you watch over them, but they're old enough to know how to behave." Bug once again glanced to the Reed and Heather. "Aren't you?"

"Yes, sir, Bug!" Reed assured.

"Yes," Heather whispered. Eva patted the girl's thin tiny shoulder and rested her head atop the fine red hair.

"Eva and I are getting married tomorrow. It will be a big party, and I'm going to need your help getting ready for it."

"What you need us to do, Bug?"

"Well," he started, glancing up at Joanna. "Mrs. Porter will tell you what you need to do." His eyes went back to the children. "And after we're married, you'll move into the house here with us. But," he grinned at the kids, "this is where I need the favor."

Their attention was stuck on him, as was Eva's. "I'm wondering if you could stay at Mr. and Mrs. Porter's house for a few more days. Just until Tuesday or so. That will give Eva and me time to get the house all ready for you."

"Oh, sure, Bug," Tucker said, sighing as if he expected something different. "We can do that. And we'll help with the party, too." He glanced at his brother and sister. "Won't we?"

"Yes," Heather and Reed agreed in unison.

The children had a few other questions, mainly about the party, that Bug answered. The Porter's two children, playing on the porch, kept peeking in, and Bug, noticing, said, "I think your friends want you to go out and play for a bit. Do you think they'll help with the party?"

"Sure they will," Tucker offered. "You remember Adam and Anna, don't you Bug? They're good kids, too."

Eva grinned at how mature Tucker acted. It was delightful, yet at the same time, she was anxious for him to be able to return to being a little boy, and have another chance to not have to grow up as quickly as he already had.

"Yes, I remember Adam and Anna, Tucker. You're right, they are good kids. You all are." Bug lifted Reed off his lap. "You go play with them, now. Eva and I have to talk about the wedding. I'll see you again before I leave."

Tucker scrambled to his feet and then waited while Heather stood up so he could take her hand and lead her to the doorway. Joanna fell in step behind them and quietly pulled the door closed. The squeals and laughter of children faintly filtered into the kitchen.

"So, what do you think?" Bug asked, his eyes still on the door.

Eva leaned over and kissed his cheek. "That you are going to be the best father ever."

"They are good kids, Eva. Real good kids."

His voice was so heartfelt, she shivered. "I know they are, Bug. I already love them dearly."

"You do?"

"Yes, I do." She wrapped an arm around his neck and leaned her head against his. "We are so very lucky to have them."

He sighed heavily. "That's what I think, too." His hand slipped over her stomach to caress her side. "Oh, Eva girl, I sure do love you."

She slid her other hand down his folded leg and ran her fingers over the top of his bare foot beneath his knee. The skin was soft and smooth. She'd never imagined a man's skin could be so silky. "I love you, too."

He tugged his foot aside. Her fingers followed it. He tugged harder. She started to giggle. "You're ticklish."

"No, I'm not," he tucked his foot all the way under his thigh.

She found it, tickling the bottom of his sole with the tips of her fingers. "Yes, you are."

His fingers dug into her side. She yelped as her skin puckered. He lightly pinched her, making her giggle harder. "You are, too," he acknowledged.

"No," she let out a little squeal at the sensation rippling up her side. "I'm not."

Still tickling her side, he flipped around and grabbed her other side. She tried to wiggle away, but couldn't. The delightful spasms he created in her sides held her captive. She went for his sides. He squirmed and she burrowed her fingers deeper, running the tips of her fingers up to his armpits.

"Hey!" He twisted, but didn't stop teasing her sides.

Laughing, she reclined, flat on the floor, and kept tickling his sides. He straddled her legs, looming over her, with eyes so dark, her breath stalled in her chest. Simultaneously, their fingers slowed. Her hands slid around his back, aiding as he leaned toward her. His hands snuck up her sides. Her breasts started to throb as his fingers brushed along the sides of them.

"Oh, Eva, tomorrow can't come soon enough, can it?" His breath tickled her lips.

"No, Bug, it can't," she agreed, parting her lips in an invitation. The connection was soft, yet demanding, and swiftly gained momentum like a rain shower that started out slow, but then exploded into a full out storm, demonstrating how ready they both were for their kisses to lead to something more.

Locked together, they kissed and touched, and Eva grew more heated by the second.

Bug rolled, pulling her until she was plastered on top of him. His heart nearly beat its way right out of his chest, not to mention other parts of his body that throbbed and screamed for release. He kissed her one last time, and then pulled his lips away, drawing air into his burning lungs.

"Oh, Eva girl," he whispered. Her delicate scent, like roses in bloom, filled his nostrils as he buried his face in her neck. Cloaked by her hair, he filled and emptied his lungs until he dragged up the final ounces left of his endurance. "You're driving me insane. You know that, don't you?"

Her giggle tickled the edge of his ear.

He laid his head back so he could see her twinkling eyes. "What do you find so funny?" His hands continued to roam up and down her sides and back. Try as he might, he couldn't stop them.

She flipped her head, making more of her hair slip out of the pins holding it up on the back of her head, and leaned over his face. "You, me. When did it become so hard for us to be together and not..."

His fingers found their way to her hair, and one by one, plucked out the tiny bits of metal. Fine, silky, strands of hair fluttered to fall around her face. "I don't know, for sure," he said, pushing the hair over her shoulders and down her back. Kissing the tip of her nose, he added, "Tomorrow seems a long way off, doesn't it?"

"Yes."

The somber tone in her voice had him wrapping his arms around her.

"So very long," she added as she laid her cheek against his.

He held her, letting both of their bodies cool down as they lay on the hard kitchen floor. It may have been the sounds of people outside, or the stiff wood beneath them, either way, at the same time they shifted. Bug released his hold, and Eva slid off. The separation left him chilly—like a part of him was all of a sudden striped away. He rose to his feet, and held her wrists as she did the same. Then, because he needed just one more hug, he pulled her against his chest.

"We still need to talk, Eva girl."

"I know." She sighed heavily. "This is just so much more fun." Her head snapped up and she grinned. "Isn't it?"

He kissed her lips, quickly so he wouldn't be tempted to carry her upstairs—as if that was possible—and then took her hand to lead her to a chair.

"You sit," she instructed near the table. "I'll get us some lemonade. Joanna made some earlier."

None to gently, Bug plopped onto a chair. Still fighting the burning urges deep in his core, he tugged his eyes from her departing form. Tiny hair pins were scattered across the floor, and he moved off the chair to gather them up. They were sitting in a pile on the table when she set two glasses on the table and took a seat on the chair next to his.

"Thank you," she said, glancing at the pins.

"Thank you," he offered, lifting one of the glasses.

She giggled again.

"Now, what's so funny?"

"You, me. A minute ago we were rolling on the floor, and now we're sitting here like two proper strangers, thanking one another." She took a sip of her lemonade.

Without taking a swallow, he set his glass down. "We're far from strangers, Eva."

"I know. It was just a comparison."

Bug nodded. The lemonade was good. Not to tart, not to sweet. Just like Eva. He chugged the rest of the beverage and set down the empty glass. There was so much he had to tell her. Where should he start? "I came across the kids on the train from New York."

"I know," she said, twirling her glass between her fingers. "Mrs. Porter told me about it."

"There were hundreds of them, Eva. Hundreds of little kids with no families." The remembrance made him shudder. "I never saw anything like it. Some were tiny babies. And the folks at the stations..." he dragged a hand through his still damp hair. "I didn't know what to do."

"You did the right thing." She reached over and took his hand. "Tucker and Reed and Heather are wonderful kids." With her other hand she smoothed his hair back. "And we'll all get along stupendously. I know it."

A sense of unease rippled his spine. "I don't know much about being a father."

"And I don't know much about being a mother. But we'll figure it out. We have lots of family who'll help. And I've hired the Porters to stay on here."

He folded his other hand on top of their clutched ones. "You have?"

She covered his top hand with her other one. "Yes, I have. I knew we'd need the help, and they needed the jobs. It was the best possible solution. The children already know them, and it will help with their transition into our home."

Kid had told him about the storm that took out the Porter's small farm, and Bug decided he'd talk to Jonathan Porter about the arrangement, make sure the man did intend to stay on for a bit. It appeared that subject was settled, for now anyway. With a sigh, he went on to the next. "I was arrested while I was in New York."

"I know," she said, grinning.

"It wasn't funny," he insisted.

Her face grew solemn. "I'm sure it wasn't. I didn't mean to make light of it. It took some finagling, but I finally got Jack to tell me the whole story." One side of her mouth curled up adorably. "I said I wouldn't paint a picture for the judge if he didn't."

*The painting!* That was probably why the judge sent his message.

She smiled. "I was kidding of course. I'll complete the painting as soon as I get Buffalo Killer's approval. I was a bit shocked to hear about Jenny's part in your arrest."

That snapped his attention like twine pulled to hard. "Jenny's part? You know about that, too?"

"Of course I do." She slid her hands from his, and took another drink of her lemonade. "Actually, there's probably not anything I don't already know about." Handing him the glass, she continued, "I don't mean to sound pretentious, but I couldn't wait any longer for us to get married. I figured if I took care of all the...the issues separating us, there wouldn't be any reason for you to say no."

Her cheeks had turned bright red. He took a swallow from her glass and then set it down. "Say no? What made you think I'd say no?"

"A lot has changed since you—"

"What's changed?" he interrupted. "Nothing's changed."

"Yes, it has."

"What?"

"Me."

Bug froze, all except for his mind. It was running circles around itself like a dog chasing its own tail.

Chapter Eighteen

"What do you mean?" His guts were curdling.

"My surgery. I—"

A wave of relief set his mind and stomach at ease. "Eva," he said sternly, only because he wanted her full attention. "If you're about to say things have changed because you can't have children, stop right there. We talked about this in Wichita. I told you then, and I'll tell you until the day I die, that doesn't matter to me." He waved a hand toward the back door. "Besides, we already have three kids. How many more do you want?"

A tiny grin momentarily flitted across her lips. "Three is a perfect number."

"I think so, too." He touched the point of her chin. "And I love you. That's never changed. There isn't anything I want more than to marry you."

The smile returned, and stayed on her pink lips. "I love you, too."

He leaned close. "I do have one thing to ask you about."

She tipped her head so her lips almost touched his. "Oh, what's that?"

"What's up with the oil well?"

"I told you," she whispered. Her breath floated over his lips like a gentle caress. "I didn't want any reason for you to say no. You love oil. I have an oil well." Her lips touched his. "We're a perfect match."

It was more than an hour later when Bug tugged on his oil soaked boots, and then gave Eva a parting kiss before he walked down the back porch steps. They'd talked just like they had years ago.

About things that mattered to both of them and things that didn't. The smile on his face was fueled with deep-down appreciation. The kids were all in the fenced in garden with Mrs. Porter. He waved at them while walking toward the oil well.

The derrick stood out like the lighthouses that lined the eastern seaboard. How had he not seen it before? His mind circled back, telling him he'd been a little busy the last month, and not noticing a derrick shouldn't surprise him. Men swarmed the base, unloading things from the wagon. Excitement bubbled in his veins. He owned an oil well. Once again, his mind corrected him. He'd own an oil well as soon as he and Eva got married. And this was just the first. Before the end of the year, he'd have a field of them that would rival Chester's American Refinery ones.

****

Eva tried to see around Jessie's shoulder, to catch a glimpse of how the curls were forming in her hair.

"Keep your head still, I don't want to burn you," Jessie instructed, wrapping another clump of Eva's hair around the hot metal bar Lila kept heating up on the little parlor stove in the corner of the bedroom.

At first they'd all thought Lila had no idea what she was talking about, but like usual, the woman did. The hot iron made Eva's otherwise straight, flyaway hair, form into lush curls.

The women, as well as the Quinter men, had descended upon Eva's house shortly after the sun rose this morning. The steady bang, bang, bang of hammers creating tables and benches floated through the open windows, as well as the happy shouts of people setting up the wedding preparations.

Eva's heart quivered, as if it, too, couldn't quite

believe her wedding day was finally here. She'd barely slept last night. Her mind had roamed and danced, thinking of all the wonderful days to come. And of course, their wedding night. A profound, dreamy sigh left her chest.

Jessie patted her shoulder. "Happy?"

Eva grinned, afraid to nod with the hot rod twisted in her hair. "Very."

Lila, staring out the window, turned around. "Well, I can't believe you invited *her* to attend."

"Who?" Eva pretended ignorance, for she knew who Lila referred to.

"Jenny Staples. Who else?" Lila walked across the room, flouncing her mint green dress around her legs as she planted herself on the bed. "If she was after Skeeter, I'd have already ripped every hair out of her head. Especially after that little gun incident yesterday."

The violence in Lila's voice made everyone— Eva, Jessie, Randi, and Summer—turn and gape at her.

Lila rolled her eyes to the ceiling, and then pointed a finger at her sisters-in-law. "Don't any of you look at me like that! You know damn well you'd have each done the same."

The three of them, Jessie, Randi, and Summer looked at each other. Practically giddy, they nodded at one another.

Eva turned to Lila. "You and Skeeter have been married for years. Surely you're not worried about his love for you."

"Of course, I know he loves me. But, I come from a time and place were a relationship is never safe. No matter how much a man loves a woman, and vice-versa, there's always an outsider thinking they can have what's not theirs. Skeeter assures me there'll never be anyone else, and I believe him, but that doesn't stop me from making sure." She glanced to the other women. "You girls know what I'm talking about, don't you?"

Eva waited for them to react. Lila often talked about another place and time, but she'd been born and raised over near Hayes—or so she said.

Jessie handed the curling rod to Summer, who carried it across the room. "Yes, we know what you're talking about," Jessie agreed. "It wouldn't matter if I was as old and feeble as Mrs. Butterfield, I'd fight tooth and nail if another woman attempted to draw out Kid's attention."

Eva grinned at the image of Mrs. Butterfield, who was a hundred if she was a day, defending herself with her knob-headed cane.

She turned to Lila, and admitted, "That's the reason I invited her."

"What?" Lila asked. "So you can pull her hair out at the wedding?"

"No." Eva giggled. "Not that I wouldn't like to. But that won't happen. I invited her just so she could see how much Bug and I love each other. So, she'll see with her own eyes she doesn't have a hope in hell of having him."

The other girls chuckled, but Lila remained thoughtful, patting her lips with one finger. "Good thinking, girl. I'd have never thought of flaunting it." She laughed then. "I always knew you were tougher than you let on."

Her recent bout of willpower made Eva glance around the room and let her eyes land on Jessie. "I'm sorry I didn't consult you about the wedding. I...Well, I just felt it was time I stood on my own two feet and prove to Bug just how much he means to me."

Jessie's smile was filled with understanding. "I'm not upset about it. None of us are. And you've always stood on your own two feet."

"No, I haven't. Especially not where Bug is

concerned. I've always been timid."

"What are you talking about?" Lila asked, rising from the bed. "You've lived out here *alone* for years. I could never have done that. And you traveled to New York, with a fourteen-year-old. That takes gumption."

"September's a good girl," Eva defended.

"I know that, that's not what I meant. It was just the two of you, two women alone. Anyone could have taken advantage of you," Lila explained.

Eva shook her head against the tiniest tingle. "I never thought about that."

"We did," Jessie, Summer, and Randi agreed as one.

Jessie continued to poke pins in Eva's hair as she spoke. "Kid is ecstatic that you and Bug are finally getting married. You drove him crazy."

"I did?"

"Yes, you did. He said it was because of Willamina. He said the way you two traveled around—out to the badlands and to Dodge—by yourselves was extremely dangerous, and made you believe you could do anything by yourself. I thought he was going to wring Ma's neck the night she wouldn't let you get married." Jessie laid the brush on the dressing table.

A wave of guilt bit at Eva's nerve endings. "Is Ma upset with me about the wedding?"

Summer lowered a pearl necklace over Eva's head. "No, she's not. She's delighted. The only reason she stopped the wedding that night at the house was because she wanted you to stand up to Bug. She wanted him to know he was marrying a strong woman, not a shy little girl."

"She did?"

"Yes, she did. She tangled with her actions that night the whole time you were sick." Summer hooked the necklace and moved around to stand in front of Eva. "She told me she knows how much you loved Bug, and him you, and that she was sorry she stopped the wedding. But at the same time she said she promised Willamina, when it came to your wedding, you'd be in charge."

Eva tugged out the handkerchief she had tucked up her sleeve. It had been Willamina's, and had tiny blue bells embroidered around the edges. "Willamina always said women are stronger than men. That our muscles aren't as big or bulky, but that our inner strength, our willpower, can withstand much more than theirs."

The room, except for the sounds drifting in the windows, remained silent for a few minutes.

"Well," Lila said. "She's right. And I believe everything happens for a reason. Exactly when and how it's supposed to." She turned and nodded toward the other women. "Right now, I don't think I've ever seen a more beautiful bride."

The women, all four of them standing in front of Eva, moved at the same time, revealing the mirror behind them. Eva's lungs locked. The woman staring back at her in the mirror was stunning. It couldn't possibly be her.

She glanced down to decipher if the pale peach dress she wore was the same one in the mirror. Her gaze lifted. It was. Yellow and white daisies sat amongst the mass of curls flowing from her head to disappear behind her shoulders. The pearl necklace glimmered against her skin left open by the low neckline of the dress, but it was her eyes that made her gasp. They sparkled brighter than the stars at night. She'd never seen them light up her reflection like this before.

"Oh, my."

"Jenny Staples is gonna eat her own heart out," Lila whispered in Eva's ear.

She giggled, and the others joined in. Their

laughter grew, and when Ma pulled the door open, all five of them were holding their stomachs and hooting like a room full of half drunken men.

Ma crossed the room. "You look downright beautiful, Eva."

"Thank you, Ma. And thank you for the dress. I love it." She and Ma shared a joyous hug. One that lifted her happy heart even higher.

"I knew that color was perfect for you." She patted Eva's cheeks. "I sewed it three years ago, you know."

"You, did?"

Ma nodded. "I did."

Eva hugged her again. "Thank you."

Ma wiped at her eyes. "Come on, Eva girl, your groom is waiting." As they walked across the room she added, "With about as much patience as a penned up bull."

The next few minutes were a blur. The women fussed around her as Eva made her way down the stairs and out the door, and the crowd filling her front lawn might as well have been weeds for all the notice Eva took of them. With crystal clear clarity, Bug entered her vision. Her heart stalled. He was several yards ahead of her, yet, she detected his love traveling though the open space and entering her being. It had always been this way, this connection the two of them had, and she'd always known it was love, but never before this exact moment had she realized just how deeply he affected her.

His wide smile, and his hand lifting towards her, jolted her heart back into its racing mode, and she put one foot in front of the other. Without a stumble or wobble, she glided to his side.

Silence settled like nightfall on a summer's eve, without ado or bother, it simply established the start of the rest of her life.

Reverend Kirkpatrick opened his book. "Dearly

beloved, we are..."

Holding Bug's hand, absorbing the heat of his palm against hers, Eva listened to the Reverend's smooth, practiced tone. She cherished every word, for they were what would bind her and Bug together forever. Tears pricked her eyes as Bug vowed his love to her, and the droplets slid down her cheeks as she repeated her vows to him. The ring he slipped on her finger became permanent; she knew she'd never take it off. When the service ended, Bug wiped away her tears with a gentle brushing of his finger before he lowered his head to capture her lips in an extraordinary and devoted kiss.

The crowd exploded, and the noise brought her tumbling back to earth. She tightened her hold on his neck, and commanded a wild and passionate kiss that left them both breathless. Bubbling with happiness and laughing, she spun to the crowd and tossed her bouquet of garden flowers high in the air.

Renewed shouts and clapping echoed over the land as the flowers glided high overhead. The wind plucked out a few daisy petals from the clump, and then as if it hit an invisible wall, the bouquet fell. Family and friends alike grew silent as the flowers gracefully drifted downward and bounced on the ground near Ma's feet.

Ma, eyes transfixed on the flowers, picked up the spray. When her face lifted, a smile grew on her lips. Ma glanced toward Red Elk standing beside her, and then turned and winked at Eva. Laughing out loud Ma held the bouquet over her head.

The crowd cheered, and Eva turned to Bug, who kissed her quickly before he led her through the mass of people dowsing them with handfuls of wheat. They arrived on the porch, and while Bug brushed the seeds from her hair, she cleaned it away from his broad shoulders. The black suit coat fit him like a glove. Their eyes met, and he kissed her again, bringing more joyous sounds from the crowd.

The next instant, he reached down and hoisted her up. With one arm under her knees and the other around her back, he turned and carried her into the house.

"Bug!" she exclaimed, holding on as he kicked the door shut. "What are you doing? We can't—well, we shouldn't while everyone is…"

"God, I love you, Eva girl," he said and ran a trail of kisses down the side of her face.

"I love you, too, but…" She couldn't help but glance to the door again. The yard was full of people. It would be extremely rude to enclose themselves in the bedroom, especially at four in the afternoon. Yet…

Bug set her down. "Don't worry, we'll wait until after the meal."

Relieved, yet disappointed, she swayed her torso against his. "Then why did you carry me inside?"

"Because I want five minutes alone with you." His lips covered hers again. When it came to his kisses, she had no willpower, except that which kept him kissing her until she was lightheaded from lack of oxygen.

Snuggling deeper in his embrace, she asked, "What did you need?"

"Need? I have what I need in my arms."

"Why are we here then, instead of out there?" She tipped her head toward the door.

"I told you, I want five minutes alone with you."

"What for?"

"For no other reason than to hold you. To know you are truly, finally, mine."

"Hmmm," she mumbled against his chest. "Finally."

Bug held her for a bit longer and then stepped back. "I also wanted to give you this." He spun around and pointed to a box sitting on the desk by the door.

"What is it?" Her fingers trembled as she touched the wood. It was a wooden crate, with a hinged top, more than a foot square.

His cheeks held a tinge of red. "I've been trying to come up with a wedding gift. Something I could give you that you don't already have. There isn't anything I can buy, anything I could make that you don't already have." He sighed heavily. "The lady I rented from in Pennsylvania sent the things I'd left there." He nodded toward the box. "That's pretty much it."

Eva lifted the lid. The box was crammed with paper. "Bug, these are letters."

"I know."

She pulled a few out. "There has to be hundreds of them."

"I'd guess close to a thousand. I wrote one almost every day I was gone."

The writing on the front of each envelope she picked up made her heart throb. "Are they all addressed to me?"

"Yes. I wrote to you almost every night." He stood behind her, talking softly next to her shoulder. "Some are about the oil fields, or the people I met. Others are about something I'd done or seen and how I wished you were with me to see it as well. But they all tell you how much I love you. How much I missed you. And that I was doing it all for us, so that when I returned I'd be able to financially support a wife and children."

She glanced at him, and blinked through the blur. "Why didn't you ever mail them?"

"It's hard to explain. First it was because I was traveling, but then as time went on, it was because I was afraid."

"Afraid?"

"Yes, by then I had already been gone for six

months." He shook his head. "And I got to thinking, what if you found someone else. If that was the case, to mail them wouldn't have been fair to you."

"But, I wrote to you," she whispered, "and you wrote back." Once. In three years there had only been one letter from him. She gazed back down at the hundreds of letters. How different things may have been had he sent them.

"It's hard to explain, the fear I felt that is. I regret it now, but at the time, I couldn't get past it." He looped his arms around her waist, flattening his hands over her stomach. "You don't have to read them. I just wanted you to know that I thought of you every day."

She straightened the letters, closed the lid, and then spun around in his arms. "I will read every one, and cherish them always." Wrapping her arms around his neck, she kissed his lips softly. "Thank you for giving them to me." She settled a serious gaze on his face. "But everything I have is because of you."

He shook his head. "No, it isn't. You've bought it or built it with money you earned from your paintings."

She shook her head. "In one way or another, you've given me everything I have."

He frowned. "How so?"

"Most importantly, you gave me three children when I thought I'd never have any, but furthermore, when you left I was despondent. I painted a picture of you riding away, of how you'd looked back over your shoulder at me." To this day the picture she spoke of was carved in her memory. "Willamina said you'd like to see that one. Her words struck me, and from that day on I started painting everything I saw—for you. I wanted to capture everything that happened so when you returned you could see it. Whether it was a glorious sunset, or a peddler who'd

239

stopped by, I painted it for you."

"You did?"

"When Jack arrived the barn loft was full." She shrugged. "There are still several out there that I wouldn't let him take. They are for you." Looking around, she added, "Even when it came to building this house. I had it built so you would have a home ready and waiting. It's not my house, Bug, it's ours. They aren't my paintings, they're ours. Right down to the oil well. It's not mine, it's ours. That's how I've always felt. I wasn't doing any of it for me. I was doing it for us." She cupped his cheeks. "The only reason I agreed to go to the art show in New York was because I thought I might see you."

"Really?"

She nodded. "And when I did—"

His lips stopped her from finishing. When the kiss ended, he said, "Today is the first day of the rest of our lives. We have no regrets, just promises of a wonderful life together."

"You're right," she agreed. "A wonderful, wonderful life." Once again, she kissed him, demonstrating just how much he meant to her.

Unfortunately, their time alone was interrupted by the echoes of people going in and out the back door. "I guess we better join the party," Bug said, drawing his mouth from hers.

"Yes, we better," she agreed and took his hand to be led into the kitchen.

Randi was instructing a throng of people which container to carry and where to place it outdoors where Hog had been tending to a large side of beef over a smoldering pit since the wee hours of the morning.

Bug paused in the doorway, holding Eva's hand firmly in his. The turmoil filling his life the past month was over. "Need any help in here?" he asked.

"Of course not, we have it all under control."

Randi waved a hand. "You two go enjoy your guests."

The party lasted for hours, and was great fun, but to Bug, the event should have ended ten minutes after it started. He and Eva shared their first married meal with all of the guests, they cut and fed each other wedding cake, per Lila's instructions, and they partook in several dances when the music started. It was torture. Pure and simple.

Before the sun started to set, people began to leave. Bug gladly hitched and harnessed horses by the dozens, and waved gaily as the crowd dispersed. It was mainly family clearing up the front yard of makeshift tables and benches when a wagon rolled down the road.

"Who could that be?" Kid asked as he carried the other end of the stack of planks to the barn.

"I don't know," Bug answered, "But they're too late for the festivities, so they best just turn around."

Kid laughed. "A little anxious there, little brother?"

"Yes," Bug admitted without misgivings. He backed into the barn to unload the last of the boards on top of the large pile. "It's about time the rest of you left, too."

Laughing, Kid slapped his back. "We're going. But you know the women won't leave until everything's cleaned up."

"Yes, I know," Bug said. "Why do you think I'm helping?" Shaking his head, he added, "You know, Kid, every one of you, you, Skeeter, Snake, and Hog, got married in the blink of an eye. I've been trying to get the deed done for three years."

Kid nodded and hooked an arm around Bug's neck. "You got a point there, little brother."

As they walked back out the barn door, Bug's feet dug into the dirt. Kid stopped beside him. "What's wrong?"

Bug couldn't talk. His tongue was stuck on the

roof of his mouth, and his heart thumped in his heels.

"Mr. Quinter!" Mrs. King, looking as fierce as her fat lady companion from the train, stomped toward the barn.

Chapter Nineteen

"There are rules, Mr. Quinter, and laws. What you've done is illegal!" Mrs. King insisted. "It's called kidnapping."

Bug glanced around the kitchen. Every female in his family had something to say about Mrs. King's remark. The Aid Society worker ignored the voices and glared at him.

"I didn't kidnap anyone," he offered, solemnly, for he knew he hadn't followed any of the society's rules when it came to how he'd obtained the children. But the way the society went about auctioning them off was a hell of a lot worse than what he'd done. Yet, he knew he couldn't say that. It wouldn't matter even if he did, since he'd already said as much while on the train, but he didn't need to increase Mrs. King's anger.

Eva stood from where she sat on a chair in front of him. "Mrs. King," Eva said kindly. "Perhaps you and Bug and I, as well as the Porters could discuss this more comfortably in the parlor."

Ma's huff echoed in the room that had gone silent as soon as Eva stood up. The sound didn't seem to affect his new wife. She smiled at Ma. "Perhaps you'd help the others watch the children for a few minutes. Mrs. King's arrival has Tucker, Reed, and Heather extremely upset. They are outside with September." She turned to Jack then. "Elliott was supposed to be at the wedding today. I didn't see him. Could you ride to town and see what prevented his attendance?"

Jack nodded and was out the door the next

243

second. Eva turned to Randi then. "Is there any punch left? Perhaps Mrs. King would like a glass?"

Bug's head was swirling. Mrs. King wanted to take their kids away, and Eva was offering her punch? She twisted just then, and the serene smile on her face settled his nerves. She had a plan—knew what she was doing.

"Let's go to the parlor," she instructed, resting a hand on his forearm.

Believing in her, Bug took her arm and walked to the doorway. He waited with Eva as the Porters and Mrs. King made their way through the opening, and then, hand in hand, he and Eva followed.

Randi carried in a tray and set it on the table in front of the sofa before everyone was seated, and Eva, as if she was offering royalty tea, served her guests. When everyone was settled, glass in hand— his was still on the table, where he'd set it down as soon as Eva had handed it to him—Eva sat down beside him.

"Mrs. King," she started. "Thank you for traveling out here. This is something we need to get cleared up as soon as possible."

"Yes, it is, Miss—"

"Mrs. Quinter," Bug interjected, wrapping an arm about Eva's shoulders.

"Mrs. Quinter," Mrs. King corrected, and then continued, "What's happened here could cause the Children's Society to lose our license."

"We understand the repercussion," Eva said seriously, "and we are willing to do whatever is necessary to rectify the situation." She laid a hand on Bug's knee. "But you should be warned, we will not lose our children."

"They are not your children to lose. That's the problem." Mrs. King set her glass down with a solid thud.

Bug was at a loss. He trusted Eva, but at the

same time, felt he should be doing more than just sitting here. If Mrs. King was a man, he'd know how to handle this fight, but how was a man suppose to defend his family against a woman from the Children's Aid Society? An eerie sensation gripped his spine.

He lifted his gaze from Mrs. King's glass to her stern expression. "How'd you know where to find us, and the kids?"

Mrs. King's face fell, she caught it, and puckered up another grimace, but he'd seen her initial reaction.

"Mrs. King? How'd you find us?"

"You told me—"

"No," he interrupted. "I told you I lived west of Dodge. I never said exactly where."

"Well, I-we—"

His stomach erupted, this time full of anger, and deceit. "Who? Who contacted you?"

"I received a wire while in Denver," Mrs. King admitted. She glanced to the Porters and then Eva. "We are opening a division of the Children's Society out there."

"From who?"

"That doesn't really matter, Mr. Quinter, now does it?" She never looked his way.

"Yes, it does," he insisted.

"No, it doesn't." This time she settled a solid glare on him. "I'll be taking Tucker, Reed, and Heather back to Denver with me. Where they will be properly adopted by law abiding citizens."

Bug met her glare eyeball for eyeball. "You aren't taking our kids anywhere."

"Yes, I am." She stood up and slapped her hands on her hips.

He was on his feet just as fast. "No, you aren't!"

The front door flew open. Elliott Hampton and Jack burst into the house. The lawyer, limping, made his way into the parlor. "Eva, Bug, I'm sorry. My horse threw a shoe halfway from Garden City. I had to walk the last ten miles." He opened his saddle bag as he spoke. "I'm sorry to have missed the ceremony, but congratulations." Elliott offered Bug his hand.

Bug took it, and recalled that Eva had hired the man to see to the adoption. No wonder she was so confident. He grinned and pumped Elliott's hand harder. "Thanks, Elliott."

Eva, standing next to him, leaned around his shoulder. "Hello, Elliott. I'm sorry to hear of your inconvenience." She pointed to Mrs. King. "This is Mrs. King. She is from the Children's Society."

"Yes, Jack filled me in. Thank goodness he heard me shouting as he turned onto the main road." Elliott offered his hand to Mrs. King. "I'm Elliott Hampton, Attorney at Law. I'm representing Mr. and Mrs. Quinter in this case." He nodded to the Porters who also had stood up. "Let's all be seated, shall we?"

Bug assisted his wife down beside him. Worry tugged on her face, but she offered him a smile. He laid his arm around her. For as confident as she appeared, he knew her insides where shaking like a frightened kitten. He rubbed her shoulder.

"Mrs. King," Elliott said as he glanced through the papers he'd tugged out of his saddle bag. "I believe you made the trip from Denver for no reason. I have adoption papers for all three children, and they've been duly signed and notarized."

Bug's heart took flight like a rooster pheasant—cackling with glee. He squeezed Eva's shoulder.

"The children are no longer eligible for adoption, Mr. Hampton," Mrs. King stated.

Bug jolted. "Since when?"

Mrs. King didn't answer him. Instead, she kept her eyes on Elliott. "The children will be returning to

Denver with me."

Elliott looked as calm as a cat sleeping in the sun, but his words were harsh. "Mrs. King," he started. "If you so much as attempt to remove these children, I will charge you with contempt and for accepting a bribe."

The woman gasped.

Eva squeezed Bug's knee. He patted her hand reassuringly, though his insides were shuddering.

"You wouldn't," Mrs. King challenged.

"Oh, I would," Elliott assured. "I don't know how much Miss Staples offered you, but I'll find out. And so will Judge Holden."

Mrs. King's eyes bugged out of their sockets. Bug knew it. From the get go this escapade had reminded him too much of his arrest for it to be anyone else but Jenny.

"I see you've heard of the Honorable Judge Holden," Elliott said. "He's one of New York City's finest judges. And he has a soft spot when it comes to children." Elliott glanced to Eva and Bug. "Did you know, Mrs. King, that Mrs. Quinter is the judge's favorite artist, and that he and Mr. Quinter have a very tight friendship?" Elliott grinned. "He and Bug have worked together before."

Mrs. King wrung her hands together in her lap. Her demeanor grew sheepish.

"Your silence makes me believe you understand and accept the fact that Tucker, Reed, and Heather, are no longer your concern." Elliott straightened the stack of papers he'd set on the table. "They have been legally adopted by Mr. and Mrs. Quinter."

"Yes, Mr. Hampton, I understand." Mrs. King rose from her chair. "I believe I will be going now."

A tinge of regret tugged on Bug's heart. The woman had been kind on the train. He stood. "Mrs. King. Thank you for checking on the children. I'm glad you were concerned about their welfare, but I told you from the beginning there would be nothing to worry about."

She bowed her head. "Yes, you did, Mr. Quinter, and I'm sorry to have disturbed you." Mrs. King looked at Elliott then. "For the record, Mr. Hampton, I didn't accept Miss Staples's offer of money."

"You may not have," Elliott said. "But someone at the society did. You may want to check on that."

"I will, sir. As soon as I return to Denver." She nodded towards everyone else in the room. When her eyes landed on Bug, she said. "I have to admit, I'm glad it turned out this way. I knew those children had found someone who'd love them in you, Mr. Quinter. I sincerely hope you do understand that I was just doing my job."

"I do," he said, and glancing at Eva's smiling face, he added, "We do."

"Well, good day, then," Mrs. King said.

Jack walked her to the door, and Bug caught sight of his family—most of them anyway, peering into the room. He turned back to Elliott.

"I don't know what to say other than thank you, Elliott."

"Don't thank me, thank your wife." Elliott smiled at Eva. "She's the one that figured something was going to happen and had me check into every possible angle while I completed the adoption process."

Bug peered down at his wife. Eva was nibbling on her bottom lip.

"You are amazing, Eva girl," Bug said, running a knuckle over her cheek.

A grin appeared on her face. "I think we need to go talk to the children. They were very worried when they saw Mrs. King."

"So was I," Bug admitted. He kissed her, quickly, before agreeing, "Yes, let's go talk to them."

It was another hour or so before everyone else

left, including Tucker, Reed, and Heather. Bug wasn't sure if it was Ma or September who insisted the children stay at their house for a couple of days instead of staying with the Porters. Part of him wanted to protest, but the other part of him strongly wanted the time alone with Eva. He did remain silent, the grins on the kids' face said they were looking forward to getting to know their new cousins.

Eva stood beside him, waving at the final departing wagon. He tightened the arm looped around her shoulders, tugging her closer. Her head settled on his shoulder, and she let out a long sigh.

"Are you tired?" he asked. A hint of fear tickled his spine. It hadn't been that long since her surgery, and the day had been busy—exhausting even.

"No," she said. "Just content." She spun about, circling his waist with her arms. "How about you?"

"I'm content," he agreed.

"You're content, are you?" The glint of mischief in her eyes made his heart—and other significant body parts—jolt.

He leaned down until their noses bumped. "Yes. I'm content." He hooked her behind the knees, sweeping her off her feet, and spun about. "And so gall-darn excited I'm about to burst."

She giggled and wrapped her arms around his neck. Nuzzling his neck, she said, "Me, too."

He was up the steps and inside the house faster than if he'd been blasted with nitro. After kicking the door shut, he set her down and spun about.

"Where are you going?" she asked.

Snatching the key from the bowl on top of the desk, he stuck it in the front door lock. "I'm not taking any chances," he said. "We've waited too long."

"I'll lock the back door," she shouted, already running for the kitchen.

Laughing, he tossed the key back in the bowl, and followed her.

"What about the windows?" she asked, spinning around to toss the key she'd used on the kitchen counter.

He laughed harder and caught her by the waist. "I don't think we need to go that far."

Her face glowed with happiness. She tilted it up, looking him straight in the eyes. "Do me a favor?"

"Anything," he vowed.

"Call me Mrs. Quinter."

His hands slid up her back, trembling as they explored every curve beneath her dress. "Hello, Mrs. Quinter."

Giggling, she closed her eyes and leaned her head back as if she was accepting a gift from above. "I've waited a lifetime to hear that."

"Really?" He kissed her neck, and slid the tip of his tongue along the delicate line of her chin. "Mrs. Quinter?"

"Hmmm, yes, Mr. Quinter." She tipped her face forward, and her hands went to the buttons of his shirt. Plucking them through the material, she asked, "Would you like to know what else I've waited a lifetime for?"

He started working on the line of buttons trailing down her back. "Well, Mrs. Quinter, I believe it's the same thing I've been waiting for."

She tugged his shirt out of his waistband and flayed her hands over his bare chest. The gentle, soft caress had him sucking in air.

"I do believe you're right, Mr. Quinter. I do believe you're right."

He took her hands, knowing he had to stop her before his control burst, and walking backwards, drew her from the room. She followed, eyes locked on his, and smiling so serenely his heart threatened to beat its way right out of his chest.

Bug led her up the stairs and down the hall. All the while, Eva's heart swelled until taking a breath of air seemed impossible. As they entered their bedroom, she glanced over his shoulder, and stumbled. The bed covers had been folded back, exposing crisp sheets covered with pink rose petals. A bottle of wine and two glasses sat on the table beside the bed, and an array of lit candles made the ceiling twinkle as if stars shone overhead.

"Oh, Bug," she gasped. "How romantic."

His cheeks grew red. "I had a little help from Lila," he admitted.

She ran the tip of one finger down his chest, making a winding, twisting trail all the way over his hard, flat abdomen to his britches. "You'll remind me to thank her, won't you? For right now, my mind is so busy with other beautiful things I may forget how lovely the room looks."

Bug started to pull the pins from her hair. "I'll try, but you might have to remind me." His fingers paused, and he held one of the daisies from her hair before her eyes. One by one he plucked the white petals from the yellow center. "She loves me, she loves me not," he said, dropping the pieces one at a time.

Eva held her breath, hoping and praying the childhood game would hold true. It was silly, yet so significant at this moment in time she couldn't release the air in her lungs.

"Aw," he groaned, plucking the final petal. "She loves me."

She let the air escape, crumpling against his solid, strong, and divinely muscled chest. "Yes, she loves you."

****

A month in one's life span doesn't seem like a lot, but to Eva, cherishing each and every minute, it held more fascinating and treasured moments than all of the previous months of her twenty-three years combined. Being a wife and mother was more than she'd dreamed of. So much more. Every day, Bug, or Tucker, or Reed, or Heather did or said something that had her eyes misting with joy and her heart bulging with love.

She leaned back and dipped the end of her paint brush in the dab of black paint on her palette. With a quick flick of her wrist, she dotted the I of her signature.

*Eva Quinter.*

She frowned. It wasn't quite prominent enough. Touching the brush to the canvas, she made an elegant swirl beneath the full name. Eloisa Reynolds no longer existed. Never had really. It had just been a name she'd used until she obtained the one she was destined to have forevermore.

Satisfied, she dropped the brush in the small bottle of turpentine, and set the palette aside.

"That's gorgeous."

She spun about. Bug stared at the painting. The sight of him made her smile. "You've seen it before."

"I know," he said, still sounding awestruck. "But, wow, completed, it's really..." His hands settled on her shoulders, and his thumbs gently caressed her neck. "Gorgeous."

"Thank you." She pressed a cheek to his knuckles. The painting was the one of the oil derrick she'd started months ago. But in the finished product, oil blasted out of the top and rained down to the ground. In the forefront, there was she and Bug. She'd painted the moment he'd lifted her off the ground and twirled her in the air. Near their feet, seated on the ground, smiling and clapping with delight, were Tucker, Reed, and Heather.

Eva sighed. "It is gorgeous, isn't it?"

Bug kissed the side of her face. "Yes, it is." Cheek to cheek, his gaze went back to the painting.

"That's the one we need to hang above the fireplace."

"Oh, yes, let's," she agreed as she scooted off her stool. Turning around, she wrapped her arms around him. "I didn't even hear you come in." After fully delivering a welcome home kiss, and receiving one just as devoted, she asked, "How was your trip to town?"

"Good," Bug answered.

"Was there a letter from Ma? Is she enjoying her time out at Skeeter and Lila's?" The real question was, was Ma enjoying her time with Chief Red Elk, but Eva, along with her sisters-in-law, didn't think their husbands were too keen on the idea of their mother marrying again. Therefore, she along with the other girls, kept their knowledge of Ma's courtship quiet. Eva did wonder how Lila was managing with Skeeter though. She'd have to write to her tonight.

"No, no letter from Ma." Bug held up an envelope. "But I got one here from Rockefeller."

Her heart leaped. "You do? What's it say?"

"That they want every ounce of crude we can ship them."

She squealed and grabbed his neck.

He spun her around, and kissed her again. "With the five wells we already have pumping, and the other three we're drilling, that's a lot of crude, Eva girl, a lot of crude."

"Oh, I knew it! I just knew it!" She planted kisses all across his face.

He caught her lips for a quick peck. "Yes, and it's all thanks to my wildcat bride."

She giggled, loving when he called her that. "What else does the letter say?"

"Well, that he plans on making a trip out here this fall." He handed her the envelope. "Within the next month or so."

"Oh, Bug, that's so wonderful."

He pulled several other letters out of his pocket. "I got another letter from Chester. He still wants to build a refinery out here. I'm thinking about it, Eva. The area could use the jobs, and it would cut our shipping costs down to nil."

"Well, then, perhaps that's what we need to do."

He shrugged. "I just had my mind set on working with Rockefeller." Handing her the stack of envelopes he continued, "There's one from Judge Holden, too. He received your painting, and loves it, of course." His grin depicted his teasing tone.

She poked him in the ribs. "I'm glad."

"Me, too." He planted a kiss on her forehead. "He, too, is making another trip west, and wants to stop by."

"Oh, goodness, that settles that."

He frowned. "That settles what?"

It had been something she'd been thinking of lately, but hadn't brought it up. Now was as good of a time as any. "I've been thinking it's time we build a new house."

"A new house? This one's hardly old."

She walked to the windows where she could see the children, along with the Porter kids playing on the swings. "I know," she said. "But Tucker and Reed are sharing a bedroom. I think they need their own rooms. And if we're going to continuously have company, we should have a couple of guest bedrooms. Besides, the Porters could live in this one." Turning around she met his gaze. "I've been thinking we should build it on top of that big knoll. That way we could look out our bedroom window and see the oil wells."

He chuckled. "I doubt there are many women who'd want to look out their bedroom window and see oil wells."

Keeping his gaze locked on hers, she sashayed into his arms. "Well, you, Mr. Quinter, had better never find out if any other woman wants her bedroom window to overlook an oil field."

"The thought never crossed my mind," he assured, kissing her soundly.

When they separated, she asked, "So what do you think of the new house idea?"

He shook his head. Not in disagreement, but with credibility. "If you want a new house, then we'll build a new house."

She tugged his shirt out of his pants and ran her hands up his bare back. The heated, smooth skin, glided beneath her fingers, and she wiggled her torso against his. "Good," she said, nibbling on his earlobe. "For who knows when another orphan train is going to roll through Kansas."

He jerked, and stared down at her with a startled look. "Eva?"

She winked at him. "Who knows?"

## A word about the author...

Lauri Robinson lives in rural Minnesota where she and her husband spend every spare moment with their three grown sons and four (soon to be five) grandchildren. She works part time, volunteers for several organizations, and is a diehard Elvis and NASCAR fan. Her favorite getaway location is the woods of northern Minnesota on the land homesteaded by her great-grandfather.

Stop by and say hi to Lauri at
www.laurirobinson.blogspot.com

Thank you for purchasing
this Wild Rose Press publication.
For other wonderful stories of romance,
please visit our on-line bookstore at
www.thewildrosepress.com.

For questions or more information
contact us at
info@thewildrosepress.com.

The Wild Rose Press
www.TheWildRosePress.com